CALL IT TREASON

An Adam Drake Novel

SCOTT MATTHEWS

Copyright © 2015 by Scott Matthews

Published by Vinci Books 2024

All rights reserved.

No part of this book may be reproduced in any form or by any electronic or mechanical means, including information storage and retrieval systems, without written permission from the author, except for the use of brief quotations in a book review.

All characters in this work are fictitious. Any resemblance to actual persons, living or dead, is purely coincidental.

Chapter One

ADAM DRAKE SLIPPED into his office early, ahead of his secretary, wearing jeans and an Oregon Duck sweatshirt, not appropriate attire for a day in court. But then, he didn't have to appear before Judge Frank in U.S. District Court today. The opposing counsel had called the night before and caved.

His client was the world leader in the design and manufacture of thermal imaging infrared cameras and tactical imaging systems. The year before a German company had copied its long range thermal targeting system developed for the U.S. Navy and was preparing to sell it to the Iranians. Drake filed suit against the company to block the sale and demanded the return or destruction of the copied imaging systems. The German company's attorney's last minute call was to advise him they were withdrawing their opposition to Drake's motion for summary judgment.

Drake was at his desk in the office loft and left a note for his secretary to clear his calendar for the day, when he heard her unlock the back door below and walk in. Margo Benning was his first and only legal secretary, beginning with his first days in the District Attorney's office.

She had been the alpha female then, quietly asserting her control over the staffs of all the prosecuting teams, with her encyclopedic knowledge of criminal court procedures and her fierce determination to make the justice system function smoothly.

She inherited Drake, when the senior felony prosecutor she worked for died suddenly of a massive heart attack. Under her tutelage, she trained him to be the best prosecutor in the office. And when he left the D.A.'s office to start his own private practice, she went with him to make sure his office continued to perform up to her standards.

"Good morning Margo," he called down.

"You're early today. Ready for court?" she asked from the break room.

He heard her starting a pot of coffee below. The familiar sounds of water running and the bean grinder whirring promised that he would soon be enjoying a cup of his favorite Kona coffee. He decided to wait until the aroma of brewing coffee to permeate the office before telling her he was leaving for the day.

The office had been a rare book store on Portland's Riverwalk and marina before Drake purchased it and the apartment above, altering it for his needs. The lower level now had a waiting area for clients with deep brown leather sofas, a glass-enclosed conference room and Margo's work area.

The loft above had an oak desk he'd restored that served as the focal point of the room. Along one wall stood a tall bookcase, one of the few things he kept from the original bookstore. A broad window looked out over the river, where he could stand and watch sailboats and motor yachts come and go from the marina below. The view impressed his clients, which was nice, but it was the momentary relief from dealing with other people's problems it provided him that he cherished.

"Zeismann's attorney called last night," he said. "He's not opposing our motion for summary judgment."

"Congratulations! That's a nice win. Have you called our client?" He heard her heels clicking on the red oak flooring as she moved from the break room to her desk.

"I will before I leave."

"Leaving when, today?" she asked.

"As soon as I can," he said. "I'm leaving notes on some of these files for you to call. I'll be back on Monday."

When he didn't hear a response, he wasn't surprised to hear her cross the room and begin to climb the staircase to the loft.

"It's Friday, and I know you like your long weekends" she began in a patient tone when she reached the top of the stairs, "But we have a lot that needs to be done. Today."

She stood with her arms folded across her chest, favoring him with the commanding gaze she'd perfected in the D.A.'s office. She was a determined fifty two year old trim black woman, standing fit and tall at five feet four inches with tightly curled gray hair. Silver wire-rimmed reading glasses hung from a silver chain around her neck.

"There's nothing that can't wait until Monday, Margo. Mike's invited me to be his spotter tomorrow at a shooting competition down in southern Oregon. With oral argument cancelled on my motion, I can drive there today and be back Monday morning. I haven't been able to see him much since he was poisoned in San Francisco."

Margo sat down in the chair in front of his desk and scooted it closer. She sat back in the chair for a moment, then shrugged her shoulders and reached for the stack of files he was working on. "Mike, huh? Is his wife still blaming you for his being poisoned?"

"She is, and I can't blame her. The assassin *was* sent for me. I'm keeping out of sight until she forgives me."

"And I take it she won't be there this weekend, so being his spotter tomorrow gives you that opportunity."

"Exactly, and getting out of the office gives *you* a chance to spend more time with *your* husband. Do something fun with Paul?"

"He stayed home today," she said, as a fleeting frown creased her forehead. "I can't remember the last time he didn't punch in at the Sheriff's office."

"So, make these few calls for me and go be with him," Drake ordered.

He recognized the tight-lipped smile on her face, as she considered his "suggestion". It was time to hit the road, he saw, and be prepared to return for a couple of long days next week.

Chapter Two

FROM HIS PRONE position on the snow-covered ridge line, Adam Drake focused his spotting scope on the six foot square target 1,500 meters away on the other side of the valley. It was the last round of shooting in the competition between the ten men in the High Altitude Rifle Training course. He watched as the target was lowered into the scoring pit and then raised with a white shot hole disc marking the second of three shots each man was allowed.

"An "X", bull's eye, at four o'clock", Drake reported. He turned to his right and saw that Mike Casey, the CEO of Puget Sound Security and his best friend, was using the mini-joystick to make a small adjustment on the thermal sight mounted on his Precision Sniper Rifle, the new long-range weapon the United States Special Operations Command (USSOCOM) had recently added to its arsenal.

As Casey lowered the sniper rifle into position for his last shot, the instructor standing behind them quietly said, "A "10 ring" or better wins it. Make it count."

Drake turned back to his spotting scope and settled his right eye in the eye piece. He'd seen his friend shoot before when they had served together in the Middle East, but that had been ten years ago with a familiar rifle. The sniper rifle Casey was using had been loaned to him by SOCOM for evaluation and had only been sighted in that morning.

The crack of Casey's last shot echoed in the valley. It signaled the end of the four-day training course for his nine employees of Puget Sound Security, as they clustered around the instructor breathing vanishing clouds of vapor into the air.

Drake scoped the target again and saw it rise into position with another "X" at six o'clock. The shooters waited for the instructor to lower his spotting scope and make the call.

"Not bad for an old sniper, Casey," the instructor said, a former Marine sniper himself. "Two scores in the "X" ring and one just outside. Looks like you win. Head on down the trail, men. Let's get off this ridge while there's still light."

As the men headed out, the instructor turned to Casey and held out his hand to hold the PSR sniper rifle while Casey and Drake collected their equipment and stood up.

"If I'm remembering correctly, you two boys were Delta Force. I recall hearing some pretty amazing stories about some of your kills. Mike, did you let your employees know what they were up against when they each bet twenty dollars against you?"

"No, but I'm sure it's going to cost me a lot more than they lost for me to buy their dinners tonight, Gunney. Thanks for not letting on," Casey said. "Would you like to join us? We're staying at the Alpine Ridge Ranch down the road. They have great steaks at the Lodge."

Gunney shook his head. "I have another class coming in tonight, so I'll have to take a rain check, assuming the ranch is still open to the public next year. I heard they're thinking of selling to some Muslim group. Hope we don't have another terror training camp trying to set up here, like they tried over near Bly several years back."

Drake finished putting spotting scope in its case, knocked the snow off his hunting parka and pants and followed the instructor down the trail to the vans waiting for them. "Gunney, why would a

Muslim group want a working cattle ranch and resort in rural southern Oregon?"

"It's some Muslim foundation that works with troubled kids. They say they want a working ranch so the kids can learn how to work, away from the cities and drugs and stuff. You'd think they could find a place to do that for less than the twenty million dollars they've offered."

Casey caught up with them on the trail and said from behind Drake, "Steve Simpson, who owns the ranch, is a friend and his father is a client. They've never talked about selling out. Is Steve actually considering the offer?"

Gunney shrugged and said over his shoulder, "I expect he is. Twenty million's twice what that ranch is worth, but his wife's health isn't great. Selling would solve some of their problems."

As the three men walked in silence along the trail through the snow-laden ponderosa pine trees, Drake remembered the plot in late 1999 to establish a terror-training camp on the 158 acre Dog Cry Ranch near Bly, Oregon.

James Ujaama, a small-time crook from Seattle, Washington, had conned one-armed, one-eyed London cleric, Abu Hamza al-Masri, into setting up a training camp for Islamic fighters on American soil. The plan fell apart when al-Qaeda fighter Oussama Kassir, with ties to Khalid Sheikh Mohammed, the mastermind of the 9/11 terror attacks, flew to the ranch and found there were no recruits or weapons there yet for the jihad. Within a month of his arrival, Kassir abandoned the dream of training terrorists on the ranch and fled to Seattle. Both Ujaama and Kassir were now serving life sentences in prison after their convictions.

When they arrived at the trailhead, two white 15-passenger GMC vans were idling in the twilight and the PSS executive protection team members were loading their gear and scrambling into the warmth of the vehicles.

Drake and Casey shook hands and said goodbye to their instructor from Oregon Top Gun, loaded their gear in the back of the lead van and climbed into the open seats behind their driver.

"Next year, you'll have to come down and take one of the courses," Casey said. "It's not the close-quarters-battle shooting range we trained at in Delta Force, but it's as close as you'll get in the civilian world. It would do you good to brush up."

"What makes you think I need to brush up?" Drake asked and smiled.

"Just saying, with the way you keep running into trouble it couldn't hurt."

Drake settled back in his seat and pulled off his gloves. He couldn't argue with his friend. In the last year, he'd been involved in three confrontations that had resulted in his shooting and killing terrorists on American soil. They had all deserved to die, and he wasn't losing sleep over their deaths, but it wasn't the life he'd longed for when he left the military.

And the life he longed for certainly didn't involve brushing up on his CQB skills in a civilian version of Delta's "House of Horrors".

Chapter Three

AFTER A ROWDY and raucous thirty-minute drive to the Aspen Ridge Ranch, with bets being made for the competition next year, the PSS employees split up and headed to their respective cabins. Drake showered and changed his clothes in the cabin he shared with Mike Casey and two of his employees, and walked alone on a path that bordered a vast white meadow to the Lodge to meet Casey for dinner.

The crunch of snow under his Nike hiking boots and the star-filled sky made Drake smile as he approached the warm glow of the log building. He'd grown up in Oregon and skiied its mountains. Tonight he loved feeling the familiar bite of snow-cold air on his cheeks again.

Drake knocked the snow off his boots, using the boot scraper on the deck near the front door, and stepped into the warm bustle of the Lodge. A fire was burning in the huge river-rock fireplace at the far end of the main room and several of the PSS employees were sitting in the leather chairs and sofa in front of it. Beyond the check-in counter on the right, was the dining room and beyond that a carved wooden sign that beckoned him to the Buffalo Saloon.

Casey waved to him from the door of the saloon. "Let's have a drink before dinner. "There's someone I want you to meet," he said as Drake approached across the expanse of red oak flooring of the lodge. On the way, he passed the dining room and saw that it was already two thirds full of guests seated for dinner.

Drake hung his coat on a peg under a row of white cowboy hats and Casey led him to the bar and introduced him to Steve Simpson, the owner of the resort.

"Steve's dad was a client of Puget Sound Security when I took over the business. He manufactured avionics for helicopters in California and since I flew helicopters we became friends. That's how I met Steve, before he graduated U.C. Davis in Animal Science and bought this old ranch. He's turned it into quite an operation since then."

Drake shook hands with Simpson and asked, "Has it always been a dude ranch?"

Steve Simpson smiled. "This didn't become Aspen Ridge Ranch and resort until seventeen years after we bought it. It's always been known locally as Fishhole Creek Ranch, and always been a real cattle ranch. We've lived here for forty years."

Casey waved the bartender over and said, "Why don't we grab a drink and find a table. I want to ask Steve about this offer on his ranch."

When they had placed their order, the three men sat in a red leather booth under a stuffed head of a huge black buffalo on the wall above them.

"Bill Bradford, the instructor over at Oregon Top Gun, said you were considering an offer to sell the ranch. Is that true?" Casey asked.

Steve Simpson nodded his head. "Word gets around pretty fast around out here. Yes, we do have an offer, and it's a fantastic one. Considering it is too mild a description, though. It's haunting me."

"Why is it haunting you, Steve? I didn't think you'd ever sell the ranch," Casey said.

Simpson leaned forward. "If Carrie was healthy, Mike, I never would. But she needs treatment she can't get around here, so selling the ranch makes sense. I just can't stand the thought of this place being owned by some foundation for Muslim youth. The ranch is isolated. It requires a dedicated owner to keep it going, and I don't see a bunch of troubled city kids getting the job done."

"What's the name of the foundation?" Drake asked.

"They call themselves the American Muslim Youth Camps Foundation, out of Washington, D.C.," Simpson said. "A local realtor in Klamath Falls presented the offer. I've never met any of them until today. Two of their representatives are here to tour the ranch."

"They're here right now?" Casey asked.

"The two guys in suits, having dinner in the other room. They're staying here at the Lodge tonight."

"Have you had anyone check them out?" Drake asked.

Simpson shook his head. "No, but I was thinking of asking Mike to do it."

Casey looked at Drake before asking, "Do you have an attorney to help you?"

"I haven't decided to accept the offer. Do I need one?" Simpson said.

"Is that something you could help Steve with, Adam?"

"Yes, but I think Steve would be better served by using an attorney around here someone who specializes in ranch real estate. He doesn't need to pay me to travel down from Portland to handle negotiations."

"Couldn't you do that from your office, without needing to travel here?" Casey asked.

"I like to negotiate face-to-face, Mike."

"That's okay," Simpson said. "I've got an attorney in Klamath Falls I've used before. Why don't we head in for dinner, it's getting late. I don't want you guys to miss out on getting some of our mesquite barbequed tri-tip or ribs."

Drake and Casey carried their drinks behind their host into the dining room, where he seated them at a table next to a window, looking out on the meadow. Half of the other tables were occupied by Casey's executive protection team members.

After a quick glance at his menu, Casey looked up and studied Drake when they were alone, "Why don't you want to help Steve?"

"Mike, I like Steve but he doesn't need me. There are plenty of good attorneys in this part of the state. If he needs a referral, I'm happy to give him some names."

"He doesn't need a good attorney. He needs someone who understands the likes of those two guys sitting over there," Casey said with a nod in the direction of the only two men in the dining room wearing suits.

Drake raised his tumbler of bourbon to his lips and turned his head slightly to see the men. They definitely looked to be of Arab descent, but American in appearance, beardless and wearing suits and ties. They were talking quietly, and one of them nodded to Drake when he noticed he was being watched.

"Mike, why don't you order some wine. I'll be right back."

Drake left the dining room and walked into and then back out of the men's room. The two suits were sitting at a table close to the open entrance to the dining room. Drake selected a resort brochure and stood just outside the entrance studying it.

When he'd walked by the two men, he'd heard them speaking Arabic, with what sounded to him to be in the Egyptian dialect.

Leaning his back against the wall, he strained to hear their words. He knew that fifty percent of words in the Egyptian dialect weren't Arabic, from the language training he'd received before deployment in the Middle East. He knew he wouldn't be able to understand everything he heard. but he was sure that when he walked by he'd heard a name he recognized.

And there it was again— "Sheikh Qasseer."

Drake walked quickly back to his table and picked up the glass of red wine Casey had ordered for him. After a taste, he put the glass down and leaned forward with his elbows on the table, looking over at the two men in suits.

"I've changed my mind. I'll help Steve," Drake told his friend. "There's a chance our instructor's fear of another terrorist training camp setting up here in southern Oregon might be justified. Those two were talking about Sheikh Qasseer, the radical cleric and founder of the Army of Allah, the terrorist organization."

Chapter Four

DRAKE LEFT the Alpine Ridge Ranch Sunday morning for the drive home to his farm in the heart of the Oregon wine country. He'd asked Mike Casey to have the competitive intelligence section of his company, Puget Sound Security, dig up everything it could about the American Muslim Youth Project Foundation and any possible connection to Sheikh Qasseer.

On any other day, he would have enjoyed driving the Lake of the Woods Highway past the southern end of Klamath Lake, through the Sky Lakes Wilderness to reach Medford, and then turn north on I-5 in his silver Porsche 993. But today he couldn't stop thinking about the two Arab men at the resort and the possibility that they had some connection to the Sheikh from Bahrain.

The Army of Allah in America had been established in 1980 when Qasseer visited New York. It was made up mostly of African-Americans who had converted to Islam and was a paramilitary organization. Working through front groups, the terror group had established terror training camps throughout the country that had been connected to numerous assassinations, murders and other acts of violence.

What bothered Drake the most was that Qasseer was a Shia

muslim and the two men he'd seen at the resort appeared to be Egyptian. Egypt was the home of the Muslim Brotherhood, the father of modern Islamic terrorism, and was Sunni muslim. While the two terror groups were philosophically aligned, their religious differences in the past had kept them from working together. If they had joined forces for some reason, their marriage didn't bode well for America.

It began snowing lightly as he drove past the Lake of the Woods and the white silence settled over his car. The thought of terrorists setting up camp in America reminded him of one of his favorite songs from Creedence Clearwater Revival, "Run Through the Jungle", and the song's refrain... *"the devil's on the loose, better run through the jungle."*

Drake took his iPod out of the glove box, attached it to his upgraded Becker radio, selected his favorite CCR album and cranked up the volume. When the first drum beats of the song filled the interior, he cracked the window an inch and increased his speed.

After four hours of driving in the rain on I-5 and one fast drive-thru for a cup of coffee in Roseburg, Drake was home. He drove up the long sloping gravel driveway of his forty acre farm outside of Dundee, Oregon and pulled his Porsche, covered in winter road grime, into the garage behind his house.

The "garage" was actually a building that had been built behind his old gray limestone farmhouse, to serve as a tasting room and winery by a Connecticut dentist with a dream of making the best pinot noir wine in the world. After spending a small fortune preparing and planting thirty acres of pinot and chardonnay grape vines on the gently sloping tract, he grew tired of farming and depleting the small fortune he'd inherited, and abandoned the farm to return to the east coast.

He retrieved his canvass duffel bag from the bonnet of the Porsche and walked across the gray stamped concrete parking area in the light rain to the back porch of the farmhouse. In the mud room on the other side of the door, he heard Lancer, his German Shepherd, barking to welcome him home.

"Hi, old buddy," he said as he stepped inside and was greeted by his tail-wagging dog. Drake knelt down and received a wet-tongued kiss on his face as he scratched behind Lancer's ears. "Did you keep the deer out of the vineyard while I was gone?"

Drake took two tenderloin filets out of the refrigerator and opened a bottle of wine before he turned on the gas fireplace in the kitchen. Sharing a small steak with Lancer when he'd been away for a day or had become a tradition, one he knew not to break if he wanted a good night's sleep. Otherwise, Lancer would stand beside his bed, with his head resting on the side of his bed, until he got up and prepared Lancer a reward for guarding their home.

Before he headed to his bedroom to unpack his duffel bag, Drake saw that the message light was blinking on the digital handset receiver on the counter. When he pushed the play button, he heard subdued voice of his secretary, Margo Benning.

"I didn't want to bother you until you returned, but I won't be in to work Monday. Paul's had some bad news and I need to go with him to see his doctor tomorrow morning. Hope you had fun with Mike this weekend. I'll be in as soon as I can."

That wasn't the Margo he knew. She was a rock. He'd never heard her shaken by anything in the seven years they had worked together, except the news that his wife had been diagnosed with cancer. Margo and her husband had been married for twenty five or twenty six years, and were as solid and loving a couple as any he knew.

Drake hit return call and waited for Margo to answer.

"Hi boss," she said.

"What's going on, Margo?"

He heard the catch in her voice.

"Paul has prostate cancer. We're meeting his oncologist tomorrow, to decide on the best course of treatment."

"I'm so sorry, Margo. How's Paul handling the news?"

"He's worried about missing work and finding someone to take over his duties in the Sheriff's Department. He won't admit it, but I know he's scared."

"That sounds like Paul. Don't worry about the office, Margo.

Take as much time as you need and let me know what the doctor says, okay?"

"Sure. I'll see you tomorrow."

Drake sat and stared at the wall. Paul had become a good friend over the years he and Margo had worked together. Hearing he had cancer brought back all the memories and horror of watching his own spouse suffer, and then die.

Chapter Five

MONDAY MORNING, Drake drove the 48 miles from his farm to his law office, deep in thought. Cancer was an enemy that lost as many fights as it won these days, but from his experience the toll it took on both its victim and the victim's family and friends was devastating. He'd hoped he would never have to go through it again, but he knew that was wishful thinking.

Drake pulled onto SW Harbor drive and into the parking garage behind his office on RiverPlace, a promenade lined with shops and restaurants that ran along the Willamette River in downtown Portland.

He parked in his reserved space and took the stairs down to the back door of his office. It was dark inside, with just the light from the windows filtering through the fog hanging over the river outside. When he turned the lights on, he saw that Margo's desk was clear, except for a yellow Post-It. It was dated the day before with a message, "Call me if we haven't talked".

He started a pot of coffee in the break room and grabbed the pink message slips in his in-box before walking up the short flight of stairs to his loft office. Three messages were to be returned immediately, another of Margo's messages said, but he knew that "Immediately" was third on her priority list behind "Urgent" and "Do This Right Now".

While he waited for the coffee to brew downstairs, he called Puget Sound Security in Seattle and asked to speak to Mr. Casey.

"Good morning, Counselor. Nice to see you made into work," Mike Casey said.

"It's 8:30. Bet you didn't run five miles and fight traffic in a forty-minute commute this morning," Drake challenged.

"That's the beauty of living three miles from my office. What's up?"

"Did your research guys come up with anything on the American Muslim Youth Camps or Sheikh Qasseer?"

"Let me check. There's a file on my secretary's desk from research. I'll get it."

Drake put his phone on speaker and used the remote to turn on the flat screen TV on the wall while he waited. Fox News was interviewing a Senator about America's use of drones in Africa.

Casey returned and said, "I'll send this down as an attachment, cause you're going to want to read this. The American Muslim Youth Camp Foundation is a new foundation that was formed last year. The board of directors has a number of D.C. heavy hitters, including Mr. Big himself, John Prescott of the Prescott Group. The foundation's mission statement has the usual dedication to helping troubled youth, blah, blah, blah, "by providing a real ranch experience away from the distractions of city life, and the discrimination American Muslim youth experience there."

"Is there anything about Sheikh Qasseer?"

"Hold on, I'm reading as fast as I can. I don't see his name mentioned. And there's nothing about where the foundation gets its money. I'll send this back to Research. They should have looked into the finances for a group like this."

Drake caught the running Breaking News FOX banner on the TV in his peripheral vision and turned to stare. A 747-8 Boeing Dreamliner had just been shot down taking off from LAX in Los Angeles, on its way to Japan. 451 passengers and crew and no expected survivors.

"You still there?" Casey asked.

"Turn on your TV, FOX News. A jetliner's been shot down in Los Angeles."

A young Latina news reporter from a FOX affiliate was struggling to maintain her composure. Footage shot from a news helicopter was showing widespread debris scattered on the surface of the Pacific about a mile from shore. Black and white LAPD helicopters were keeping the news helicopters at a distance from the crash site.

"My God," Casey said quietly.

"The 747-8's a fairly new jetliner. I thought it had on-board counter measures to protect it against heat-seeking ground-to-air missiles."

"The airlines don't like to talk about it, but most of them do use a flare release system or even C-Music, the newer commercial multi-spectral infrared countermeasure system. Theoretically this wasn't supposed to happen, if the systems were operational."

Drake turned up the volume on his TV.

"*...several eye-witnesses report seeing an object streaking toward the jetliner before it exploded and fell into the sea. They say the object traveled vertically as well as horizontally, and that it turned in flight and veered toward the plane.*"

"She's sure being careful not to call it a missile," Casey commented.

"Or mention terrorism," Drake added. "Let's see how long it takes the government to ground all commercial flights when they conclude this was a missile that took down the plane. They might call it terrorism, but watch them make sure they mention the possibility that it's domestic terrorism."

"We wouldn't want to suggest that terrorists are still a threat, with the President saying we've got al-Qaeda on the run because he's killed so many of its leaders with our drones."

"When did you become such a cynic?" Drake asked.

"Don't get me started. We haven't fought a war to win it since WWII."

"If this is a new wave of terrorism, we better start fighting like we mean it," Drake said. "When people are afraid to fly, we're well on our way to losing again."

After he finished talking with Casey, Drake kept the TV on with the volume turned down the rest of the day. No official in a position to know reported anything that suggested the American public was in danger of a another commercial airliner being shot down but, just to be safe until the government's investigation was complete, commercial air travel was going to be suspended for the next couple of days.

Chapter Six

JOHN PRESCOTT TURNED AWAY from the TV monitor on the wall and stood with his arms folded across his chest. The view from his corner office at the intersection of 11th and K Street afforded him a magnificent view of the Washington, D.C. skyline.

He was reminded once again that anything was possible if you knew the right people in this city. And he knew the right people; one of them just called him from the White House.

The conversation had lasted exactly five seconds: *make sure Los Angeles doesn't screw things up!*

Prescott turned to his desk and buzzed his secretary. "Tell Mark Hassan to come see me," he ordered.

As one of Washington's most powerful lobbyists, he had created the Prescott Group to serve the interests of the progressive power elite. Running point for the administration's secret plan to unfreeze the assets of the ousted Muslim Brotherhood in Egypt, however, was stretching his allegiance to the breaking point.

He remained standing at his desk when the head of his Middle East division knocked once at his door and entered.

"I don't want this plane going down in Los Angeles to impact Senator Boykin's bill to restore Muslim Brotherhood assets in any way," Prescott said. "Make sure the Post plays up the possibility that this is domestic terrorism. The rest of the media will follow the Post, especially with the way Homeland Security keeps calling so many groups domestic terrorists. Then I want you to meet with all of the co-signers of Boykin's bill. Remind them the contributions they received from our Arab Renewal Super Pac. Now is not the time for them to go wobbly on us."

Hassan grinned. "Shall I let them know where the Pac's money came from?"

"That won't be necessary. I think most of them suspect that already, but there's no need to confirm their suspicions, just yet. Let me know if anyone's thinking of changing their vote on the bill. That's all, Mark."

Prescott poured a glass of ice water from the stainless steel pitcher on his back bar and sat down at his glass-topped desk. He had an hour before his meeting at the Willard Hotel for a drink with Senator Boykin, and he needed to know the latest information on the downed jetliner. Boykin was a five-term senator from Missouri who didn't face the voters for another two years, but who always had his finger in the air to tell which way the wind was blowing. Supporting the Arab Spring had been good politics a year ago, but the riots in Cairo had taken the bloom off that rose.

He turned around to the top drawer of his back bar and took out an encrypted iPhone. His encryption service advertised that his conversations were protected, but didn't feel he could take any chances with the call he now had to make. The man he was calling shouldn't be on anyone's surveillance list, but you never knew how far the NSA's program reached. Even to the director of Homeland Security.

"John, I told you not to call me on this phone."

"Sorry, Micah, it couldn't wait. Has your agency determined how that jetliner was brought down?"

"A MANPAD, one of the man-portable air-defense system missiles. It was left at a picnic area at a beach just west of the airport."

"A surface-to-air missile launcher was left behind for someone to find? They wanted you to know who they are. Have you identified them yet?"

"The MANPAD's a Soviet SA-24, like the ones turning up in Syria that went missing in Libya."

"You mean the ones you've been accused of smuggling out of Libya, and providing to the Syrian rebels?"

"There's no evidence of that," the director said defensively, "But it's possible."

"I don't suppose the President wants that to get out."

"That's the kind of leak that will get you killed, John."

"But you don't know who's behind this, do you?"

"Not yet, John. Call me at home from now on."

Prescott looked out through the glass façade of the architectural landmark he owned and stared at the dark gray clouds hanging over the city. It didn't look like it was going to snow, but it was still cold enough in early March for that to happen.

He was going to have to be very careful with Senator Boykin's bill, if he wanted to deliver on the promise he had made the White House. A lot of money had made its way into the coffers of the Arab Renewal Super Pac from U.S. subsidiaries of foreign investment firms owned by Arab investors. The foreign contributions were illegal, both hard to prove and prosecute, but they weren't heavily scrutinized when they were made to members of Congress.

Prescott had successfully navigated the stormy waters of American politics throughout his career, and he wasn't about to let his ship sink because some terrorist was interfering with his plans.

Chapter Seven

BEFORE MARK HASSAN left his office to meet with a friendly reporter for the Post, he first sent a text message to his cousin to meet at their regular place. The Tabard Inn was his cousin's favorite in Washington whenever he visited, and the bar was a great place for a quiet conversation.

Hassan arrived by cab and found a small table at the back of the bar. He knew from experience that his cousin would be watching for a tail from somewhere nearby, for at least fifteen minutes before he entered. Old habits die hard, and Mohamed Hassan had operated safely in Europe and America for most of his life after his father was tortured and died in an Egyptian jail. Since then, Mohamed had served proudly as the Brotherhood's most secret and successful terrorist.

His first Scotch was almost gone by the time Mohamed Hassan walked to his table. Although he was older than Mark, Mohamed could be his twin brother, dressed as if he was in a black cashmere overcoat, gray scarf and Savile Row suit.

After they exchanged the traditional double cheek-kiss greeting, both men sat and smiled at each other.

"I hope this meeting is necessary, brother," Mohamed Hassan said softly.

"The Los Angeles jetliner being shot down could jeopardize our effort to restore your assets. Is the Brotherhood responsible in any way?" Mark Hassan asked directly.

Mohamed shook his head. "It's not us. I don't know about the others, but we haven't heard anything. Is it possible your sheikh is acting out again?"

"He's not *my* sheikh," Mark Hassan said through clenched teeth. "I've helped him purchase land for his camps, but that's all."

"Perhaps you should ask his people, then, if they know anything. *His* camps are used to train *his* Army of Allah. He's been warned not to strike here, but he's ignored our warnings in the past."

"If Sheikh Qasseer is behind this, will the Brotherhood act against him?"

The older Hassan shook his head. "Not directly, but there are other ways. Let me know if you learn anything," Mohamed Hassan said, as he stood and walked out of the bar.

Mark Hassan signaled for a second Scotch and considered his options. Mohamed had always prided himself on the elaborate schemes he executed for the Brotherhood. But those previous plans were nothing, compared to the operation Mohamed was currently orchestrating in the United States.

Mohamed had worked tirelessly with Mark's father, a Georgetown professor of Middle East history, to fine tune and implement the Muslim Brotherhood's 1982 "Project", a sophisticated long term campaign of cultural jihad to conquer the West. The influence they'd developed over the last thirty years now reached into the White House, and to every other important governmental agency, and especially Congress.

With advisors whispering in the ear of the President, it had been relatively easy to encourage his backing of the Muslim Brotherhood's presidential candidate in the last Egyptian election. But the subsequent ouster of their president by the army, and the freezing of the Brotherhood's assets, had severely crippled their plans. That was why it was so important to make sure the members of Congress, who had so readily accepted money from the Arab Renewal Super Pac, continued to support Senator Boykin's bill.

John Prescott, his boss, might have guessed the request from the White House to manage the Boykin Bill would involve more than just a public relations effort to save face for the President, in the midst of the Arab Spring. The White House had, indeed, hailed free elections in Egypt, as proof that democracy could work anywhere. But the president knew the Brotherhood's real purpose was to restore a worldwide totalitarian Islamic caliphate.

Hassan knew from his cousin that the President, without Prescott's knowledge, had also benefitted from foreign Muslim Brotherhood money that had made its way into his campaign coffers. There was no way, therefore, the president could have ignored the demand of the Brotherhood to restore its assets.

Before he met with the reporter from the Post, however, he had to know if anyone involved with the American Muslim Youth Camp Foundation was involved in shooting down the jetliner.

He turned his chair toward the window and called the man who ran the largest of the Foundation's camps 340 miles in western Virginia.

"Assalamu Alaykum, Brother Jameel," Mark Hassam said in greeting.

"And peace be upon you also, Brother Mark," Jameel Marcus answered. "Heard you buying more land for us."

"We made an offer out west. I haven't heard from the owner's attorney yet."

"More camps are needed. People begging to join us."

"How are things, Jameel?"

"Fifty young men, who seem receptive. Could use more money to spread around, though."

"I'll see what I can do. How are the other camps doing?"

"Okay. We the biggest, but they're doing okay?"

"Anyone out west, say in California, who's graduated and found his way?

"That my highest hope, and I believe one has," Jameel Marcus answered, adopting a line from the Muslim Brotherhood's creed to answer the veiled question.

"All right, my Brother, keep up the good work."

Damn, thought Mark Hassan, as he slipped his phone into his coat pocket. Jameel, a black felon who had converted to Islam while in prison and still talked like the ghetto kid that he was, had just confirmed his worst fear. Jameel, the smart and a gifted soldier in the Army of Allah, was confirming that Sheikh Qasseer was responsible for bringing down the jetliner in Los Angeles.

He needed to find out, fast, if anyone else had made the connection. If they had, was there was still a way to paint this as an act of some lone wolf domestic terrorist. The press was gullible, he knew from experience, but it would need some evidence to get the spin started.

Hassan left a twenty on the table and walked out to hail a cab. It was time to meet the distinguished member of the Fourth Estate, who owed him a favor.

Chapter Eight

DRAKE WAS in his office early Tuesday morning, going over the attorney's twelve-page purchase proposal to buy the Alpine Ridge Ranch, when his secretary came in. Margo and her husband lived in Drake's old condo directly above the office, with a private back stairway that connected the two units.

"Good morning, Margo," Drake said from the loft. "Grab a cup of coffee and come join me."

When she walked up and sat in front of his desk, her red and puffy eyes told him that the treatment the oncologist recommended for her husband was more aggressive than she'd hoped it would be.

"I'm guessing you didn't sleep well last night," he said.

Margo sipped her coffee. "Good guess. They want to operate."

"How soon?"

"The day after tomorrow. They're going to do a radical retropubic prostatectomy."

"I'm sorry to hear that, Margo. Go take care of Paul. There's nothing here that won't keep until after his surgery."

"He's at work. He wants to make sure all of his cases are reassigned to detectives he likes. So, you're stuck with me for the day. What are you working on?" she asked.

"Mike asked me to help a friend of his evaluate an offer on the ranch where we stayed Saturday night. Why don't you go through this and break out the contingencies for me. The attorney who drafted this must charge by the page and the hour."

She stood and glanced quickly at the letter he handed her. "What's the American Muslim Youth Camp Foundation?"

"That's a good question. I've asked Mike to have his research people look into it. We're not sure who they are, or where they get the money to buy a place like this."

Margo took the purchase proposal and headed back to her desk.

Drake sat back in his chair and reviewed the notes he'd made while reviewing the purchase proposal. There were so many contingencies enumerated in the proposal that the slightest interference in the way the foundation wanted to operate the ranch would allow them to back out of the deal and get their money back. There was no way he could approve the deal, especially if the foundation had any relationship at all with Sheik Qasseer.

And why would so many of the big hitters in Washington get involved and serve on the board of a foundation like this, he wondered. He hadn't heard that helping troubled muslim youth was the latest *cause celeb* in the capital.

There was one sure way to find out what was going on in Washington, and that was to call his father-in-law, the senior U.S. Senator from Oregon. Accounting for the time difference between left and right coast, he saw that he might reach the Senator before he left his office for lunch.

Drake found the Senator's office number on his contact list and called.

"Senator Hazelton's office, may I help you?"

"Yes, please tell the Senator his son-in-law is calling."

Drake hadn't seen the Senator and his wife, Meredith, since Christmas when they'd been in Oregon for the holidays.

"Adam, sorry to keep you waiting," Senator Hazelton apologized.

"I'm the one interrupting your day, Senator," Drake said. "Do you have a minute, or should I call you at home tonight?"

"Fire away. I'm having a working lunch here in the office. I have as much time as you need."

"I have a new client," Drake explained, "Who's received an offer for his ranch down near Lakeview. The potential buyer is the American Muslim Youth Camp Foundation. Know anything about the foundation?"

"Give me a second to close my door," Senator Hazelton said, "and we'll talk."

Drake heard the Senator clearing his room and then returning to the phone.

"I don't believe in coincidences, Adam. That foundation is what we're working on right now. Congressman Rodecker, from our Second District, came to see me. He's getting pressure from a lobbyist for that foundation to support a bill he doesn't like. The lobbyist mentioned during their meeting the foundation was trying to buy a ranch in his district, and that he'd appreciate any help the congressman could provide."

"What kind of pressure?"

"Rodecker received a campaign donation from the foundation. The subtle quid pro quo was that if he voted for Senator Boykin's bill when it reached the House, they'd make sure no one ever questioned where the donation came from."

"What's a Republican Congressman doing receiving campaign contributions from a group like this, and what's the Boykin bill?"

"This foundation doesn't need to worry about getting support from the other side of the aisle, so it concentrates on our side," Senator Hazelton said. "And Senator Boykin's bill will release all U.S. frozen assets of the Muslim Brotherhood at the request of the new Egyptian government."

"I see," Drake said. "Do you know a lawyer by the name of Mark Hassan, with the Prescott Group?"

"I do. Why?" the senator asked.

"He's the lawyer making the offer for my client's ranch?"

"Have you met him?"

"There's no need to meet him," Drake answered. "The offer is unacceptable. I can tell him that from here."

"Let me suggest you come here to tell him that. Suggest that you might be willing to negotiate, if he's still interested," Senator Hazelton said. "Hassan's the one pressuring Congressman Rodecker. You might be able to help me figure out what's going on with this foundation, and this bill his firm is quarterbacking for Senator Boykin."

"I can't right now, Senator, with commercial flights grounded. Besides, Margo's husband is having prostate surgery the day after tomorrow, and I need to be there for her. Maybe I could come in a couple of days, or so."

"Just come as soon as you can, then," Senator Hazelton requested. "There's something that smells about all of this."

Drake nodded in agreement as he ended the call.

Senator Hazelton was the chairman of the Senate Intelligence Committee. If he had reason to be suspicious of the American Muslim Youth Camps Foundation, Drake's suspicions were confirmed. It was time to meet its lawyer.

Chapter Nine

JOHN PRESCOTT STEPPED out of the elevator on the top floor of his building and entered the lobby of his firm with a big smile on his face. He greeted his receptionist by name and walked to where his secretary stood at her desk. She handed him the morning's phone messages and a copy of the Washington Post newspaper.

When she had helped him off with his overcoat and hung it in the closet in his office, he sat down at his desk to read the Post. The story above the fold revealed that the FBI was looking for an Iraqi vet with PTSD in California as a "possible" person of interest in the downed jetliner investigation. While the vet wasn't called "a person of interest" yet, the story strongly implied that he was and would be apprehended soon.

Mark Hassan had called the night before and reported on his meeting with the reporter from the Post. Hassan assured him that he would be pleased with the story that was going to run, and he had have to say that he was. It was crazy how corrupted the press had become.

Prescott finished the Post story and was reviewing his scheduled appointments for the day, when his secretary knocked lightly on the door. The White House was calling on line one.

"I'll send a car for you," a now familiar voice commanded. "Meet me at Off the Record in an hour."

Prescott started to respond that the famous bar at the Hat-Adams Hotel didn't open until 11:30 a.m., when his summoner ended the call. But Layla Nebit would know that. He also knew that when the bar opened to the public didn't mean a thing to the Princess of Power in the West Wing.

He had enough time for two phone calls he needed to make before his meeting. The first was to Mark Hassan.

"I've been summoned to meet with Layla Nebit in an hour. How are we coming on Senator Boykin's bill?" he asked.

"The Senate won't be a problem, as expected. The House is wary of the bill, but most of the Representatives have been contacted by Muslim spokesman in their districts we've coordinated with. I think the majority of them are afraid of being called Islamophobes. There are a few new members in the House who are organizing opposition. I'm still worried about them," Mark Hassan reported.

"How many are there?"

"Five."

"What do we have that we can use against them?"

"They've all received small contributions from the American Muslim Youth Camps Foundation, but that's all we have so far."

"Do what you need to do to crush them," Prescott ordered. "Get back to me by the end of the day. I'll tell Nebit we have it handled. Don't make me a liar."

Prescott's second call was to his source in the FBI.

"Let me guess," Josiah Bennett, the deputy director of the FBI's Counterterrorism Division said, "you have a lunch meeting and you need to know what we've learned about the jetliner."

Prescott faked surprise. "Josiah, I'm appalled that you would think that. I thought we might have lunch sometime this week."

"If you're buying, of course. Now, what is it you want to know, John?"

"Have you found the vet you're looking for?"

"Damn reporters," Bennett snorted. "I have no idea how that

story got started. There is no vet with PTSD that we have any reason to believe was involved with bringing down that jetliner. The MANPAD tube we found was a Soviet SA-24. No one wants to say the "T" word, but this has foreign terrorist involvement written all over it."

"How long before that gets out?" Prescott asked.

The way this White House controls the media, who knows."

"All right, thanks, Josiah. I'll be in touch."

Prescott sat back in his chair. When he'd arrived an hour ago, he thought the prospects for the Boykin bill looked good. Now, they were starting to look as bleak as the gray winter day outside.

Layla Nebit was not going to like what he had to tell her. When the manhunt focused on foreign terrorism, any link the White House had to the Muslim Brotherhood would become toxic, including Laya Nebit's past.

The press had looked the other way when her family's ties to the Brotherhood were first rumored, and then seized upon by talk radio and conservative pundits. But they wouldn't this time. They would sharpen their claws when terrorism became the story of the day. The fact that she was one of the most powerful people in D.C. would only postpone the inevitable for so long.

The trick, he knew, was going to be keeping the White House happy, until he found a back door he could sneak out of. At the moment, however, all he could see was a solid brick wall as long as he was seen as Layla Nebit's lap boy. Maybe it was time to change that perception.

Prescott walked through the lobby of the Hay-Adams Hotel and made his way downstairs to the Off The Record bar. She was sitting alone and he was stunned to see her slender hand wrapped around the stem of a martini glass.

Nebit signaled to the bartender to bring another for Prescott, before he sat down.

"We have a problem," she said, and handed him a plain manila folder. "No one outside the White House has seen this."

Prescott opened the folder and stared at the single page inside. *In the name of Allah, the most merciful, you have been warned.*

Unless all of the demands listed below are fulfilled, your planes will continue to fall from the sky.

1. Stop supplying the rebels in Syria.
2. End all financial and military aid to Israel.
3. End the President's drone program immediately.
4. Release all Guantanamo detainees immediately.

There are 49 remaining SA-24's in America.
To make sure that you understand this message, another will be used today.
Allah's Sword

"When did you get this?" he asked.

"It was on the back seat of my limousine this morning," she said. "I have no idea how it got there."

Prescott waited for the bartender to leave after his martini was delivered and took a drink. "My god, Layla. What's the President going to do?"

"Hoping this isn't real," she said, with a tight smile. "He's screaming at the Director of National Intelligence at the moment. I had to leave."

She's looking for a way to distance herself from this disaster too, Prescott thought. *Maybe there is a way we can both survive this.* "What do you need from me?" he said.

She finished off her martini and leaned closer. "You know this town, John. What options will we have if another plane is shot down?"

Chapter Ten

DRAKE WAS RUNNING along Worden Road a half mile from his farm early Wednesday morning when his watch vibrated and signaled that he'd received an email. He wasn't sure about the new Dick Tracy gadget. His secretary insisted that he try it out, so he'd stay in better touch with the office.

He'd decided to take the morning off and get in a good run. He needed to find a way to get to Washington as soon as possible, but he figured the message would wait until he finished his five mile run.

"Come on Lancer," he said to his dog running beside him, "I'll race you home."

Drake watched as Lancer put his head down and sped off. *Show off*, he thought.

Drake increased his pace and chased after his dog. When he reached the long gravel driveway leading up to his house, Lancer was waiting with his tail wagging, ready to play again.

"Stay," Drake commanded and jogged up the two-hundred-yard driveway. When he was fifty yards from the old stone farmhouse, he whistled for Lancer to join him and sprinted for home.

He'd reached the first step on the back porch and before he

could turn around, felt a not-so-gentle nudge on his right glute, as Lancer tagged him.

"Looks like you lost, big guy," he laughed, as he scratched behind his dog's ears. "Maybe that will stop your gloating when we reach the driveway on our run."

Drake opened the door and followed Lancer through the mud room to the kitchen, where he opened a can of grain-free protein dog food for his companion before checking his email message. It wasn't from his secretary. It was from a woman he was looking forward to seeing again soon in D.C.

"CALL ME. IT'S IMPORTANT"

Drake hit speed dial #7.

"Hi Liz," he said. "What's up?"

"Congressman Rodecker's in the hospital," Liz Strobel said. "Senator Hazelton wants you here as soon as possible."

Drake sat down at his kitchen table and asked, "What's happened?"

"He was beaten and left unconscious on the steps of the Lincoln Memorial. He's in the ICU."

"Liz, if he's unconscious, what can I do?" Drake asked. "The Senator just wanted me to talk with him."

"You will, when he's conscious," she said. "But we think this wasn't a random beating. Someone stuffed a copy of Senator Boykin's bill in the pocket of his jacket with "Read It!" written in red. He was being warned."

Drake paused, and took a deep breath. "Okay, tell the Senator I'll be there as soon as I can. Are you okay?"

"I'm fine," she said, and then added, "I miss you."

He was surprised by her directness and wasn't sure how to respond. He remembered the kiss she'd given him in San Francisco, as well as the guilt he felt about liking her kiss.

"I'll let you know when I'm arriving, Liz," he said and ended the call.

In the small bathroom off the old study he was now using as his bedroom, Drake ran cold water over his face and stared into the ice blue eyes looking back at him in the mirror. Since his wife, Kay, had died two years ago, Liz Strobel was the only woman he'd been attracted to.

She'd been the executive assistant to the Director of Homeland Security when they'd met. Tall and beautiful and smart, she was now the senior advisor for intelligence and homeland security on his father-in-law's Senate staff.

Drake dried his face, ran fingers through his hair, and pointed at the mirror. Get a grip, he told himself. One kiss doesn't mean you're in love, so don't get all worked up over it. Kay had told him before she died to find someone. and was probably laughing at him right now, saying "I told you not to worry about it, you big lug."

I'm not there yet, Kay, he thought, *but I'm trying to work on it.*

Drake stripped down and took a shower. The stinging hot water started to relax the muscles in his legs and back, and the oxygenated steamy air fueled the formulation of a plan in his mind.

When he was dressed, he called his friend, Mike Casey, in Seattle.

"Mike, do you have a protection team currently available?" he asked.

"Who's the protectee?"

"Oregon Congressman Rodecker," Drake said. "Liz just called and said he's in a hospital in D.C. Someone's playing hardball about a bill he's fighting."

"How many men will he need?" Casey asked.

"Two for now," Drake said. "I'll know if more are needed when I get there."

"How soon do you need them?"

"Can you fly them there tomorrow?" Drake asked, and then added, "With a brief stopover in Portland to pick me up?"

"The Gulfstream just got back from a run to Hawaii. I can have it there in the morning. You need me to ride shotgun for you?" Casey asked.

Drake laughed. "I don't think your wife would appreciate me asking, after what happened in San Francisco."

"Well, Megan does think the lady assassin who poisoned me by mistake was a hooker coming to your room," Casey chortled. "How long do you think you'll need the team?"

"I have no way of knowing, Mike."

"Tell you what," Casey said, "I've always wanted to see the cherry trees in bloom in the capital. There's business I can do while I'm there. Buy me dinner at some extravagantly expensive restaurant and I'll discount the travel expense for your Congressman."

"You're on," Drake said. "Text me your ETA and bring along whatever your research guys were able to dig up about the American Muslim Youth Camps Foundation. We'll kill two birds with one trip to D.C."

Chapter Eleven

RETURNING from his meeting at the Hay-Adams with Layla Nebit, John Prescott had sequestered himself in his office to think about what, if any, options the president had if the terrorist group calling itself Allah's Sword shot down another jetliner.

He concluded the options were limited, in terms of national security. But that wasn't his worry. The United States didn't meet the demands of terrorists, at least openly, and wouldn't start doing it now.

The President's problem, however, from a PR perspective, was the perception that he was soft on terrorism, even with his drone program.

The option that kept floating to the surface of his mind, as simple as it sounded, was finding someone to blame. Some nation or group that would draw attention from the Muslim Brotherhood and Senator Boykin's bill. Focus the media and world attention on an enemy everyone could agree on, like Syria.

Prescott ran through the givens he had to work with:

- The U.S. had supported the Syrian rebels against the abusive Assad regime.

- Syrian rebels had been the recipient of the MANPAD shoulder-fired missiles that America had collected in Libya and secretly into to Syria.
- Many of those MANPADS had fallen into the hands of Assad's forces.
- Syria had turned to Russia for help and got the President to blink, convincing Assad that the President was afraid of challenging Russia.
- Who, then, would deny that Assad was crazy and reckless enough, after gassing his own people and giving the finger to the West, to shoot down some American jetliners in retaliation for America's support of the rebels he was fighting, when he knew Putin had his back?

Syria was the perfect patsy. It provided the generals in the Pentagon a righteous reason to strike at Syria. The White House would just have to find a way to make the world believe the Syrian leader was responsible for the attacks.

Prescott fine tuned his plan for another hour before he called Layla Nebit at the White House, and invited her to meet him at the Hay-Adams the next day.

―――

DOWN THE HALLWAY in another office, Mark Hassan berated Jameel Marcus for the way his men had dealt with Congressman Rodecker. He stood behind his desk, facing an original watercolor painting of the perfection of the Egyptian Pyramids on the wall, and struggling to calm himself.

"I ask you to rough him up, not put him in the hospital, Jameel!"

"That cracker put his self in the hospital! He should know better than fight back."

Hassan took a deep breath. "Call off your men on the other four. That's an order. I'll find another way."

"Hassan, I don't take orders from you," Jameel hissed. "I do you favors when I want to. When it works for *US*! It's time for jihad,

Hassan. You want to join the fighting', you call me. Otherwise, stay the hell away."

Hassan let the beauty of his painting sooth his anger for a minute, then sat down and called his contact in the NSA on an encrypted iPhone.

"Carl, this is Mark Hassan. We met at a fundraiser Layla Nebit hosted. My firm lobbied against some of the bills that were aimed at putting you guys out of business."

"I remember, Mr. Hassan," Carl Sumner said. "What can I do for you?"

"We're helping the White House with Senator Boykin's bill. They're interested in knowing about any opposition the bill is facing."

"Send me the names. I'll see what I can do."

"Thank you, Carl. I'll make sure Ms. Nebit knows you were helpful."

Carl Sumner was an ambitious young climber in the NSA. Hassan knew that when Layla Nebit introduced Sumner to the Prescott Group, she was passing him along as a valuable resource. No one played the game better than she did, even John Prescott, and using her name in D.C. was almost as good as having a executive order from the President.

THE HAPPY HOUR crowd had filled the Off the Record bar at the Hay-Adams Hotel by the time Layla Nebit made her way to Prescott's table, stopping at a dozen tables to exchange greetings with her unofficial constituency. She had the President's ear and bestowed blessings on the few she favored, while everyone else hoped to be counted among the few. That desire to be considered an insider gave Nebit an immense amount of power.

Prescott wasn't jealous. He'd seen presidential power players come and go, and knew how quickly their power waned when their reign was over. But Layla Nebit was different. Her power didn't just exist because she had the run of the White House, as a derivative of her close personal relationship to the president. Nebit's power existed because of the genuine fear she created in people, Prescott included.

Layla Nebit had been born in Egypt, the daughter of the former Egyptian Ambassador to the United Nations and her mother, an Egyptian movie star. She stayed in the U.S. when her father retired and returned to Egypt, and became an American citizen. Before her father left for Egypt with her mother, Layla had already inherited a keen understanding of geopolitics and, from her mother, a grasp of the ancient and great power an intelligent woman could have over men.

But it was also her ties to the upper echelon of the Muslim Brotherhood when she was younger that gave her power. Before the recent rise to power of the Muslim Brotherhood in Egypt, Prescott had lobbied for the Egyptian government. From the records the government maintained on the outlaw organization, he'd been able to confirm Nebit's ties to the Muslim Brotherhood. He also accepted recent reports of people mysteriously disappearing who crossed her as true and convincing evidence that her relationship with the original terrorist organization was still strong, and not to be overlooked.

And now, here she was, the president's closest and most beautiful advisor, sitting down at his table and making everyone in the place envy him.

"I hope you're worth the money we pay you," she warned preemptively, "because the second jetliner was shot down twenty minutes ago. The networks are covering us for now and not releasing everything they know. They know this isn't just another disturbed vet, it's terrorism. What are our options?"

Chapter Twelve

THE PUGET SOUND Security Gulfstream G450 landed at the Washington Dulles International Airport. It taxied to the Landmark Aviation services hub, where Mike Casey had arranged for the plane to be serviced and parked for the duration of their stay.

Two white Chevy Tahoe's, rented on-site from Hertz, were quickly loaded with gear and luggage for the drive to Georgetown University Hospital, where Congressman Rodecker was still in the ICU.

"Liz will meet us at the hospital," Drake said in the lead Tahoe, as he and Mike Casey drove out of the parking lot. "She thinks they'll be able to move the Congressman to a private room tomorrow."

"Why would anyone want to put a Congressman in the hospital over his vote on a bill?" Casey asked. "Why not just unleash the IRS on him, or start a rumor that he was a child molester or something."

Drake shrugged. "Maybe it doesn't have anything to do with his vote. D.C.'s a tough town, sure. But if the senator thinks Rodecker needs protection, there's more to it than just random violence."

GPS directed Drake onto I-66 from the airport, then over the

Francis Scott Key Memorial Bridge to M Street and the campus of Georgetown University.

When they drove into the parking lot, east of the main red brick building of the hospital, they found Liz Strobel waiting for them at the main entrance to the first floor lobby. She gave each of them a hug and led them to the bank of elevators.

"Thank you for coming so quickly," she said. "The Congressman's in the Neurosurgical Intensive Care Unit in a coma. They're monitoring his intercranial pressure to see if he needs surgery. If the pressure continues to ease, he'll be moved to a private room tonight."

Drake held the door open for her when the elevator arrived, and asked, "How bad is it, Liz?"

She punched the button for the sixth floor and said, "It's bad. He took a vicious stomping, judging from the bruising and marks on his head and body. Broken ribs, contusions everywhere, and the subdural hematoma causing the coma."

"Why does the senator think he still needs protection?" Mike Casey asked.

"Because he can identify his attacker or attackers," she said. "His defensive wounds indicate that he put up a pretty good fight before he went down."

"I brought two of my best protectors, Liz," Casey said. "He'll be safe in here. One of them will be with him round the clock."

"Thanks Mike," she said as they reached the sixth floor and the Neurosurgical ICU. "I'll introduce you and your men to hospital security, and then let's go to the café on the second floor where we can talk."

Drake watched as she introduced Casey and his two men to hospital security in the hallway. The PSS protection team consisted of a former Army Ranger and a former Marine Force Recon. Both were dressed in blazers, button-down shirts without ties and gray slacks. They still looked to be, however, every bit the spit and shine soldiers they had recently been. Puget Sound Security was known for hiring the best of the best when they left the military, and these two men were no exception.

Standing alone back by himself during the introductions, Drake felt the cold dread of the place penetrate his senses; the smells, the controlled movements of the nurses as they rushed about, the grief and panic on the faces of family and friends sitting in the waiting area. His mother had been a nurse and she had died in a place like this when a drunk teenager ran a stop sign and T-boned her car. He'd been a high school senior then and he remembered that hospital all too well.

He saw Liz Strobel shake the hands of both of Casey's men and then walk to him with Casey in tow.

"Let's go get some coffee and I'll tell you what we know," she said, as they re-entered the elevator and rode down to the café.

After a quick trip through the cashier's line, they were seated around a table near the window.

"How's your new job?" Drake asked Strobel.

She pushed her hair back over her left ear before saying, "Your father-in-law's a wonderful man, Adam. He's pretty much allowing me to handle my work as his liaison with the Senate Intelligence committee as I see fit. I know most of the staff on the committee from my work at DHS. So, working for a senior Senator makes my job pretty easy."

Mike Casey leaned toward her and asked, "What can you tell us about the two jetliners, Liz?"

"We know that a vet with PTSD isn't responsible," she said firmly.

"I didn't believe for a second," Casey bristled. "Our enemy kills innocents, not us."

Strobel conceded the point with a nod of her head. "The launch tube for a Russian SA-24 was found on the beach in L.A., just west of the airport. We think it's one of the ones we rounded up in Libya that wound up in the hands of the Syrian rebels."

Drake raised his hands in surrender. "We'll never learn, will we," Drake said. "You would think after providing arms to bin Laden in Afghanistan to fight the Russians, and then having those same weapons used against us in Iraq, we'd stop arming our enemies. Has anyone claimed responsibility for the plane yet?"

"DHS is briefing the Senator's Intelligence committee tomorrow, but so far I haven't heard that anyone has."

Casey stood and said, "If you'll excuse me, I need to find a place for us to stay. Any recommendations, Liz?"

"The Georgetown University Hotel is here on campus. There's a Holiday Inn a half a mile away, and the Savoy Suites Hotel about a mile away. My choice would be the Savoy."

When Casey left to make room reservations, Liz put her hand on Drake's arm and said, "Senator Hazelton said to tell you you're welcome to stay with them, and there's room for Mike as well. He wants you to come over for dinner tonight, if you're available. There are some things he wants to discuss with you in private."

"Will you be there?" Drake asked.

Strobel smiled and said, "I think private means private. You need to see your in-laws tonight. I offered to take you to dinner when you were in D.C., so pick a night."

Chapter Thirteen

AFTER CHECKING with Casey to make sure the Congressman was well-guarded, Drake took a shower and donned a sports coat and tie at the Savoy in the room he was sharing with Mike Casey. Appropriately dressed for dinner with a senior United States Senator, even if he was his father-in-law, Drake took one of the rented Tahoes and drove a short distance to N Street NW, in Georgetown.

It was the first time he'd been to his in-laws new home, and he was impressed. It was a white brick, two story row house built in the Federal architectural style. Its stately look fit the Hazeltons; classy and understated, unlike so much of the capital architecture.

Drake rang the doorbell at the top of a short flight of stairs and was warmly greeted by his mother-in-law, Meredith Hazelton, when she opened the door.

"Oh honey," she said, as she kissed him on the cheek and slipped her arm through his, pulling him into her house, "come in. I'm so glad you're here."

"Me too," Drake said, as he stepped inside. "Your home's a beauty."

"It is, isn't it," she beamed. "It was built in 1900, but it's been completely remodeled. Come, I'll show you around."

Drake followed as she led him through the first floor, and then up the stairs to the family area on the second floor. There were two separate bedroom suites at either end of the floor, she pointed out, with a common area that served as the family room in the middle. Across the room from the built-in entertainment center on the north side of the floor, was a closed mahogany four-panel door on the opposite south side.

Meredith Hazelton motioned to the door for Drake to go in. "The Senator wanted a word with you in the library before dinner. I'll come get you when it's ready."

Senator Hazelton was sitting in a brown leather chair, with an opened bottle of bourbon on a round glass-topped iron end table beside him. He looked up from a file he was reading and stood.

"Thanks for getting here so quickly, Adam," the senator walked over and welcomed him with a hug. "Care for a drink?"

"Sure," Drake said, as he looked around the room while his father-in-law walked to a wet bar at the far end of the den. Floor-to-ceiling bookshelves covered both walls, filled with an extensive collection of first edition books on American history, politics and the Constitution.

"I've added a few new ones since I moved the collection here from Portland," Senator Hazelton said, returning with a Bourbon glass etched with an "H".

Drake poured himself two fingers of the amber whiskey and sat on the leather sofa facing the senator. "I asked Mike Casey to bring a two-man protection detail for Congressman Rodecker. He'll be guarded for as long as he's in the hospital if you think that's necessary."

"Sadly, I'm afraid it might be," the senator said, shaking his head. "There are five young Turks in Congress, all newly elected and rebellious as hell. They're working to rally opposition to the Boykin bill. Before Roger Rodecker was attacked, the other four had thought they were being followed. So, this wasn't a random attack. Someone was trying to intimidate all of them."

"Is this bill that important?"

"It is for the Muslim Brotherhood, certainly. Our releasing its assets would send a clear signal to the generals in Egypt, that they may not have the support here they think they have."

"But won't strong arm tactics only strengthen opposition to the bill?" Drake asked.

"Sure," the senator nodded. "It doesn't make a lot of sense, but there are a lot of things going on that don't make much sense. But the Muslim Brotherhood has quietly exerted their influence before, without resorting to this type of behavior."

"Their democratically-elected president, though, hadn't been dethroned either," Drake pointed out.

Senator Hazelton raised his glass and conceded the point. "So, with that said, why are terrorists hitting us now?"

Before Drake answered, the senator's wife knocked on the door and announced that dinner was ready.

As both men stood, Drake looked his father-in-law squarely in the eye and said, "Because they're not afraid of us. Congress has allowed the president, unchecked, to undue everything we've fought for since 9/11."

"That's not fair, Adam, even if it appears to be true," Senator Hazelton said and motioned for Drake to walk ahead of him as they left the library. "As Commander in Chief, the President has the authority to bring our troops home, whenever he decides it's time. The Constitution only gives us the power to declare war and authorize expenditures for it. But **WWII** was the last time Congress actually declared war. Since then, presidents have pretty much done what they please with our use of force around the world."

"I didn't mean any disrespect, Senator," Drake stopped and said before walking down the stairs. "But when I see the president wanting to sit down with our enemies and negotiate his way to peace without a word of protest from Congress, I want to throw up.

Drake started down, then turned on the first step and said, "This is an enemy you can't trust, Senator! President Jefferson understood that in 1801 and created a navy to kick some Islamic butt in Tripoli. We need to keep doing the same until *they* beg for peace, not us."

When the two men reached the bottom of the stairs, Drake felt he'd said too much. He didn't know what Congress did or didn't do to oppose the president's foreign policy in the Middle East. But he did know, and he did understand the enemy. He wasn't sure that most politicians did.

If shooting down jetliners and killing innocent people didn't wake people up from their post-9/11 slumber, he thought, God help America.

Chapter Fourteen

WHEN MOHAMED HASSAN operated in America, he conducted his official business as an investment banker. His firm's Washington, D.C, executive offices were in the historic Evening Star Building on Pennsylvania Avenue, 2,500 feet from the White House.

As Washington worked to become the new Wall Street, after the collapse of Lehman Brothers in 2008, most major investment firms had opened offices there, to facilitate the demands of the government for financial intelligence that ranged from inside information on prospective deals, major financial firm's new hires, and even executive compensations. The American capital became *the* place to operate as an international investment banking firm, like Hassan's Gulf Alliance Capital of London.

Washington had also become a necessary base of operation for the Muslim Brotherhood, well before the eruption of the so-called Arab Spring. For the most part, the *West* that Islamists vowed to destroy was the Great Satan America. More so than its European puppets. To defeat your enemy you had to know your enemy, and Mohamed Hassan had come to know his enemy very well. He had taken as his lover the one woman in America who knew all of its secrets; Layla Nebit, the personal advisor of the president.

Hassan drove his black Gembala Porsche 911 this night from the first-floor underground parking level of the Evening Star Building out onto Pennsylvania Avenue and headed to Layla Nebit's ultra-chic millionaire condo in Georgetown. The two had been lovers since her seduction in London, when she had accompanied the president on a visit with the Prime Minister prior to a G12 conference.

Layla opened her door with a glass of champagne for him. She was wearing a black sheer lace robe that did little to hide her black bra and panties.

"You're late," she pouted.

"I see you're ready for bed."

"This isn't just for you, Mohamed. I get tired of wearing business clothes all day."

"Of, course," he said. "And you would *never* dress like this for anyone in the White House."

She reached up and started to undue his necktie. "Of course not, not with this in mind," she said, as she pulled him inside.

Later, as they sat up against the pillows arranged along the black satin headboard of her bed and finished the last of the Veuve Champagne Cliq she preferred, he asked, "Is the president still willing to support our bill?"

Layla set her empty champagne flute on the night stand and snuggled against him. "He wants to, but with these demands from **Allah's Sword** and the country's policy of not negotiating with terrorists, he doesn't see how he can do anything that will appear to favor the Brotherhood."

"But doesn't he realize," Mohamed said patiently, "that if it's discovered the MANPADs being used are the ones he'd gathered up in Libya and then supplied to the rebels in Syria, that he'll be blamed? That's what Iran and the shias wants! They want to embarrass America for being on the wrong side and fighting against Assad and Hezbollah in Syria. He needs to help us fight them."

Hassan knew that Nebit was a Sunni and supported the Muslim Brotherhood. Her family in Egypt had been closely tied to them in earlier days. But of late, she seemed to be more concerned with politics in her adopted country than the jihad they were both committed to.

Hassan set his champagne glass down and lightly traced the curve of her breast against his chest with the tips of his fingers. "If the president was convinced Iran was responsible for shooting down the jetliners, would he be willing to take action against it? Would he see *it* was the enemy, and allow us to help him?"

"It's possible," she said, as she smiled up and slipped her hand slowly down his chest. "But he would have to be certain Iran was behind this."

Hassan allowed Layla to satisfy her curiosity beneath the sheets and prepared himself to satiate his slightly drunken lover.

WHEN HE WAS sure the exhausted Layla wouldn't wake up soon, Hassan slipped out of her bed. He made his way in the dark to the sofa nearest the balcony, retrieved his clothes and then moved silently down the hall to her office.

Her white MacBook Pro was sleeping on her desk, and opened quickly to the file that contained her White House notes. He'd obtained her password from a keystroke device that he'd used on the laptop not long after their affair began. Layla was the president's most-trusted advisor and confidante and, while she was a brilliant political strategist, she was also remarkably naïve about her role in the civilization jihad they'd begun over thirty years ago.

She had been tasked by the Muslim Brotherhood to direct and influence the affairs of state, by utilizing her close relationship with the current president. The Muslim Brotherhood's plan to destroy Western civilization from within; by presenting Islam as an honorable alternative to the excesses of the West, and by exploiting the destructive policies of cultural relativism, multiculturalism and diversity, and intolerant political correctness, until the American *idea* no longer worked.

In this, she had been remarkably successful. Far more successful than the leadership of the Muslim Brotherhood had dreamed possible in any of their lifetimes. America was untethering itself from its historic underpinnings and was adrift. It was floundering in its choppy sea of secularism.

But there was also a war being fought in the Middle East, between the aggressive and belligerent Shia Islamist movement, sponsored by Iran and led by Hezbollah, and the more patient Sunni jihadists who had the long view of securing the world for Islam.

The Shia's of Iran could not be allowed to dominate the Middle East, or undue everything he and Layla and the Muslim Brotherhood had achieved in America.

And that was what **Allah's Sword** was doing by shooting down jetliners. His plan had been to sell MANPADs to Sheikh Qaseem and replenish the Brotherhood's coffers. But it had not been to tarnish the image of Islam in America for a lifetime.

While Layla had her job, his job was to make sure Iran and Syria took the blame. He fervently hoped Layla's notes from her meetings with the president he was downloading onto his flash drive would show him how to do just that.

Chapter Fifteen

THE UPROAR across the country was instantaneous, when the major networks broke the news Friday morning. It was confirmed, by an anonymous administration source, that the second jetliner Wednesday evening had also been intentionally shot down.

"CLOSE THE AIRPORTS!" the Washington Post demanded.

"AIRLINES THREATEN FLIGHT **CANCELLATIONS IF SAFETY CAN'T BE GUARANTEED"** the L.A. Times warned.

"PRESIDENT PROMISES JUSTICE! **CONSIDERS MARTIAL LAW,** the New York Times assured the nation.

RADIO TALK SHOW hosts were more critical.

. . .

"IF THIS PRESIDENT *wasn't blind, he'd see that al Qaeda isn't*
 on the run. It's attacking us here because he didn't finish
 the job over there," a former Congressman from a flyover state
 opined.

"TRY *and negotiate your way out of this one, Mr. President,*"
 another challenged him.

DRAKE WAS HAVING breakfast in the Savoy Suites Hotel restaurant with Mike Casey as he scanned the front page of the Post.

"You think they know who they're looking for?" Drake asked, refilling his coffee cup from the carafe on their table.

Casey spread a generous amount of strawberry jam on his toast and said, "Not unless some group's stupid enough to take credit for the two planes. The FBI keeps a close eye on the known terrorist groups operating here."

"That's not going to help much with our open-border policy. Any terrorist with a shoulder-fired missile who wants to pay us a visit can find a way in. More than a million of the man-portable air defense system missiles have been manufactured in the world. Gadhafi alone had 20,000 of them, and 15,000 of his stockpile are reported missing in Libya."

"Well, if the airlines stop flying and the economy slams to a halt," Casey said, pointing to the headline on the paper Drake had just put down, "they'd better find these guys quick. When the funerals start showing up on TV, people will be in the streets if this drags on for very long."

Drake just shook his head. "Then imagine what will happen if martial law is declared."

"I can't," Casey said. "But, if that happens, I'm going to be back home with Megan and the kids."

"About us getting home," Drake asked, "What's the latest on Congressman Rodecker?" Drake asked. "Is he still in a coma?"

Casey took his cell phone out and called his protection team leader at the hospital. "I'll check."

The other tables in the restaurant were being used, for the most part, by businessmen and women in the capital, to do business in one form or another. No one seemed overly concerned about the threat to their safety. If they were aware, they certainly appeared to have complete faith in their government's ability to protect them.

Casey finished the call. "They think he's coming around. We should get over there."

Drake signed for their breakfast and asked for their Tahoe to be brought up. It was cold when they got outside to wait beside the valet stand. But the sky was clear and held the promise of a bright spring day.

At the hospital, Casey led the way to the Congressman's private room on the sixth floor. Both men from the protection detail were standing in the hall outside the room.

"The doctor and his team are inside," Ryan Mitchell, the former Army Ranger said. "They're bringing him out of his coma. I just got here to change watch with Brad, but he says the nurse he's been flirting with told him we should be able to talk with him soon."

"That's good news," Casey said. "You two go get some coffee. Drake and I will stay here and talk with the doctor when he comes out."

Before the two protectors reached the elevator down the hall, the door to the congressman's suite opened and a young nurse stepped out.

"Doctor Wah will be out shortly," she informed them. "You'll be allowed a few minutes with the Congressman, but don't expect much. As I told Brad, the man you had guarding him, he might not be coherent right away. We understand that you need to speak with him, but please don't agitate him. He's been badly beaten."

Drake watched her walk away. "Your Brad has good taste."

"I only hire the best," Casey said, with a grin. He was still grinning when the doctor joined them.

"Since you're not family," Dr. Wah said curtly, "I can only give you a general accounting of his condition. He is conscious, in great pain. He was beaten savagely, but he will recover in time. He may not remember anything about the attack. Please do not pressure him to remember. You may see him, but only for a few minutes."

With that, the diminutive doctor turned and followed the nurse down the hall.

Drake and Casey entered Congressman Rodecker's room and stood beside his bed. One nurse was checking the bandages on his head, while another nurse was writing notes on his chart.

His face was swollen and bruised, but his eyes were open and followed them intently.

Drake leaned down and introduced himself. "My name is Adam Drake. I'm Senator Hazelton's son-in-law. This is Mike Casey from Puget Sound Security. His men have been here protecting you, in case your attacker returned. Can you help us identify him?"

Rodecker nodded slightly and spoke softly through swollen lips. "Twenties, black." After two deep breaths, he continued, "Ragged beard, diamond in both ears." Another pause, then, "He yelled that "Akbar" thing.. and I smelled marijuana."

The beeping of the heart rate monitor accelerated and the nurse at the foot of the bed waved for them to leave.

"That's enough, out," she said, as she shooed them out the door.

In the hallway Casey said, "That's not much to go on."

"No, but it points in one direction, doesn't it," Drake responded.

Chapter Sixteen

JOHN PRESCOTT WAS ESCORTED to the Navy Mess on the ground floor of the West Wing of the White House, where he found Laya Nebit eating lunch. She was sitting at the head of a long table in the Ward Room of the mess, making notes on a legal pad next to plate of Salad Nicoise. The red of the seared tuna nearly matched the color of the dark mahogany paneling in the small, private room.

Nebit took off her purple reading glasses and looked up at Prescott. "I thought you should know the president is holding a press conference this afternoon. I've spent the morning going over the points I want him to make."

Prescott pulled out a chair and sat down. There wasn't another place setting on the table, and he clearly hadn't been invited to join her for lunch. "Are you going to blame Syria and Iran for shooting down the two airliners?"

"He knows the idea was yours," she said. "So, for your sake, it had better work. He will announce that he's sending another aircraft carrier and three more guided-missile cruisers to the Mediterranean. He will display the discarded tube from the Russian SA-24 MANPAD, and say we have clear evidence that it belonged to Hezbollah in Syria. He will also warn that any interference by

Russia, in any action he may be forced to take in Syria, would be an act of war."

Prescott sat back, stunned. "Layla, I never suggested that we go to war. I was thinking about a leak from some anonymous administration source, that you're just looking into the possibility that Syria was responsible. The media would run with it and deflect attention away from any security lapses that may have occurred."

"He's getting killed in the polls, John," Nebit said firmly." He needs to appear to be an angry leader, who won't let innocent Americans be killed without someone being held accountable."

"For god's sake Layla, we don't have any evidence that Syria's involved. What will he do if the threat of war doesn't work, and another airliner's shot down? He'll be forced to take action."

"Nebit dismissed his concern with a wave of her hand. "We've got that covered. We're going to protect all our major airports with drones. We'll be able to spot any threat and take them out with the Sidewinder missiles they'll carry. The Air Force assured us they can handle it."

Prescott focused on an oil painting of Valley Forge on the wall behind Nebit's head. He knew how Americans were going to react with armed surveillance drones flying over all the major airports. They didn't trust the government as it was, without armed drones flying over their heads.

"What do you want me to do?" he asked quietly.

Nebit picked up her reading glasses and put them back on. "Use the time you have to get ahead of this. Let your media contacts know that the president is confident the actions he's prepared to take against Syria will end this crisis. Create the narrative that will make him look like our savior. You've done it before."

When she began making notes again on her legal pad, Prescott dismissed himself and walked out of the Navy Mess without an escort. He knew his way, but wondered how many more times he'd be invited back if this fool's errand he was being sent on didn't work.

Prescott's reputation as an insider, a power broker that made things happen in Washington, would not survive if the gambit they were playing failed. It was bad enough that the president was willing to go along with Nebit's plan to support a bill to release the holdings of the Muslim Brotherhood in America.

But trying to "wag the dog", by blaming Syria to divert attention from a failure to defend the homeland, and risk war with Syria and its ally Russia, was madness. And Prescott knew, without a doubt, that Layla Nebit would make sure he was outed as the man behind the plan, if it failed.

As soon as he was alone in the back of his black Mercedes S600, he called his friend, Barry Marshall, the new executive editor of the Washington Post. Layla Nebit might have the ear of the president, but he had the ear of the one man who could salvage his reputation if she tried to destroy him.

"Barry, we need to have lunch today," Prescott said when his friend took his call. "Something big is in the wind. You need to know which way it's blowing."

While he waited for his friend to confirm arrangements for lunch, Prescott sat back and considered how far he was willing to go to sabotage the president's plan to risk war just to improve his poll numbers. Outright betrayal was out of the question, but something had to be done. Something that would give the president an out and still demonstrate that he could be trusted to protect the country.

When his car was driving down the ramp to the underground parking at the Prescott Building, he decided what he had to do. He would reach out to his liaison with the Muslim Brotherhood, the man who arranged for the funds he received to lobby for the Brotherhood in America. If anyone could find out who was responsible for shooting down the two planes, this man could.

Chapter Seventeen

RYAN WALKER, was an international banker with offices around the world, handled the transfer of funds from abroad for the lobbying Prescott did for Muslim interests in America. While Walker had never admitted the money he funneled to the Prescott Group came from the Muslim Brotherhood, Prescott was sure that it did. Especially after he received the last five million dollars, to lobby for Senator Boykin's bill.

Prescott told his secretary to hold his calls and get a hold of Ryan Walker when he stopped briefly at her desk. Alone in the sanctity of his executive lair, where he'd accomplished so much for himself and his clients, he stood staring at the dome of the capitol in the distance, focusing his thoughts. He would have to choose his words carefully with Ryan Walker.

When the intercom beeped, his secretary reported that Walker was in London. Prescott took out his encrypted iPhone, found the banker's number, and sat at his desk while he waited for the call to go through.

"Mr. Prescott, how are things in America?" Walker asked cheerfully. "I was coming to Washington next week, but decided to wait until someone stops shooting down your planes."

"I'm sorry to hear that, Mr. Walker. I was looking forward to hearing how things are in the rest of the world."

"The rest of the world, Mr. Prescott, is waiting for your president to make America safe enough for us to travel there."

"And how do you think he should do that, Mr. Walker? Invade Syria? Carpet bomb the Middle East? Blame North Korea or Venezuela or Russia?"

Walker chuckled. "Oh come, Mr. Prescott.! I'm sure there are defense contractors who would pay you handsomely to warmonger for actions like that. But I think you would do well to concentrate your efforts a little closer to home."

Prescott paused. If Walker knew who was shooting airliners out of the sky, would he share the information? Did the man really know something, or was just trying to appear to be worldly and wise?

"And how close to home would that be, Mr. Walker?"

"Right down the hall from your office, Mr. Prescott. Ask your man Hassan," Walker said. "Now, I have a dinner to attend and I assume you have what you called for. Good evening, Mr. Prescott."

John Prescott sat looking at the message on the screen of his phone, telling him the call had ended. What in the world did Walker mean?

Mark Hassan headed his Middle East division. He was responsible for the lobbying work they did for Middle Eastern clients, clients who had business with the government or American companies. Hassan was Egyptian by birth, certainly, but he'd grown up in America, the son of a Georgetown University professor of Middle East history. Mark Hassan was a bright young man, but his work was limited to clients Prescott had brought in, and he knew them all personally. None of them, he quickly hoped, would know anything about the deranged idiots who were shooting down airliners and killing hundreds of people.

He leaned forward and jabbed the button for Mark Hassan's extension on his phone set.

When Hassan appeared at his door a minute later, Prescott waved him in.

"Take a seat."

Mark Hassan unbuttoned his black cashmere blazer and sat in one of the two leather chairs in front of Prescott's expansive cherry wood desk. Prescott studied him for a long minute.

"Mark, you've headed my Middle East division for five years now. You've done all that I have asked you to do, and our clients like you. Do you like it here?"

He watched the young man blink twice, as he considered where the conversation might be going.

"Yes, I like working for you. I hope you don't doubt that, Mr. Prescott."

"Sometimes an ambitious young man like yourself is asked to work with a client that engages in activities that might not be a good fit for our book of business. That young man might not want to jeopardize his own position and be tempted to keep his mouth shut, when he learns about things that client is doing. It's a natural thing, something I understand. But it's something I also cannot allow to happen. You understand that I trust."

"Certainly," Mark Hassan said and shifted his position in his chair.

"Then, tell me if there is a client I should be worried about."

Hassan maintained eye contact, but his eyes squinted just a little and he pressed his lips together a little tighter than he normally did.

"Why do you think you should be worried about any of our clients?" Hassan asked.

"Because I just had a conversation with an acquaintance in London, who intimated that you might know who's responsible for shooting down these airliners."

He watched as Hassan looked up at the ceiling for a moment, then slowly let out his breath before looking across the desk. Prescott felt his stomach tighten, as if he was about to be slugged in the gut.

"I think the American Muslim Youth Camps Foundation might be Sheeikh Qasseer's front for terrorist training camps in America," Hassan said. "There's a possibility the man who runs his largest camp, in West Virginia, is involved."

Prescott thought he knew all about the troublesome cleric from Bahrain. He was on the board of the man's damn foundation that raised money to operate the camps. Now he was being told that he may have been duped, by his Muslim Brotherhood clients, to help that same sheikh who was attacking the country.

Chapter Eighteen

THE LATE MORNING temperature had warmed to 12 degrees by the time Drake left the hospital with Mike Casey and drove downtown.

"Drop me off at the Prescott Building. I'll drop in on the attorney with the client who wants to buy the Alpine Ridge Ranch," Drake said. "I may as well use the time before we meet Liz for lunch. Why don't you go see some of the sights you've been talking about. Pick me up here in an hour."

"Roger that," Casey said. "I'll go see how the cherry trees are doing along the Tidal Basin. If this cold snap stays around too long, those blossoms might take a hit and I won't get to see them in bloom."

"If they survive and the airports don't reopen," Drake added, "a lot of people aren't going to be able to fly here and see them bloom either. The National Cherry Blossom Festival kicks off in just two weeks."

Casey was driving down Wisconsin Avenue NW and rubbernecking so much at all of the sights, Drake was about to ask him to change places and let him drive.

"That's the Old Stone House," Casey said, as they drove by. "It's the oldest house in Washington, built in 1765."

"What did you do, buy a guidebook for the capital?" Drake asked.

"Damn straight. Had to have something to read, and I love this place. There's so much history."

"Would you want to live here?"

"No way!" Casey snorted. "I couldn't afford it. Half the members of Congress are millionaires and the other half want to be. The counties surrounding the capital are the wealthiest in the whole country."

"Think of all the new clients you could add," Drake suggested. "Security work for all of our politicians, government contracts. You'd soon be among the wealthy yourself."

"Nice try, friend, but I'm happy in Seattle."

They turned onto Pennsylvania Avenue NW and swept around Washington Circle and onto K Street NW.

"The Prescott Building is at the intersection of 11th and K Street," Drake said. "Drop me off out front. It won't take me long to hear this guy's pitch about turning the resort into a Muslim youth camp."

"I thought the offer was so generous the owners wanted to sell."

"The offer is generous, but there are so many contingencies this Foundation could walk away from the place anytime they want. Their proposal's too one-sided."

"Well, good luck. Go do your lawyer thing, while I have some fun," Casey said and pulled to the curb in front of the impressive Prescott Building.

Drake paused in front of the Prescott Building before entering and admired the sight of a spectacular black 2012 Gemballa Porsche 911 parked at curbside. The owner of the car, if he worked in the building, was either very brave or very rich to leave such a car unattended.

Gemballa was a German company that tuned and modified one of the world's finest sports cars, with its own aftermarket parts, to produce a true supercar. Seeing the Porsche beauty made him want to return to Oregon and take a scenic drive somewhere in his own 911.

Seeing that the Prescott Group was the only tenant on the top floor, Drake took the elevator up and walked out to meet a receptionist in the center of a large atrium. The roof above was composed of blue-tinted triangles of glass to reflect and cool the sun's rays, while bathing the entry in a calm, serene light.

"May I help you, sir?" the young receptionist asked.

"I'm here to see Mark Hassan."

"Do you have an appointment with Mr. Hassan?"

Drake smiled. "If he's in, tell him I'm here about his offer to buy a ranch in Oregon."

"May I tell him your name, sir?"

Drake was tempted to imitate James Bond and say "Drake, Adam Drake". "Tell him Mr. Drake would like to see him," he said instead.

While he turned to look around at the collection of modern art displayed on the walls, the receptionist softly relayed his request to Mr. Hassan's secretary.

"Mr. Hassan will be with you shortly, Mr. Drake. Would you like an espresso while you wait?"

"No thank you," he said. If Hassan was anything like the attorneys he was used to seeing, the offer of coffee was meant to provide time to quickly review a file or let the visitor know whose turf he was playing on. He found the Post and an assortment of magazines on an end table, next to a plush white leather sofa, and took a seat.

The front page of the Post was doing its best, he saw, to provide cover for the president during the current crisis. One headline announced that the Federal Aviation Administration hadn't recovery the flight recorders from the two downed airliners and could not explain the crashes at the current time.

Another reported that Army psychiatrists were being interviewed for leads about vets with PTSD that could be suspects. They apparently weren't concerned about the time-honored doctor-patient privilege that still existed.

The last story, below the fold, cautioned that an unnamed but reliable counterterrorism expert was advising the White House that with the decapitation of al-Qaeda and the unsophisticated abilities of the lesser remaining terrorist groups, a rogue nation might well be responsible.

That's great, Drake thought. Ignore the obvious threat, because we took a victory lap when bin Laden was killed and start looking for a new boogie man to blame. The enemy has told us directly and boldly who it is. Why can't we finally have the courage to declare war on radical Islam?

He tossed the paper down and looked up to see a slender man in his early twenties approaching.

"Mr. Drake, I'm Mr. Hassan's assistant. I'll take you to him."

Drake followed past a ceremonial conference room on full display with its massive oak conference table and black leather chairs, and down a long hallway. Open secretarial workspaces fronted each office, and an interior window behind the secretary allowed a view inside to the attorney and beyond to the skyline of the city.

Hassan's assistant stopped in front of a secretary's desk at the northwest corner office and announced that Mr. Drake was there to see Mr. Hassan.

Drake was ushered in and introduced to Mark Hassan. He noted the man's supreme confidence, as the attorney walked around his desk to shake hands.

"I didn't know you were in town. I trust you didn't come all this way just to respond to the offer we made on the Alpine Ridge Ranch. Please, have a seat."

"I'm here on other business," Drake said, as he sat down and faced Hassan. "When I have the opportunity, I like to meet my opponents."

Hassan sat as well and rocked back in his brown leather executive chair. About the same age as Drake, he looked like a young version of Omar Sharif. Straight black hair, parted, over intense brown eyes and a thick black, neatly trimmed moustache.

"Why would you consider me an adversary, Mr. Drake? The offer I made your client is more than generous?"

"Perhaps it is because it is so generous. Perhaps you felt that my client would overlook some of the conditions you've insisted on."

"Such as?" Hassan asked, as he continued rocking in his chair.

"The agreement that the land sale contract is voidable if, at some future time, the activity of operating a youth camp is determined to violate any zoning code, use restriction or other requirement, county, state or federal. That's vague, don't you think?"

Hassan leaned forward and fingered a gold signature ring on his right hand. "Are you familiar with our youth camps?"

"You mean the camps of American Muslim Youth Camp Foundation?"

"Of course I meant the foundation's youth camps," Hassan said curtly. "I'm on the board, but you probably knew that. You didn't answer my question."

"No, I'm not familiar with your camps, other than what I've read about them," Drake said, wondering why Hassan had become defensive and a little hostile.

"Perhaps you should visit one of our camps before you believe what you read, Mr. Drake. Opening a Muslim youth camp has become almost as difficult as building a new mosque. America professes to welcome all races and religions, unless you happen to be Muslim, and then the resistance develops. If the foundation is going to spend the kind of money we're offering your client, we need to know the camp has a future, free of endless litigation. How long will you be in D.C.?"

"Undetermined, why?" Drake asked.

"Visit a camp, judge for yourself," Hassan said. "One of our largest is nearby in West Virginia. You can drive there in a couple of hours. If you don't feel comfortable with what you see, reject our offer and we'll find another property."

"I think that's a good idea, Hassan," Drake as he stood. "Just so you know, I've spent my share of time in the Middle East, and I consider a number of Muslims my friends. I don't judge you or your religion by what appears in the papers. But I also don't overlook the actions of Muslims fanatics either. Here's my card. Email me directions and I'll visit your camp tomorrow."

When he reached to door of Hassan's office, Drake turned. "In case you haven't heard, Congressman Rodecker is out of his coma. He probably won't be available for a vote on the bill you were lobbying him for, if it comes up anytime soon. He was able to identify his attacker, and I'll be sticking around until he's caught."

Drake left Hassan's office satisfied that Hassan knew he wasn't afraid to call a spade a spade. He had sensed in the man a smoldering anger. Mark Hassan might be a peace-loving Muslim, but Drake's alarm bells were ringing in his ears.

Chapter Nineteen

DRAKE AND MIKE Casey met Liz Strobel at the Old Ebbitt Grill across the street from the White House for lunch. She was sitting in a red velvet booth, waving at them as they entered the historic watering hole.

Both men paused briefly when they reached her table, before Drake slid in beside her and let his taller friend have the other side of the booth to himself.

"From the look on your face," Drake said, "I'd say you're not having a great morning. What's going on?"

"Buy me a glass of wine and I'll tell you," Liz said with a tight smile.

Drake waved to a nearby waiter. "Is this about the Senate Intelligence briefing this morning?" he asked, before turning to the waiter to order a glass of pinot gris and two Sam Adams Boston Lagers.

"I'm so damn mad at the moment," she began, "I'm not sure where to start, and this isn't the place. You'll hear some of it this afternoon if you listen to the president's press conference. But that won't be close to the whole story."

"Does the public ever get the *whole story*?" Casey asked.

"They might not get all of it," she said, "but what they do get is usually true. If what I'm hearing is accurate," Strobel paused and then held up the glass of wine that had just arrived, "the old saying "in wine there is truth" is more reliable than anything the president will tell the country today."

Their waiter returned and recited the day's special menu items and asked if they were ready to order. They weren't and studied their menus before Drake leaned closer and said, "Despite the frown on your face Liz, you look wonderful. Let's enjoy lunch and tell us what you can later."

With a nod and a thumbs up, she agreed and asked, "Mike, what's catching your eye?"

"Well, since you asked, I'm thinking grilled Fillet Mignon, a side of Clyde's chili and a Caesar salad for starters."

"Nothing's changed, Liz," Drake said, "that's his idea of a light lunch."

They both laughed and continued to do so when they saw that Casey was, indeed, still looking over his menu.

After an hour of small talk, and enjoying an order of crab cakes for her and a platter of Chesapeake Bay fried oysters for him, they waited for their check as Casey finished off a slice of cheesecake.

"Why don't we walk to Lafayette Square and talk before I call you a cab," Drake suggested when he'd paid their bill.

Outside, the three walked arm-in-arm to the park. Liz Strobel told them as much as she could about the intelligence briefing that morning.

"SA-24 MANPADS shot down the two airliners, but no group is claiming responsibility. There's no chatter, no SIGINT or HUMINT and none of our allies know anything either. Despite a complete lack of evidence, however, the White House considers Syria, acting as Iran's proxy, to be the most likely responsible party. He's going to send another carrier and more missile cruisers to the Mediterranean, while warning Russia not to interfere if he decides to act," she explained.

"Syria's not that stupid!" Casey exclaimed. "Even if Iran gave them a nuke, that wouldn't keep us from leveling their miserable country with cruise missiles and they know it."

"I don't think Iran is that stupid either," Strobel added.

"So what does the president do if can't find someone other than Syria to blame?" Drake asked. "He'll be forced to act, and that'll mean war."

"It won't be the first time he's acted before he thought about the consequences," Casey said.

The three stopped for a light to cross the street.

Stobel shook her head and said, "All they think about are the polls. He's getting clobbered because he hasn't prevented two planes from being shot down. But there are 500,000 MANPADS in the world, and thousands of them on the black market. God only knows how many of them are in terrorist hands. This has always been our worst nightmare."

They crossed the street and approached Lafayette Square.

Drake stopped and said, "This doesn't make any sense, in so many ways. Could there be someone playing us?"

"Someone, like who, Adam?" Strobel asked, as she turned to face him and keep her back to the cold wind blowing across the square.

Drake shrugged his shoulders and said, "I don't know, Russia so Putin can storm in and become the savior of the Middle East. Maybe China, so they can get us in a fight and sit back and watch us bleed, as part of their doctrine of unrestricted warfare. Why not North Korea, just for the hell of it."

They finally stopped at the statue of General Rochambeau, the Revolutionary War hero, in the southwest corner of Lafayette Square.

Drake took Strobel's hand to reassure her that he understood her frustration. "Look, I'm driving to West Virginia tomorrow to check something out. Why don't you come with me? It's a two hour drive, we'll see some country and I'll have you back in time for that dinner you promised me."

"Don't worry about me being left alone, Liz," Casey whined. "I'll visit a museum or something and then get something from room service and watch pay-for-view or something. I'll be fine."

"What do you say, Liz?" Drake asked. "It might get your mind off things."

She patted Casey on the cheek and mouthed "You poor thing" and said, "I'll go on two conditions; one, if Senator Hazelton doesn't need me to stay in the capital."

"And the other condition?" Drake asked.

"We take my car, and I'll let you drive part of the way."

"Poor thing," Casey poked his friend in the ribs. "She probably drives a Prius."

"It's time he learns to appreciate American cars, Mike. I bought a Cadillac CTS-VSPORT, because I love to drive," she said jauntily and patted Drake on his shoulder. "We'll see if he can handle a woman's car that's better than his old 911."

Drake graciously withstood the dig. Now there were two reasons to look forward to tomorrow.

Chapter Twenty

DRAKE ROSE EARLY Saturday morning and got a good workout in the hotel's fitness center, then returned to his room to shower, shave and dress for the day. After a light breakfast with Mike Casey in the restaurant downstairs, he was in the lobby waiting for his ride to West Virginia.

The night before, he'd gone online to see what kind of car Liz had bought and was intrigued. The Cadillac CTS V Coupe was a rocket ship, with 556 supercharged horsepower, a tuned chassis designed for the racecourse complete with Brembo brakes and Recaro seats. Capable of 0-60 miles per hour in four seconds, the car did, indeed, have the performance specs to outperform his old Porsche 993.

It lacked the charisma of his classic, of course, but if it performed as well as promised, he couldn't wait to drive it. If he got the chance, that was. His companion had seized the high ground for the day by demanding that they drive her car. And in doing so, his admiration for her amped up a notch.

He knew that she was an FBI agent before she'd been chosen to serve as the executive assistant to the Director of Homeland Security. He also knew that it hadn't been her good looks, as good as they were, that gave her the edge in competing with her male counterparts; she was fearless. When she'd been wounded by shattered glass from a sniper's bullet last summer in Oregon, she'd refused to seek medical attention. Then she coordinated the efforts that prevented a terrorist's nuclear demolition device from blowing up a dam in the mountains. Estimated potential casualties from the breached dam were a hundred thousand people killed in the valley below.

Two quick honks of a car's horn brought Drake's thoughts to the present. He walked out of the lobby to the hotel's porte-cochere and into the bite of the 20-degree morning air, and was glad he'd worn jeans and a white cable knit sweater under his jacket.

The silver metallic CTS V Coupe idling outside, with the smiling and beautiful woman behind the wheel, was amazing. With a two-fingered salute to her, he circled the car from the front to rear, admiring it. The sharp angles of its aerodynamic design, the red brake calipers behind the spokes of the 19 inch wheels mounted with Michelin Sport tires, and the center-mounted dual exhaust pipes at the rear made him think of a stealth fighter ready to take off down the highway.

Drake opened the passenger door and slid into the black and yellow leather seat.

"Wow!" he said. "This is some car."

"Good morning to you, too," she said.

"Sorry. Good morning, Liz."

"Some women would be hurt to think a man was more impressed with a car than its driver. But, since I happen to like most cars more than the men who drive them, I'll give you a pass this time."

"How long have you had it?" he asked.

"A couple of months and six thousand miles, to be exact," she said after looking at the odometer. "I needed something to compensate for the less-than-exciting work I'm doing. Care to give me directions before we head out?"

"We're driving to Romney, West Virginia, about 120 miles west of here. This youth camp is in the mountains nearby."

He watched her deftly enter the location in the navigation system and then drive away from the hotel.

Low-hanging gray clouds hinted at the possibility of snow, making him appreciate the warm cabin of the car and the soft leather of its interior. The clouds also reminded him that he had promised to take her skiing in Oregon.

"When do you think you'll be able to come to Oregon?" he asked, quickly regretting the opening it gave her to slip back into work mode.

"Not until we find out who's shooting down our airliners, and the airports open again. If the president goes after Syria, who knows how soon anyone will be able to enjoy a ski vacation. Boy, I miss my old job," she pounded on the steering wheel. "At DHS, I was able to do something helpful in a crisis. Now, I just sit on the sidelines and watch."

Drake doubted that Liz Strobel ever sat on the sidelines. He glanced over and saw she was clenching her jaw and gripping the steering wheel so tightly her knuckles were white.

With two hours on the road ahead of them, Drake steered the conversation away from work and asked her about her taste in music, where she worked out, her family and friends and her favorite restaurants. By the time they reached Winchester, Virginia, a little over halfway to their destination, she was smiling and promising him a meal he'd never forget when they returned to D.C. that night.

With a quick look his way, she abruptly slowed and pulled into the parking lot of a roadside fruit market advertising the best apples in all of Virginia.

"Would you like to drive the rest of the way?" she asked.

He answered by quickly shedding his seat belt, getting out and around the rear of the CTS-VCoupe by the time her car door was just opening. He waited patiently for her to exit, then settled into the performance driving seat, snugged the seat belt tight and waited for her to do the same. This wasn't your daddy's caddy and he was anxious to try it out.

Just as he prepared to pull back onto the highway, the upper corner of his rear-view mirror signaled that something was in the car's blind spot. When he turned to check, the black 2012 Gemballa Porsche 911 he'd seen parked outside the Prescott Building the day before flashed by.

Chapter Twenty-One

THEY FOLLOWED the black Porsche from Winchester, Virginia, to Romney, West Virginia. Drake wanted to open the Cadillac up to see what its race-tuned suspension and 556 horsepower could do, but seeing the other car for the second time in as many days made him curious. Finding it on the same road to the American Muslim Youth camp made him suspicious.

Drake drove at the unbelievably slow speed limit behind the Porsche. When they reached the outskirts of Romney, he let the sleek sports car continue through the downtown. He had planned on stopping for lunch and pulled off in front of Table 41, a popular restaurant housed in an old pharmacy. The manager at the Savoy Suite Hotel had recommended the chicken salad and hamburgers as the best in town.

He didn't believe in coincidences, but then the Porsche hadn't been following them. They had been following it. The only way someone could be tailing them from in front, was if that someone their destination. As far as he knew, only Mark Hassan with the Prescott Group, and Mike Casey, knew he was visiting the youth camp today. And Mark Hassan had no interest in tailing him to make sure he'd visited the camp; the camp's director would be able to confirm his visit.

He escorted Liz into the restaurant, where they were seated beside a long bar that once had served as a soda fountain. A bank of drawers, with the various drug names still on them, complimented the masterfully restored original woodwork in the warm interior. And as recommended, they ordered chicken salad and a chicken salad sandwich accompanied with two glasses of pinot gris for lunch.

An hour later, they followed the directions from their waitress and drove north out of town on Hwy. 5 into the hills. They found the gravel road she described and drove up it until they reached a warning sign that prohibited trespassing onto the American Muslim Youth Camp of West Virginia.

Drake pulled off the road and stopped before heading up a steep driveway lined by thick undergrowth. "This is pretty isolated for a youth camp," he said. "If these Muslim kids are coming here from big cities, they're going to suffer culture shock out here in the boonies."

"Maybe that's what they want," Strobel observed, "to get them as far away from the influences of the gangs and drugs in the inner cities."

"Guess we'll soon find out," Drake said, and pointed to four young black men walking down the driveway toward them. They were all growing beards and wore plain black T-shirts, jeans, and army-style combat boots. They fanned out in a line and blocked the driveway.

"Stay inside," he said. "They don't look like they were expecting us."

Drake got out and started to approach the welcoming party.

The tallest of the four standing in the middle of the line held up his hand.

"See the sign, man. No trespassing."

"Trespass is an unlawful intrusion on someone's land without the permission of its owner," Drake said calmly. "So, this isn't trespassing."

Alpha-boy just stared and pulled out a cheap flip phone.

"Tell Jameel Marcus that Adam Drake is here to see him," Drake said and walked back to the car. When alpha-boy finished his short conversation with someone, the four young men turned and walked slowly up the drive, four abreast.

"I guess that means we're supposed to follow them," he said.

Fifty yards up the dirt driveway, the land leveled out onto a plateau of ten acres or more, surrounded by thick forest. On the south side of the gravel driveway, a wide dirt road that looked like a rural landing strip ended at a cluster of older buildings that included an old barn and a shop.

Liz scanned the perimeter of the plateau. "It looks like they have the top of this mountain all to themselves," she said. "These kids won't be bothering the neighbors."

Drake followed slowly behind his escorts. "This reminds me of an old hunting lodge that's seen its better day. Except for satellite dishes on two of the building, the ATV's parked in a row in front of the barn, and the three new corrugated steel Quonset huts lined up like barracks over there."

"This foundation has some big money behind it," Strobel said, "if all their camps look like this."

The line of escorts stopped in front of the largest of the main buildings, a two-story log cabin with a front porch that spanned the width of the first floor. Two men stood on each side of the front door with their arms across their chests, posed like Black Panthers outside a polling place.

"Why am I getting a feeling that Muslim youth who come here are being trained to be more than just model citizens," Drake asked.

"It could be they're hired security to keep people like us out," Strobel offered optimistically.

Drake tried to think of a witty comeback, as a well-muscled black man wearing khakis and a white shirt with the sleeves rolled up strode out and walked to their car. His hair was close-cropped, and his wire rim glasses were pushed up over his forehead. He was clean shaven and sported diamonds in each ear.

"Mr. Drake, my name is Jameel Marcus," he said, as he reached in through the open window of the Cadillac to shake hands, "Hassan told me you might visit today. Come inside."

While the man's eyes seemed friendly enough, his crushing handshake sent a subtle warning he was not a man to mess around with.

They were led inside to an office that was Spartan, but well-equipped with two computer monitors on a gray metal desk, a flat screen TV on the wall behind the desk, a commercial-size copier/printer/fax machine and a bank of four gray metal file cabinets.

Marcus took his seat behind the desk and motioned them to two metal folding chairs in front of the desk.

"Why are you here?" the man asked. "The foundation's brochure explains what we do."

"Yes," Drake answered. "It says you work with Muslim youth. Where are they?"

"Out hiking on one of our nature trails."

"How many youths are here, currently?"

"Each barrack sleeps twenty, plus the counselors. All three barracks are full."

"That's a lot of bodies. What do they do when they're not out hiking?" Drake pressed.

"We teach 'em how to cope in America, as Muslims," Jameel said curtly. "Teach 'em skills they need to survive."

Drake turned to Strobel and asked if she had any questions.

"Do you live here year-round, Mr. Marcus?" she asked.

"Why is that important?" he asked. "You come here to see the camp, or interrogate me?"

Liz leaned forward and said, "I work for U.S. Senator Hazelton, Mr. Marcus. If you're here all the time, I thought I might arrange a visit for some members of Congress, to acquaint them with your work."

Jameel Marcus pointedly looked at the military-style watch on his left wrist and stood. "Doubt that be good for the boys, having a bunch of politicians out here. Talk to the foundation if you want. I have something I need to take care of. The boys will escort you back to the road."

They followed him out and watched him march off to the large shop next to the camp's old barn. Inside, several young men were working on the inside of a fairly new delivery van, hanging sheets of metallic-looking polyurethane.

When they got to Strobel's CTS-VCoupe, Drake held out the keys to her.

"Go ahead and drive," she said. "I'm going to call my assistant and get her started investigating Marcus and these camps. Something's not right."

Chapter Twenty-Two

TWO HUNDRED YARDS down the gravel road from the training camp, Mohamed Hassan trained his Zeiss binoculars on the silver CTS-VCoupe as it headed back to town. When it turned the corner and drove out of sight, he laid the binoculars down beside his Sig P226 pistol with a threaded barrel, for the sound suppressor he preferred to use, and drove to the driveway.

The same four Muslim men who had escorted the silver Cadillac onto the property turned as they heard the purr of the Gemballa Porsche 911. When he lowered the driver's side window, they recognized him and waved him on.

Hassan drove slowly to keep from raising dust along the long driveway and pulled off in front of the shop, where Jameel Marcus standing with several of his men.

Hassan got out, stretched and walked to greet Marcus. "Assalamu `alaykum," he said.

"Ua alaykum us salaam," Marcus returned.

Hassan walked to the back of the white step van and watched the men inside covering the walls and ceiling with sheets of infrared heat shield polyurethane.

Marcus joined him. "It will be finished by tonight."

"Let's talk inside," Hassan said, and turned toward the camp's office in the log cabin. Marcus followed a couple of steps behind him.

"Close the door," Hassan ordered when they were alone in the office. "Show me where you will fire the missile."

Marcus sat at his desk and brought up a map of an airport on his computer.

"Across the river from the airport is a park," he said, pointing to one of the monitors he turned so Hassan could see. "It was a plantation before the Americans used it as a fort to keep the British from using the river for transportation in their Revolutionary War."

"Will you have any trouble getting the step van into the park?"

"No, the park is open to the public from dawn to dusk each day."

"When does the sun set tomorrow?"

"Sunset is 6:10 pm."

"And when does the target take off?"

"Scheduled departure is 4:55 pm."

Hassan nodded his head approvingly. "You have done well, my friend. Who will fire the missile? Is he well trained?"

"I will. I was trained on the SA-24 in Pakistan. We can't train here with these missiles, but I remember."

"When will you leave?"

"Early tomorrow," Marcus reported. "We have arranged to pick up supplies for the camp in Baltimore, from our regular supplier. The van will be loaded to help conceal our weapons if we're stopped. Then we'll continue on to the park. The boxes of supplies will shield me when the tailgate is raised. When we return, the load of supplies will validate our travel."

Hassan studied his young accomplice for a moment. "Are you and your men prepared to do what is necessary, if you are captured?"

Marcus stood and smiled across the desk at Hassan. "Isn't martyrdom every Muslim's dream? Don't worry, we will do our duty."

Hassan considered the response and then returned the smile.

"Good. Walk me to my car and tell me about the visitors who just left."

Marcus held the door open for Hassan and then followed him outside. "You mean the attorney and his woman?"

"Have you had any others since they left?" Hassan asked.

"You've been watching us."

"I am careful, Marcus. That's why I have survived in this war we fight."

"Your cousin Mark sent him here. He wanted to see one of our camps. He asked where all our young Muslims were, and what they do here."

Hassan continued on to his car and turned when he got there. "And what did you tell him?"

"I told him the truth. We teach them the skills they need to survive."

Hassan opened the door of his black 911 that was now covered with a fine coat of dust. He lowered the window when he was seated and said, "I will tell the Sheikh of your good work. Perhaps we will work together again, *Inshallah.*"

Driving as slowly as the Porsche would allow, Mohamed Hassan looked back in the rearview mirror at the foolish young Shia warrior who had not yet learned how to tell a friend from a foe. By the time he realized he was being set up, it would be too late.

Chapter Twenty-Three

DRAKE WATCHED for the black Gemballa Porsche 911, parked on Marshall Lane, a half block off Main Street in Romney, West Virginia. When they'd pulled onto the road leaving the youth camp thirty minutes ago, he'd seen the reflection from either a rifle scope or binoculars from the black car two hundred yards or so back up the road.

Seeing the same car three times in the last two days wasn't a coincidence.

"Thanks for letting me drive back to D.C., Liz," he said. "When we get the license number for the Porsche, see if you can work your magic and find out who's following us."

"There's no magic involved. I still have contacts in the Department of Homeland Security who do favors for me occasionally."

"How's your old boss, Secretary Rallings, doing?"

"He's on his ranch in Montana recovering from his heart attack. He won't admit it, but I think the stress of worrying about the next terrorist attack is what caused his heart condition. His wife says he's restless and bored, but otherwise doing fine."

"He should be glad he's not involved in this crisis. The president has a history of letting Cabinet members take the fall when things don't go well."

Drake was reaching into the pocket of his jacket for his Samsung Galaxy 6, when he saw the black Porsche drive by out on Main Street.

"When I pull out," he said, "use my phone and take a picture of his license plate. You'll be able to expand the picture enough to read it."

He waited until the other car was three blocks away before he followed it. As Main Street ended and became Highway 50, Strobel took three pictures in rapid succession, checked them and said she had it. Drake fell back and let the Porsche pull ahead another hundred yards.

"It's a New York plate," Strobel said, as she took out her iPhone and searched her contact list for her friend at DHS. "Let's see who this guy is."

Drake listened as she greeted her friend and then asked him to run the New York plate on the black Porsche. While she was on hold waiting for the owner's ID, Drake couldn't resist the temptation.

"How good a friend is he?" he asked.

Strobel turned and smiled. "What makes you think it's a him?"

"I heard his voice. It's either a him, or a her with a very deep voice and a moustache."

"Do deep voices and moustaches go together?"

"They do if the voice on the other end belongs to a woman."

Strobel hit him in the chest and held out her hand. "Pen," she mouthed as her *friend* came back with the owner's ID.

"Mohamed Hassan," she repeated and then, "New York, New York. Thank you, David, I owe you one. Tell your wife hello for me."

"For your information," she said to Drake, "David does have a moustache and he's very good looking. Jealous?"

"I always wanted to grow a good 'stache, but couldn't stand the way it tickled my nose," he said as he ignored her tease. "You think you could see if your assistant can learn anything else about Mohamed Hassan?"

As she called her assistant, he caught her smiling out of the corner of his eye. Drake relaxed and forced himself to concentrate on keeping his distance from the black Porsche and keeping his eyes on the road.

They drove for another ten minutes without speaking until Liz's assistant began her report on one Mohamed Hassan. Drake saw her raise her eyebrows with a puzzled expression when he glanced her way.

"Why did Interpol flag him, does it say?" she asked, and after a pause as she listened, said, "Okay, see if you can find out where he's staying in D.C. I'll see if my former counterpart in the NYPD Counterterrorism Bureau has anything on him. Thanks, Kerry."

"Well," Drake said," this just keeps getting better and better. Who is this guy, Liz?"

"No one seems to know. He's apparently an investment banker from London, with known ties to the Muslim Brotherhood. Interpol's not sure if he's just a money man for them, or he's been involved in some of their operations. His travels seem to match up with several assassinations around the world, but that's all they have on him so far."

"Why in the world is he following us? There's nothing we're doing that would interest the Muslim Brotherhood?"

"You don't spend enough time in Washington," she said. "The Muslim Brotherhood and their front organizations are everywhere, and they're interested in everything Muslim. There's one man on the Advisory Council of DHS and the White House routinely asks for their advice on Middle East policy. They're working very hard to get "democracy" and former President Morsi restored to power in Egypt.

"So, you're suggesting he might have followed us we're looking into the American Muslim Youth Camp Foundation and its bid to buy a ranch in Oregon?"

"Or," she said, "Maybe they have some interest in this West Virginia youth camp."

"If Mohamed Hassan is Muslim Brotherhood, a youth camp in

West Virginia would seem to be small potatoes for someone who travels the world like he has."

Strobel thought a moment. "Of course, we don't know if Mohamed Hassan is driving his Porsche. He could have loaned it to someone."

Drake considered that for a moment. "I saw this black Gemballa Porsche 911 the first time, parked across the street from the Prescott Building when I went there to meet with the attorney for the American Muslim Youth Camp Foundation, Mark Hassan. And I guess it might just be a coincidence they're both named Hassan."

"If there's a connection," she cautioned, "You'd better find out before your client sells his ranch."

"If there's a connection and Mohamed Hassan is who Interpol thinks he might be, we'd better find out what he's doing here in West Virginia," Drake warned.

Chapter Twenty-Four

IT WAS five thirty when they got back to Washington, on a cold Saturday evening. Strobel had made dinner reservations at a French restaurant near Union Square she promised would make him forget the weather when she dropped him off at his hotel.

Drake found Mike Casey waiting for him in the bar.

"Have you heard how the president is going to get the airports open again?" Casey said and waved to the TV above the bar.

Drake sat next to his friend. "No, we didn't have the radio on in Liz's car."

"He's going to protect the major airports with armed drones. The Air Force has assured him they can identify and eliminate any threat before a terrorist can launch a MANPAD."

"Will that work?" Drake asked. "You're the pilot."

Casey raised his hands, palms up, and said, "Who knows, it's never been done before. I wouldn't want to be the general that told the president it would, if another plane goes down."

Casey motioned for the bartender to bring a beer for Drake and some peanuts.

"Did you find a safe place for Congressman to stay when he's released," Drake asked.

"He's one of the new ones, who live in their offices while they're here, doing the people's work," Casey explained. "He doesn't have an apartment, so we're working on it."

"I could ask Senator Hazelton if he can stay with him," Drake suggested. "He's the one who asked us to come and protect him. If he's still worried about the Congressman's safety, he can arrange for someone else to protect him so you can get back to Seattle."

Casey turned to Drake and grinned. "Do I sense that you're trying to get rid of me? Maybe so you'll have more time to spend with Liz?"

"I just spent the day with her, Mike. That's more time than I've spent with a woman since Kay died. I don't need more time."

"Why are you going to dinner with her tonight, then?"

"Because, she made me promise last year in San Francisco that she could take me to dinner when I was in town. I couldn't say no."

Casey took a handful of peanuts and threw a couple in his mouth. "You know, it's okay to like her. Kay would have wanted you to move on."

Drake sighed and finished his beer. "I know, but I don't want to talk about it, okay? When do you need to get back to Seattle?"

"I called Megan while you were gone. I told her I'd be home as soon as possible, next week probably, when we're finished here."

"If I stay on, when you leave with your team, can you loan me a few things from the armory you keep on your Gulfstream?" Drake asked.

"What happened, did some redneck in West Virginia give you a bad time today?"

"Right reason, but it wasn't a redneck."

"Probably plenty of them still around there," Casey said. "You know how that term was used, in the 1920's and 1930's?"

"Am I about to learn?"

Casey nodded, "Indeed you are. Striking coal miners in West Virginia wore red hanker chiefs around their necks or arms as part of their informal uniforms. Hench the term, "rednecks."

"How long have you waited to tell someone that?" Drake asked, shaking his head.

"Thought you needed to know, before you embarrassed yourself someday. Lawyers aren't the only ones who know a few things. So," Casey continued, "If it wasn't a redneck, who was it that got you thinking you needed some weaponry?"

"A black Muslim, on top of a mountain in the middle of nowhere, at the youth camp we visited. We didn't see any inner-city youth, but we were greeted by a welcoming committee. They looked a lot like the new Black Panthers."

Casey ordered them another round of beers. "It sounds like Congressman Rodecker was spot on to try and head off the sale of your friend's ranch. Some of his constituents were nervous about another terror training camp being set up like the one near Bly in 2002."

"Did he tell you about that in the hospital?"

"He's been trying to figure out why he was attacked," Casey said. "He thinks it was more than just his opposition to the Boykin bill. He thinks it might be the zoning change he was helping the ranchers get the county to adopt."

"Interesting," Drake said. "The attorney at the Prescott Group said he drafted the land sale contract with contingencies because of the possibility of zoning changes."

"So, my principal, the Congressman, might not be safe after all," Casey said. "I think I'll swap in a new protection team tomorrow, just in case."

"And I'll ask Liz to keep digging up anything she can on the American Muslim Youth Camp Foundation. The camp in West Virginia cost someone a pretty penny, and it's not the only camp they operate."

"Would you like me to see if my favorite IT employee can come with anything?" Casey asked.

"Mike, this could get messy. I don't want you or Kevin, your young hacker, to get crossways with the feds over this. Our government seems to go out of its way to make sure the rights of American Muslims aren't violated."

Casey huffed. "I doubt this foundation has security that's better than the Pentagon, or the IRS. Kevin visited both of them without being detected before he came to work for me. He won't get caught."

"It's your call, just be careful," Drake warned. "There's no need for you or your company to be tied up in a DOJ lawsuit for the next ten years."

Chapter Twenty-Five

DRAKE DROVE the rented white Tahoe to a French bistro on Massachusetts Avenue to keep his dinner date. When he got there, he was surprised to find a parking spot on the street in front of the popular restaurant. He was early and looked around for her silver CTS-VCoupe, but he didn't see it parked anywhere nearby. The bistro was, however, close to her Senate office, so it was possible she'd walked and was inside.

The temperature had fallen below freezing and he was glad he'd brought his black wool topcoat on the trip. Wearing it over his black wool suit, with a white shirt and a red tie, he was moderately warm by the time he crossed the wide sidewalk and outside patio area to reach the front door.

French cuisine wasn't his favorite fare, but he was looking forward to the evening as he checked his coat and asked if Ms. Strobel had arrived. When he was told she hadn't, he followed his hostess to the adjacent bar and ordered a ten-year-old Eagle Rare Bourbon Whiskey.

The evening crowd waiting for their tables in the bar was a mix of couples out on a Saturday night and power players working hard to impress their guests. Drake had seen it all before, as smooth lobbyists were overly solicitous of their clients, and couples without huge expense accounts attempted to relax as they anticipated spending more in a night than they'd spend on food in a week.

He focused on the amber liquid in his glass. It was a delicious whiskey, one that could become a favorite with its dry, spicy finish.

As he set his whiskey down and looked toward the hostess stand, he saw Liz walk in. The view was as delicious as the whiskey he'd just savored. She was wearing a red three-quarter length wool coat with a black feather-like scarf. When she was helped with her coat, he saw she was wearing a short v-neck black sheath dress that allowed an enticing view of cleavage and leg. Her auburn blond hair was pulled back in a ponytail, and diamond stud earrings sparkled on her ears.

Drake waved and stood to seat her when she reached his table.

"Did you walk?" he asked when he noticed her bright pink cheeks.

"It was only a couple of blocks," she said as Drake pulled out her chair. "I stopped by my office to see if my assistant had anything new for us about the youth foundation."

When he leaned down to push her chair in, he smelled the fresh and flowery fragrance of her hair. "Would you like a cocktail or glass of wine?" he said close to her ear.

"A vodka gimlet would be nice," she looked up and said with a wink, "I'm feeling festive tonight."

MOHAMED HASSAN SAT in the passenger seat of his cousin's dark blue AMG Mercedes, parked outside the French bistro where the attorney from Oregon was having dinner. They'd followed him from his hotel.

Mohamed's iPhone was held to his ear, as he heard the attorney's date telling him about the bottle of wine she'd just ordered for their dinner.

"*Domaine du Pegau Chateauneuf-du-Pape is a Rhone region blend of reds I think you'll like. It's not a pinot, but try it.*"

"Can you hear them?" Mark Hassan asked, watching Drake and the woman through a pair of binoculars as they sat at a window table in the Red Room of the Bistro Cacao.

"Perfectly," Mohamed said. "The Q Bug you had the waiter slip into the fold of the drape behind the attorney allows me to hear them as if I'm standing at their table."

The Q Bug was the world's smallest voice transmitter. Its SIM card was activated when Mohamed sent it a text message and allowed him to listen to surrounding sounds over his cell phone.

"Has he said anything about visiting Jameel today?" Mark asked.

"Not yet, but be quiet," Mohamed said.

Mohamed listened intently for fifteen minutes before the conversation turned to matters more interesting than how good the pistachio crust sea bass and the grilled hanger steak tasted.

"Did your research assistant find anything interesting about the American Muslim Youth Camp Foundation?" the attorney asked.

"We know the names of the board members and locations of the rest of their camps, but that's all right now. They have 34 more of these camps spread around the country, mostly in rural areas like the one we visited."

"What about the kids they're supposed to be working with? Who are they and where do they come from?"

"The foundation doesn't list the identities of the kids who attend the camps, just that they come from the inner cities all around America. From the brochures the foundation puts out, most of them look like black inner city teenagers," the woman said.

"The camp manager said they teach them skills they need to survive. It'd like to know if those skills include how to be a good American rather than how to be a good little jihadist."

"Adam!" the woman exclaimed.

"I'm just saying. The camp manager and his Black Panther look-alikes aren't your usual camp counselors. Remember, I overheard the two foundation representatives at the ranch mention the name of Sheikh Qasseer, from Bahrain. If he's behind this philanthropic outreach to Muslim youth in America in any way, that's exactly what they might be teaching."

Mohamed swore and turned to his cousin. "We have a problem. The attorney is suspicious of the camps."

"Suspicious of what?"

Mohamed held up his hand for silence.

"If Mike's up for it, I'd like to go back to West Virginia and take another look at that camp," the attorney said.

"What could you see that we didn't see today? I doubt that they'd give you a guided tour if you asked them."

"Who says anything about asking them. Mike and I are pretty good at slipping in and out of places. We could drive there tomorrow night, see what there is to see and be back by breakfast Monday."

Mohamed had heard enough. "The attorney needs to learn that trespassing is a crime, punishable by death. Call Jameel, tell him to expect two men sneaking onto camp property tomorrow night. I don't want them leaving alive. "

AFTER SHARING dessert and a glass of Blanquette de Limoux sparkling wine, Drake was able to talk Liz into allowing him to pay for half of their dinner and drive her home.

When they pulled up to her high-rise condo building in Arlington, she leaned over and kissed him on the cheek.

"Dinner was supposed to be on me. Next time, we're eating in and I'll cook. Call me tomorrow, especially if you and Mike are traveling back to West Virginia," she said and got out.

As the doorman opened the door for her, she turned and waved.

Drake drove off, still feeling the lightness of her kiss on his cheek.

Chapter Twenty-Six

BY EIGHT O'CLOCK SUNDAY MORNING, Jameel Marcus had the stolen white 1998 GMC step van ready for the trip to Baltimore, to pick up supplies for the youth camp and then continue on to New Jersey to shoot down another jetliner.

The work on the van had been completed the night before, and the cargo space was now draped with infrared heat shield sheets of polyurethane. They'd anticipated the deployment of armed drones to protect the airports, even before their source in the White House had confirmed the president's plan and had a supply of the infrared heat shield material on hand. With their body heat signatures blocked from the infrared spying eyes of the drones flying above, they would have no trouble launching the missile undetected from inside the back of the van.

The problem was going to be leaving the scene undetected once the missile was launched. While the drone operator wouldn't be able to detect the firing of the missile, he would see the launch and know where it had come from. For that reason, two recruits would follow the van in two separate cars to the launch site. As soon as the missile was away, Marcus and his accomplice would leave the van and split up, to be be driven to a nearby residential area where the two cars would be abandoned. They would then be picked up in a rented eight passenger van that would be returned to an Alamo Rent A Car lot at the Dulles Airport on Monday.

Marcus, however, was more worried about the two men who were planning on coming to the camp that night. He had planned a reception for them, and gone over the plan with his two best men twice the night before, but needed to make sure they clearly understood their orders before he left.

Kareem and Rashid stood at ease in front of his desk. Both wore green jungle camo, black combat boots and black berets. They would each carry a folding stock AK-47 with a 30-round magazine and a holstered Beretta 92F when they hunted for the intruders that night, each leading a six-man squad similarly equipped.

"If these men set foot on this camp, anywhere on our 270 acres, I want them," he said as he pointed to a map of the camp on the top of his desk. "They will probably park somewhere off the road from Romney, somewhere along here or here. Put lookouts here and here. Capture them, do not shoot them, and bring them to the barn. I will deal with them when I return."

"What if they fire at us?" Kareem asked.

"Make sure you're not hit. I need them alive to find out how much they know."

"What should we tell the younger ones?" Rashid asked.

"Tell them they are cops who must be dealt with," Marcus directed. "That's all they need to know for now."

"Can we begin interrogating them if you haven't returned?" Kareem asked. "Might be hard to keep the young ones happy if we don't."

"You tell them to be patient. They'll get to watch and learn. Now, walk with me to the van. It's time for me to leave."

Marcus walked out of his office ahead of his two lieutenants and crossed the field to the shop where the white van was idling. Since it had been stolen in Pittsburgh, the recruits had repainted it white, changed the Pennsylvania license plates to New Jersey plates taken from a repair shop in Maryland, owned by a follower of the Sheikh, and added signage that identified it as belonging to a nonexistent produce company in southern Virginia.

The back of the van was loaded with crates of cabbage, cauliflower and kale purchased from nearby farms. One row of kale crates nearest the cab of the van concealed their weapons and the Russian SA-24 shoulder-fired anti-aircraft missile he would use.

Seeing that the crates were stored as he had directed, he pulled down the rear door of the step van and locked it before climbing in beside his driver and waving him on. There were 244 miles ahead of them, first on I-70 to Baltimore and then I-95 to Philadelphia. He needed to arrive well ahead of the scheduled departure of a Delta Boeing 767 leaving for John F. Kennedy International Airport at the end of a long weekend.

As the white van left the camp, Marcus settled back in his seat and began visualizing the jetliner as it accelerated down the runway across the Delaware River. His driver would act as his spotter and tell him when to be ready to stand in the open rear of the van and fire. The infrared heat shielding they had installed would keep the drone from seeing him before he fired. When the missile was away; drop the launch tube, exit the van and jump in one of the two escape cars parked beside the van. It would be the moment he had trained for in Pakistan, the moment he had lived for all his life. It would be his act of loving devotion to the Prophet, peace and blessings be upon him.

Chapter Twenty-Seven

AFTER AN ENERGIZING workout in the hotel's fitness center and quick showers, Drake and Casey were having breakfast and sorting out the week ahead.

Drake watched as Casey slathered his toast with butter and strawberry jam. "What are the plans for Congressman Rodecker?" he asked. "Have you decided where he'll be staying while he recovers?"

"He's making some calls. He doesn't want to impose on any of his colleagues, but staying in his office like he's been doing isn't going to work."

"How long before he's back to work?" Drake asked.

Casey finished swallowing a chunk of his toast and said, "His doctor says two to three weeks. He says one week, max."

"I can still ask the Senator if he could stay with him for a week. It would make it easy for your team to keep him safe at his house."

"Sure, go ahead and ask him," Casey said. "I'm rotating a new protection team in here tomorrow."

Drake asked a passing waitress for another glass of orange juice. "Pretty gutsy for the president to open the airports before he catches the terrorists. I wouldn't fly commercial now, unless I knew they were in custody."

"He doesn't have a choice, Adam. The cost of closing all the airports for the last four days has to be tremendous."

When Drake finished the last of his omelet, Casey set his coffee cup down and leaned forward on his elbows across the table. "Time for all the details, buddy. How was your date with Liz?"

"Mike, give it a rest, will you? She invited me to dinner. It was nice. I took her home."

"And then?"

"Like I said, it was nice. The dinner," Drake said, with a big smile. "How was your night?"

"I will find out, you know," Casey promised. "I can have Kevin hack into the security cameras at her place and know exactly when you entered and left her condo."

"How'd you know it was a condo?"

It was Casey's turn to smile. "Ve haf our vays, Capitan."

Drake knew he was bluffing but laughed anyway. "Since you think I'm having all the fun, want to join me tonight for a quick trip to West Virginia?"

"The youth camp?"

"Bingo! We were greeted by four men, not boys, who were trying hard to look menacing. The camp manager looked like the prison felons who converted to Islam in prison we dealt with back in Portland last year. He didn't exactly give us a warm welcome, and virtually no information. Besides, he had diamond studs in both ears."

Drake waited for the light to go on.

"Like the guy Congressman Rodecker described who attacked him?"

"Exactly like that guy," Drake affirmed.

Casey sat back in his chair and rested his chin on steepled fingers. "It fits, I guess. Rodecker interferes with their plans for the Oregon camp and they send him a message."

"I have a hunch there's more to it than that. I just don't know what. That's why we need to find out what it is."

"When do we go?"

"Tonight," Drake said, "If you're up for it. We can leave at nine, get there by midnight, go have a look around and be back by sunrise," Drake said.

"Will we need some of the stuff I have on the Gulfstream?"

"I don't know what to expect, so let's go in heavy. Bring my Kimber Master Carry Pro I left on the plane," Drake said. "Something more robust for you, night vision and whatever tactical comm setup your guys use. I don't plan on running into anyone, but you never know."

"Okay then," Casey said. "I'll make a run to the airport this afternoon and grab our stuff. Where will you be?"

"I need to check in with my office and see how Paul's doing. He had his prostatectomy Thursday and should be home from the hospital by now. And I think I'll pay my father-in-law a quick visit this afternoon and see if he's heard anything that could be helpful. Let's meet back here for dinner, say seven?"

"Seven it is."

Drake signed for their breakfasts and returned to their room, while Casey drove to the hospital to check in with his protection team guarding Congressman Rodecker. It was 12:00 p.m. in Washington, but 9:00 a.m. in Oregon and he knew his secretary would be with her husband, either at the hospital or at home.

He reached her at home, which was the condo located above his office. He'd let Margo and her husband live there, as part of her compensation for running his office and being the best legal assistant in the city.

"Margo, how's Paul doing? Sorry I haven't called sooner."

"He's home and sleeping and I'm fine, just a little tired. They did the robot-assisted surgery and removed some lymph nodes for testing, as well as his prostate. He's having a fit about having to have a catheter in for the next week or so, but they think they got everything. We'll know when the test results come back."

"That's great, Margo, that's great. Sorry Paul had to go through this."

"So is he. When do you think you'll be back?"

"Another couple of days," he said. "I met the lawyer handling the offer on our client's ranch and want to check some things out before I head back. Call me when you get the test results, and don't worry about things in the office. We'll get caught up as soon as I get back."

After he made sure she wasn't worrying about work in the office, and that their health insurance carrier was taking care of everything involved with her husband's cancer surgery, he hung up and called his father-in-law.

Senator Hazelton was just leaving for church but invited him to join them for lunch. There were things the Senate Intelligence Committee was hearing that Drake needed to know.

Chapter Twenty-Eight

DRAKE FOUND his in-laws sitting at a table, back away from the tall windows of The Lafayette restaurant in the historic Hay-Adams hotel. Seating by the windows offered the best view across Lafayette Square to the White House, but the tables across from the windows offered more privacy for serious conversations during the power meetings that frequently occurred there.

Senator Hazelton and his wife, Meredith, were there this Sunday for Sunday brunch and some time with their son-in-law.

Drake leaned down and kissed his mother-in-law on the cheek before sitting beside her and opposite the senator. "This is a nice surprise. How was church?" he asked.

Mrs. Hazelton rolled her eyes. "The pastor said some things I wish *some* people paid a little more attention to. The senator was too busy, however, making notes on the back of his bulletin to pay attention."

"I heard every word," Senator Hazelton said, "just as I do at every senate hearing I attend. Men can multi-task, too. We've ordered Champagne, Adam. Would you like something?"

"A Bloody Mary sounds good, thanks."

When their waiter came to take their orders, Drake studied his menu while the senator ordered his Bloody Mary.

When the waiter left, Mrs. Hazelton said, "My husband tells me you drove to West Virginia yesterday with Liz. Was this for your client you mentioned with the ranch in Oregon?"

Drake nodded that it was. "I met with the lawyer representing the buyer Friday and had some questions about the youth camps they're operating," Drake said.

"And what did you learn?" Mrs. Hazelton asked.

"I'm not sure," he answered carefully. "The camp counselors, if that's what they are, looked more like drill sergeants. They had 50 kids out on a nature walk or something, so we didn't see any of them. The camp itself is impressive, though. They've spent some money on the place."

"They probably have," Senator Hazelton said, "knowing the people on the board of the foundation. That's John Prescott over there, Washington's top lobbyist, having a chat with Layla Nebit, the woman rumored to be the president's closest advisor. Everything he's involved with is usually first class."

Drake looked in the direction the senator had glanced. Prescott was a man in his sixties, who looked like he could run for elected office on his looks alone. He didn't appear to be having a pleasant time with the woman at his table, however.

Prescott was turned away from her, looking out the window toward the White House, while the woman was sitting back looking up at the ceiling and one of the beautiful chandeliers. They weren't talking to each other and their body language reminded Drake of a married couple silently fighting.

"What's Prescott doing on the board of a foundation that works with Muslim kids from inner cities?" Drake asked the senator.

"He does a lot of lobbying for Muslim groups. He represented the Egyptian government and then the Muslim Brotherhood when they took over. I'm not sure what his relationship is at the moment, now that the military is running the country."

"By any chance," Drake asked, "Is he lobbying Senator Boykin's bill to release the Brotherhood's assets?"

"Bingo," the senator said. "He's the main lobbyist for the bill and it's being closely watched by the White House, in the person of Ms. Layla Nebit."

When their food arrived and they began eating, the conversation at their table turned to news from Oregon, Drake's plan to replant the old vineyard on his farm and March Madness. From time to time, Drake looked at the table where John Prescott and Layla Nebit sat and saw they were still disagreeing about something.

As the remnants of their brunch was being cleared from their table, Senator Hazelton ordered coffee for the three of them and pulled his chair closer to the table.

"This isn't public knowledge yet," he said to Drake, "but the word is spreading fast around Washington that some unknown terrorist group sent a written demand to the president. It says the jetliners will continue to fall from the sky unless he stops interfering in Syria, stops helping Israel, ends his drone program and releases all the Gitmo detainees. They claim to have another forty plus MANPADs in America to carry out their threat."

"Good lord," Drake said. "No wonder we're sending another carrier and cruisers to the Mediterranean. Shooting down commercial jetliners sounds like something the mullahs or Syria would do."

The senator shook his head. "The CIA isn't buying it. There's nothing that supports that conclusion," Senator Hazelton said.

"If you've been briefed on that by the CIA, certainly the president has the same intel. Why is he accusing Syria, then?" Drake asked.

"When you don't a clue about who's responsible for killing almost seven hundred innocent people, on two different commercial flights, you can't admit that. The president needs to put a face on the enemy and show people he's doing something."

"And risk war?" Meredith Hazelton exclaimed. "Even he isn't that reckless. Why would he do something like that?"

"Honey, I don't know," the senator said. "He's getting bad advice, is my best guess. He's a smart politician, but I can't see how any of this pleases his base or any of his support groups, let alone be in the best interest of the country."

"You said she's his closest advisor," Drake's mother-in-law said, looking toward Layla Nebit. "Could she be the one giving him the bad advice? She was born in Egypt, I read somewhere."

Both men watched the president's advisor as she left her table, and John Prescott remained seated. The idea that someone that close to the president could be influencing his decisions, in a way that benefitted another nation or worse, an avowed enemy of the United States, was not something neither man wanted to contemplate. It would constitute treason, at the highest level of government.

Chapter Twenty-Nine

JOHN PRESCOTT PAID for brunch and left The Lafayette. Instead of leaving the Hay-Adams, he took the stairs to the basement to find an empty booth and a quiet place, to drink and sort out the mess he was in.

He had advised Nebit of his concern that Allah's Sword, the terrorist group shooting down American planes, was somehow connected to the American Muslim Youth Camp Foundation. She had been the one who asked him to represent the foundation and later serve on its board as chairman. He had demanded to know what she knew about the people who were behind the foundation, and what her involvement with them was and continued to be.

Her response had been to look him in the eye and call him a fool, for believing anything so unthinkable. Then she told him that if he ever repeated such a thing to anyone, she would see to it that he never represented another client in Washington, or anywhere else in the country, as long as she lived.

When he reminded her that he had been in Washington longer than she had, that presidents come and go and so would she, she had coldly told him that *they* would be around forever and that he did not want *them* as an enemy.

Prescott didn't know who *they* were, but he'd never been threatened before and he didn't like it one bit. He needed to know more about Layla Nebit, and he knew a couple of people who should know.

When he entered the Off the Record, Martín, the bar's maitre d', waved him to his favorite red booth and headed his way.

"Mr. Prescott, how may I help you today," Martín asked as soon as he was seated.

"Do you still have a bottle of the thirty-year-Old Speyside Scotch, Martín?"

"I keep a bottle just for you, Mr. Prescott."

"A double then, and a pot of black coffee. I have some work to do."

Prescott took out his encrypted iPhone and found the home number for Edward Grimes, a senior counterintelligence officer in the CIA. Grimes had questioned him a couple of times about a Saudi prince he'd represented who was lobbying Congress for approval to buy a major share of American Airlines. The CIA's interest in the prince was threatening the effort, and the prince had learned that Grimes had a taste for child porn. Prescott had used the information to get Grimes to back off, and reminded the man of their secret from time to time when he needed information.

"Edward, John Prescott. I need a few minutes of your time."

"Give me a minute. I have company," Grimes said.

"Entertaining yourself, or do you really have company, Edward," Prescott asked.

"Screw you, Prescott. What do you want?"

"Everything you have on Layla Nebit, and any relationship she may have with the Muslim Brotherhood. I need it today."

"I'm home and it's Sunday. How am I supposed to do that?"

"You go to your office and get what I need. Or would you rather provoke me and lose your job, so you can stay home every day and watch your movies?"

He heard Grimes take two deep breaths and waited for a response.

"Good," Prescott said when there wasn't one. "Get back to me tonight."

He hoisted the tumbler of amber whisky in a mock toast to the slimy spook and sat back to wait for the long finish of butterscotch in his mouth. Layla Nebit might have the president's ear, but money ruled Washington and he controlled the flow of it through one of the biggest spigots in the city.

What he needed was a way to insulate himself from the fallout that was surely to come, if the American Muslim Youth Camp Foundation was somehow involved with the terrorists shooting down the jetliners. And if Layla Nebit and the Muslim Brotherhood were tied to it as well, he had to get ahead of whatever game they were playing. The question was how to do it.

Mark Mohamed, the head of his Middle East division, had an unconfirmed suspicion that the foundation he was somehow involved in the terrorist attacks. How he had come to that suspicion wasn't clear, but knowing more, theorectically, imposed a burden to share the information with the FBI or Homeland Security.

If Layla Nebit was involved with the Muslim Brotherhood, and they were involved with some terrorist plot, knowledge of that involvement would be difficult to prove. She was a master tactician, as her mentoring the president through his run for the White House had proven. He didn't believe she would allow herself to be directly implicated, but he did know a little of her history. If there were connections, they would be deeply buried in her past.

There wouldn't be many people who would know of those connections. But he did know of one man who might; the same man who'd suggested he ask his own employee, Mark Hassan about the terrorists responsible for shooting down the jetliners. The man who was the conduit of the money he received for the American Muslim Youth Camp Foundation, the London banker, Ryan Walker. Prescott had always suspected the man might have a cozy relationship with the Muslim Brotherhood himself.

Prescott finished his whisky and poured his first cup of the Blue Mountain Jamaican coffee the bar served. He would need to be very careful when he called the banker. If Walker was threatened by questions about Layla Nebit, or the Muslim Brotherhood, it could pose a risk to his own safety. On the other hand, doing nothing might pose the same risk.

He found the number for the banker on his contact list, considered the time difference between Washington and London, and made the call.

"Mr. Prescott," Walker answered. "I was just thinking of you and your predicament."

"My predicament?"

"May we speak freely, Mr. Prescott?"

"My phone is encrypted. Is yours?"

"That's not what I meant," the banker said. "I asked if you were prepared to be honest with me, if I ask you some questions."

"I believe I always have been honest with you."

"I'll accept that assurance for now. So, tell me, what have you learned from your employee about the planes that are being shot down?"

"He suspects that the foundation for the Muslim youth camps is somehow involved."

"What do you suspect, Mr. Prescott?"

"That he may be right, but that Laya Nebit may also be involved."

"And why do you suspect that?"

Prescott paused, before jumping in with both feet. "She's the one who got me involved with the foundation. She also threatened me an hour ago, when I asked her what she knew about the people behind the foundation and what her relationship with them was."

There was no response for an uncomfortably long time, until the banker finally said, "That was not wise on your part. You should have come to me first."

"Do you have that information?" Prescott asked.

"Information of that sort is very valuable, and very dangerous."

"If you have the information, is it something I need to know?"

"Only if you value your life, I'm afraid."

"Name your price, Mr. Walker."

When he did, Prescott drew a deep breath and said goodbye to his plan to buy the villa in Antigua he'd been coveting.

"I'll have the information delivered to your office by noon tomorrow," the banker said. "Consider how you use it wisely."

Chapter Thirty

JAMEEL MARCUS, camp commander and leader of *Allah's Sword* brigade of Sheikh Qasseer's *Army of Allah*, directed his driver to park the white van beside a picnic grove in the 44-acre Red Bank Battlefield Park in New Jersey, across the Delaware River from the Philadelphia International Airport. The van was nosed into a designated parking spot so that it provided a clear view, out the rear of the van, to the airport runways and the planes taking off and landing there.

The drive to Baltimore to deliver the load of produce had been uneventful. They'd even had time to stop and pick up some barbequed chicken at a little red barbeque shack north of the city. From there, they continued on to Philadelphia and crossed over the river on the Commodore Berry Bridge into New Jersey to reach their destination.

He had determined early on in their planning that the park was a popular place for delivery and commercial drivers to open a lunch box and spend a quiet hour.

Marcus got out of the van and walked around, kicking the tires and stretching. It was cold, with the cooling that came late in the afternoon in March, and there wasn't anything that obstructed the view across the river. The fog that frequently formed along the river was holding off, and what little wind there was wouldn't bother the flight of the missile.

Now, it was just a matter of timing, and patience. The Delta Boeing 767 that was his target was scheduled to depart at 4:25 p.m. By then, tours of the adjacent and historic Georgian-style house on the old Red Bank Plantation would have ended, and the tour staff would have left. The park would remain open, however, and on most occasions, when they'd checked, there were only a few cars still in the park. If anyone paid them any attention, they would only be able to later report that a driver and his companion had appeared to be taking a nap in their van before moving on.

Across the river in the airport, Mohamed Hassan had arranged for a spotter to call him when the target was pulling away from its gate. He'd never met the spotter and didn't need to. Mohamed Hassan had told him that all he needed to know was that the man would say "*Inshallah, it departs.*" The spotter would then call again when the plane reached the end of the runway before taking off and say "*Inshallah, it flies.*"

By then, he would be positioned in the rear of the step van, with the Russian shoulder-fired missile resting on his shoulder. The tailgate would be raised and his driver would be standing by the side of the van on the ground.

Marcus checked his watch. It was 4:00 p.m. He slipped out of his seat and walked back to the closest row of crates. The lids of the two crates had been modified to hold the missile. Nailed together, with a cradle formed by the connected ends of the crates, the two crates would have passed inspection by even the nosiest of inspectors, unless they were opened.

With the familiarity that came with hours of practice preparing to fire the missile, he took the dark green launch tube out of its cradle and hoisted it to his shoulder. He moved his eye in position to imagine that he was sighting down the iron sights, ready to pull the trigger.

"Jameel, quick," his driver yelled, "a park ranger is coming."

"Calm down. Do as we practiced it. Ask him if there's a problem. If he says the park's closing, thank him and act like you finishing your paperwork on the clip board on the dash. He'll leave."

Marcus put the missile back in its cradle and closed the lid. He checked his watch. 4:07 p.m. There was still plenty of time. He crouched behind the seat of the driver, where he couldn't be seen by the park ranger, and waited.

His driver rolled down his window and asked, "Is there a problem, officer?"

"Just checking to make sure you're okay. Saw that you've been here awhile."

"My boss wants all his paperwork filled out before I return the van. I was running late on my route and stopped to finish all his forms. It's crazy how many there are, but I'll be finished soon."

"No problem, have a good day," the ranger said and turned to leave.

Marcus said, "Keep an eye on him and tell me when he's gone. We're minutes away."

His watch read 4:19 p.m. He expected a call from the spotter in minutes.

At 4:20 p.m., his cell phone vibrated in his pocket.

"Inshallah, it departs."

Marcus put his phone on the speaker and set it on the crate he'd been sitting on.

"Has he left?" he asked.

"He's pulling away just now," his driver said.

"Is the escape car here yet?"

"It's sitting in the next picnic area. It just flashed its lights."

"Get out and get ready to open the tailgate."

He knew the driver would go to the rear of the van and act like he was checking the locking lever on the tailgate to make sure it was closed.

"Inshallah, it flies."

"Now," Marcus shouted, and stepped around the crates until he stood directly behind the tailgate.

The tailgate flew up and he looked out toward the southwest-northeast runway where he knew the Delta flight leaving for JFK was taxiing. He held the Russian SA-24 shoulder-fired air defense missile on his shoulder and readied it to fire in the automatic mode that was required for fast-moving targets.

He saw the Boeing 767 accelerate down the runway and start to lift off. He waited until it was a hundred feet high as it flashed by and adjusted his aim for lead and elevation. When he was sure of his sighting, he pulled the trigger and the missile was away.

Without waiting to see that he had hit his target, he dropped the launch tube back in its cradle, closed the lid on the modified crates and jumped out of the van. Marcus waited as his ride raced up, then jumped in as it slowed and then sped off.

His driver ran around to lock the tailgate and then jumped back in the cab to drive the van out of the park to a salvage yard. By midnight, the white van would be stripped down and then crushed to keep it from ever being found.

As he opened the door of the Dodge Charger that stopped beside him, he heard the explosion that signaled the death of Delta Boeing 767 at the end of its short flight.

Chapter Thirty-One

DRAKE WAS in his hotel room, studying a Google Earth map the camp site in West Virginia, while Casey was at the airport gathering equipment, when his friend called him.

"Turn on the TV," Casey said. "They hit us again."

Drake found the remote control on the nightstand and turned on the news at Fox 5, WTTG.

A breathless young reporter stood on the bank of the river, with flashing red

lights bobbing on boats over her shoulder.

"Eyewitnesses report seeing an explosion on the plane's right wing

engine shortly after takeoff. The plane nosed over and plunged into

Delaware River near Camden, New Jersey. Rescue efforts are under-

way for the 355 passengers on board the downed Boeing 767.

We have an unconfirmed report from a New Jersey state

Trooper saying that he saw something streaking up from the
New Jersey side of the river just before the explosion. Police
are searching the area around the Red Bank Battlefield Park."

"Are you on your way back?" Drake asked.

"Thirty minutes away," Casey reported.

"I'll call Liz and find out what she's heard." He searched his contact list and found her home number.

"You have your TV on?" he asked when she answered.

"Yes, the senator just called. These bastards!"

"Have you heard anything from your contacts at DHS or the FBI?"

"Beyond rumors, no," she said. "No one wants to confirm anything, but the talk is that a demand was made on the president from something calling itself *Allah's Sword*. There's supposed to be a list of things the terrorists want."

"Is *Allah's Sword* some Iranian or Syrian group?"

"No one's connected them to either country."

"Then why send a carrier to Syria?"

"Maybe he thinks he can scare them into backing off?" she suggested.

"I can't believe that's his answer to all of this," Drake said with disgust. "Is that all he's got?"

"I can confirm that he's ordered armed drones to protect our major airports."

"Philadelphia International Airport must have been left off the list," Drake said. "Liz, Mike's headed back to the hotel. Would you like to join is for dinner here at seven?"

"I'll be there," she said, "and I'll make some calls before then."

Drake paced in front of the flat screen on the wall. There would be major panic in America, when it was learned that armed drones were flying overhead. Even progressive Democrats would join the ranks of outraged libertarians and conservatives in protest. It was one thing for the NSA to spy on Americans, and say it was protecting us from possible terrorist strikes. It was quite another to fly armed drones overhead with the same explanation, when scenes of collateral damage from errant drone strikes in Afghanistan and Pakistan were so prominently featured on the nightly news.

And the airports would have to be closed again. Paralyzing domestic air travel would cause further damage to the economy that had already been weakened by the first shutdown. Business would scream, and amid the shock all the funerals being held for the passengers who had died, who would continue to fly when the president couldn't guarantee that it was safe.

Whoever was behind this understood America. After 9/11, we had struck out around the world at a new enemy. The enemy knew that if we were hit again and our blood was boiling, we would do the same thing again. Just as the president was threatening to do by ordering the Navy to head to the Mediterranean.

He could only conclude that we were being played. The question was by whom, and for what purpose. The possibilities, however, were now too numerous to name. American foreign policy had turned from "Peace through Strength" to "Peace through Diplomacy", and our enemies were very good at talking.

With the same angry frustration he'd felt when he left the army, when America had settled on a negotiated settlement of the war he'd been fighting, instead of victory, Drake left the room and headed downstairs to the bar to wait for Casey.

The mood of the patrons he found there was close to his own.

"What the hell," one man said as he thrust his mug toward the TV and sloshed his beer over the bar. "Why can't we stop these SOB's?"

"Because we're afraid to round up all the rag heads in the country and put them in camps, like we did the Japs," the man beside him answered.

Drake saw a number of others who had heard the comment nod in agreement. The sentiment was one he expected to hear in some biker bar. But when people were angry and felt threatened, baser emotions prevailed.

He spotted an empty table in the back and stopped to order a bottle of Sam Adams. As he opened a tab and gave the bartender his room number, Mike Casey walked through the hotel lobby and waved. He held up the bottle of beer the bartender handed him asked for another for his friend.

"If the traffic streaming out of Dulles is any indication," Casey said, "I'd say the airlines are in for a rough time."

"Did the president close down air travel again?" Drake asked.

"Not that I heard, but he didn't have to. Who in their right mind would fly the not-so-friendly-skies now?"

A waitress dropped off another bottle of beer and a dish of peanuts at their table, and Casey scooped up a handful.

"I invited Liz to join us for dinner," Drake said. "She's making some calls to find out the latest intel the government has on these guys."

Casey quickly finished his beer and signaled for another. "A small wager says she won't learn a thing. I think we're clueless on this one."

"Or, they know exactly what's going on and don't want the rest of us to know."

"Why would they do that?" Casey asked. "You'd think they would want the public's help identifying these guys/"

"Could be a number of things," Drake said. "There are a lot on MANPADs on the black market, especially after the ones in Gaddafi's arsenal went missing when we helped topple him.

Or, maybe the White House and Congress don't want it known they quietly stopped funding research on MANPAD defenses for civilian air travel.

After terrorists tried to shoot down that Israeli jetliner in 2002, several agencies were ordered to come up with an answer to the threat. They spent 276 million dollars on research, and then pulled the plug on the research. They decided the threat probability was low, and they found the price of installing defensive equipment on the airline fleets was too expensive."

"How do you know that?" Casey asked.

"I read a lot. The guy who keeps Lancer when I'm gone is a retired United Airlines pilot. He told me about it."

"I guess you wouldn't want to tell voters the threat probability is low now, after three jetliners in a week have been shot down."

"Not if you want to stay in office," Drake said. "Easier to blame Syria."

They watched what looked to be the futile efforts of the first responders to find survivors, until Drake broke the gloomy spell. "Did you get the equipment for tonight?"

"All locked and loaded in my Tahoe. I told my guys we'd leave the keys to the Tahoe you've been driving at the front desk, if they need it tonight."

"All locked and loaded for what?" Liz Strobel asked, as she walked up behind them.

Casey looked to Drake with raised eyebrows. "Just an old army expression," he deflected.

"I'll tell you about it over dinner," Drake said, "After you tell me what you were able to learn."

"The White House is in full panic mode," she said, "And there's a lot of finger pointing going on. The president is said to be considering his options, whatever that means."

Chapter Thirty-Two

AFTER BEING SUMMONED AGAIN to meet with Layla Nebit, John Prescott was delivered by limousine to the West Wing of the White House. He was then escorted by the Secret Service to her office, where he found her watching the coverage of the tragedy outside Philadelphia on the Delaware River.

"He wants some new ideas," she said, without taking her eyes off the TV. "Your last brainchild hasn't done us much good."

Prescott sat in the chair in front of her desk and struggled to remain calm. He was a lobbyist, not a military strategist or national security advisor. Surely the president had plenty of advice from men better qualified than he was. What game was the woman playing?

"What have you learned about *Allah's Sword?*" he asked.

"They haven't contacted us again. The CIA hasn't heard of them and the combined efforts of DHS and FBI haven't turned up anything useful. Why do you think I'm asking you? If those idiots had an original thought, would I be calling you?"

"Layla, you're from that part of the world. Isn't there someone you could reach out to who might know something? A rumor they've heard, or even a suspicion about who's behind this?"

When her dark brown eyes bore into his, he knew he'd crossed into enemy territory. If she had connections in the Middle East, she clearly wasn't going to talk about them. And given the current crisis, she didn't want to be told that being born in Egypt had anything to do with what was going on.

"I hope you didn't mean to suggest that I would know anyone who might even remotely be responsible for this," she said.

"No, Layla, I didn't. But you are the one who got me in touch with the sponsors for the youth camp foundation. I've never met any of them, but I believe you have. They must know people in the region who might be helpful."

She slammed her hand down on her desk. "That's enough! I didn't bring you here to tell me to solve this crisis on my own. That's what I pay you to do."

"You don't pay me to do anything," Prescott snapped and stood.

"Sit back down!" she hissed. "Every time you're paid as the chairman of the American Muslim Youth Camp Foundation, I pay you. Every time you tell someone you work closely with the White House, I pay you. When the president asks for your support on a bill because I tell him to, and you wind up being interviewed by NBC getting free publicity, I pay you. You're starting to sound like you don't appreciate that much, John. Do you want to sever our relationship, is that what you want? Because if it is, you may as well close your office and crawl back to Chicago. That's all you'll be able to do when I get through with you."

He had never wanted to strangle anyone as much as he wanted to wrap his hands around her little neck, and watch her eyes bulge when she couldn't draw another breath. She had an office in the White House and the president liked her, but she didn't know who she was threatening. He had a long memory. And he knew where the bodies were buried in the capital's body politic.

Prescott forced himself to relax and said, "How about using the State Department to go back channel to Iran and see if they know anything? It may cost you something in your negotiating with them on their nuclear program, but if you don't end this soon, it will be a long time before your party ever wins another election."

The one thing he knew she understood was the number one rule of politics; once you have power, do whatever it takes to keep it. He had to give her that. Whether she was clever enough to elevate her game from domestic politics to the worldwide stage was yet to be seen.

He watched her consider his suggestion. When she leaned forward and pressed a button on her phone console and said, "Tell the president I need to see him", he knew he had won, for the moment.

"Call me tomorrow morning," she said over her shoulder, as she walked out and left him sitting in front of her desk "The Secret Service will show you out."

Prescott followed his Secret Service escort back to his waiting Lincoln limousine and climbed in back. Layla Nebit was not going to drive him back to Chicago, because he was going to make sure he kicked her skinny butt out of the White House first. The material banker Walker was sending him tomorrow, hopefully, would give the ammunition he needed to get the job done. If not, there had to be others who could dig into her past for him.

One man came to mind. Prescott picked up the phone from the console on the floor and called Edward Grimes, senior counterintelligence officer in the CIA.

"What do you have for me, Grimes?" he asked.

"I'm in my office. I'll have it for you in an hour or so."

"What's the holdup? I need it now."

"The holdup is that some of her files are classified above my level. The ones that aren't are heavily redacted."

"Can you get the classified files?"

"If I do, it will trace right back to my desk."

"If my hunch is right," Prescott said, "you'll probably get a promotion out of it."

"Or a bullet in the back of my head," Grimes said. "Someone here's covering for her."

"Just get me the files, Grimes. Bring them to my office, I'll be working late tonight," Prescott ordered and hung up.

So, the CIA had files on Layla Nebit. It might just be that it kept files on everyone close to the president in the White House. Even so, what did it mean that hers was highly classified? Something was in play, and he needed to know what it was.

Chapter Thirty-Three

DESPITE A DINNER-LONG PLEA from Liz to join Drake and Casey to revisit the youth camp, she finally accepted the decision for her to remain in Washington. If something went wrong, they would need someone who knew what they were doing and why.

Casey had procured weapons, night vision goggles and tactical communication gear from his company's Gulfstream, stopped at a local convenience store for bottled water, beef jerky and a variety of energy drinks for the trip. The borrowed gear was from the supply of equipment stored on the jet for executive protection work his men occasionally had to do on the spur of the moment. The choice of nourishments was entirely his own.

Neither man had packed clothing for a night-time hike through the back country of West Virginia, so a quick stop at the nearest Walmart was necessary. They each selected insulated camouflage parkas and pants, waterproof hiking boots, thermal socks and underwear and black Gore Tex watch caps. The goal was to look like local hunters who were out poaching on the camp at night if they were caught. They didn't expect to be caught, of course, but they'd both seen enough action in the military to know you always prepared for the unexpected.

Drake had studied the terrain surrounding the camp from the Google Earth mapping and satellite views. He'd found a dirt road that ran close to the camp on the side farthest from the buildings and Quonset hut sleeping quarters. By the time they arrived in Romney and found their way to the dirt road, all the kids and counselors should be sleeping, if they were lucky. Drake hadn't seen dogs on the property, which made him happy when he recalled the last time he'd been chased by a pack of Dobermans. Casey had been able to pick off the dogs just in time with his sniper rifle, but Drake's memory of the night was not a fond one.

"What's the plan if we run into any of these yahoos?" Casey asked from behind the steering wheel of the Tahoe. "We'll be trespassing on their property."

"We should be able to see them long before they see us. If they see us first, they'd have to be using equipment like ours. If they are, this camp isn't what it claims to be and we'll explain ourselves to the authorities later. Escape and evasion with no casualties will be our rule of engagement. Let them shoot first, and then we'll defend ourselves if necessary."

"You really think it might come to that?" Casey asked.

"Oh yeah, I'd say there's a good possibility, Mike. The camp manager fits the description of the man who beat up Congressman Rodecker. The welcoming party that met us looked and acted like they've had military training of some sort. They sure didn't look like camp counselors."

They had been on the road for an hour when Casey asked Drake to get into the Igloo cooler on the floor behind his seat and get out some jerky for him.

"This does bring back some memories," he said. "Must be why my stomach's growling."

"Why, because you think you're not going to eat for a while?" Drake asked. They had served together in Delta Force and Casey had been a sniper who more than once had saved him with a shot from a camouflaged hide he'd been in for days on the side of a hill a half mile away.

Casey turned with a smile. "Nah, I think it's the anticipation of having a little fun with these boys. All the excitement of a good little skirmish, and we don't have to fly halfway around the world for it."

They stopped in Winchester, Virginia, to trade places and drove on through the night to Romney, West Virginia. Drake pulled over at a truck stop just outside the town to get a hot cup of coffee and use the restroom.

"In case anyone asks," Drake said, as they walked to the restaurant, "we're going to a hunting preserve south of here to hunt hogs tomorrow."

Casey held the door open for him and asked, "Where did you come up with that?"

"This is rural West Virginia," Drake pointed out. "Guys wandering around in hunting garb late at night get noticed. Having a good reason to be on the road might come in handy.

Two men sat eating chili dogs and drinking coffee at one of the picnic tables in a small eating area, and a young man sat at another table playing a game on an iPad, with an energy drink in front of him. No one looked up when they entered.

"I don't think anyone here cares a whit that we're passing through," Casey said quietly.

Drake ordered two large black coffees and paid for them and the hand full of Snicker candy bars his ever-hungry friend had picked up.

As soon as they left, the young man clicked out of the game he was playing, walked to a window looking out on the parking lot and sent a text message:

Two men just left the truck stop. One matches the picture you sent.

They're dressed as hunters, driving a white Chevy Tahoe.

Chapter Thirty-Four

IT TOOK Drake half an hour to drive from the truck stop to the northeast corner of the youth camp property for their insertion into the property. He parked the Tahoe in a wide spot of the road, under a Red Spruce tree, and helped Casey unload their equipment from two tactical duffel bags.

First, Drake strapped on his Kimber Master Carry Pro .45 in its leather belt holster, and then slipped his Harsey Tactical folding knife in the pocket of his parka. Next, he took out the night vision goggles in his bag.

"These are very cool," Casey said. "I got them from L3 Warrior Systems. This is the AN/PSQ-36 Fusion Goggle System. It allows you to switch from 100%-night vision to 100% thermal imaging whenever you want. Catch sight of someone, then lose him, and switch to thermal to relocate him. You might find the one guy now has three more standing behind him."

"I thought these were only available to the military," Drake said, as he examined the goggles.

"I still have connections," Casey said proudly. "How do you think I got a hold of that Special Forces Precision Sniper Rifle I used in Oregon at the Top Gun training last month? Most of the Special Forces units don't even have that rifle yet."

Drake put the goggle headset on and turned the system on. "This is something," he said as he switched from image intensification to thermal imaging.

Casey strapped on his preferred Colt M45 CQBP pistol in a drop leg holster and slung a tactical rifle across his chest in a tactical harness. "And this is a Les Baer "Police Special" tactical rifle I'm trying out for the company."

"You sound like a kid in a candy shop," Drake said, "trying out any piece of new gear that catches your eye."

That made Casey laugh. "You're catching on, amigo. I love my job. Why don't you join me? Come be my in-house corporate attorney. You could help me evaluate all the cool new stuff vendors keep trying to sell me."

Drake checked his watch, put on his black watch cap and started across the road. "Let's go, Mike. We can talk about it later. I'd like to be out of here before the sun comes up."

The road provided the northeast boundary of the youth camp and ran along a heavily wooded section of Red Spruce. From the Google Earth views Drake had seen, beyond the fifty yards or so of trees, the property opened onto a small flat meadow about the size of a football field before it rose steeply to the top of the camp and the buildings there.

Drake signaled for Casey to follow on his right flank and moved into the cover of the forest. The spruce needles on the ground provided a soft and scented surface that allowed them to move quietly through the area. When they reached the edge of the meadow, both men stopped and stared ahead.

The sight was a familiar one. At the far end of the meadow, a shooting range was backstopped by the steep slope rising above it. Targets were set close to the firing line for pistols, on a range set in front of a bank that had been dug into the bottom of the hill.

To the left of the shooting range was a PT area, complete with an overhead climbing ladder, a 20-foot rope climbing wall, a sand-floored fighting pit lined with sand bags and a crude roofless "shooting house" made of green-painted plywood walls. An equipment shed stood to the right of the "shooting house".

"Looks like they're training these kids to be good little soldiers," Drake heard Casey say through the bone conduction microphone in his ear canal that attached to the Motorola 2200 Combat Radio on his belt they were both wearing.

"The camp manager said they were teaching them skills they needed to survive. He forgot to mention it was survival on the battlefield."

Drake vectored the meadow, looking to see if any of the soldiers-in-training were lurking about.

"You see anyone?" he asked Casey.

"Not down here. Look up on the ridge."

Drake saw movement on the ridgeline behind a line of trees. When he switched to thermal imaging in his goggles, saw the red center mass of bodies spaced every twenty yards along the ridgeline. Their extremities were shades of green and blue, and in flashes he saw faces in white where heat escaped in the cold from their uncovered faces. When he switched back to night vision, he saw they were armed.

"You see what they're carrying, Mike?"

"Looks like AK-74's to me. Are they practicing guard duty or waiting for us?"

"Only one way to find out. I'll go left, you go right. Let's see how close we can get. Their reaction will give them away."

Drake moved from tree to tree until he reached the side of the meadow and started toward the PT area at the far end.

"You ready to advance?" he asked.

"Ready when you are," Casey answered.

Drake sprinted to a spruce twenty yards away at the side of the meadow and stopped. He looked across the meadow and saw Casey find his own tree to hide behind.

In the next ten minutes, they leap-frogged along the sides of the meadow until Drake reached the climbing ladder and Casey was behind the equipment shed on the other side.

"What now, Kemo Sabe?" Casey asked.

"There's a path leading from this side of the PT area to the ridge above. They would expect to us to use it. Let's meet at the shooting range and see about that slope below the ridgeline."

Drake ran to the climbing wall and crouched down behind it. From there, he watched Casey dart to a raised platform at the far end of the shooting range. It looked like the camp used a range master on a platform to maintain range safety, which meant the kids here were getting a better training than most of the jihadi camps in the Middle East he'd seen.

"Mike," he said softly, "work around your side of the range. I'll meet you behind the middle of those target stands."

Drake got there first. The ridgeline rose sixty or seventy feet above the meadow where more red spruce stood sentinel. The slope up to the ridgeline was thickly covered with an evergreen shrub he recognized as a species of rhododendron, standing six to ten feet tall.

"When we get up there," Casey said, when he moved next to Drake and looked up, "we'll be right under them. If they turn those 47's on us, these rhodies won't provide much cover."

"Then what about just poking the hive, see how it reacts?"

"Poking them with what?"

"I've got Crimson Trace laser grips on my Kimber," Drake said. "I could sneak a little closer and light one up. Put a red dot, center mass, on one and watch."

"And you might start a war. They're not going to know you don't intend to shoot."

"If I'm right about this place, they *will* come after us, but they won't shoot. They'll want to catch us and find out how much we know."

"Hell of a way to confirm your suspicion."

"Do you have a better idea?" Drake asked.

"No."

"When we get through these rhodies, find a place to cover me. Be on the side of the slope above of the shed where you took cover. I'll get as close as I can, mark one with my laser and join you as fast as I can. If they come after me, they'll come down the trail over there. We'll make our way out the way you came in and watch from the forest."

"Rules of engagement?" Casey asked.

"Survive, escape and evade."

Chapter Thirty-Five

DRAKE MOVED UP THE SLOPE, picking his way around tall, wild rhododendron plants. The earth was soft, and he was able to move quietly, stopping every ten yards to search for movement. If he didn't see any, he switched from the green-tinted night vision view to thermal view by reaching up and switching his NIV goggles. If it was clear, he moved on.

The steep slope leveled off above him and a stand of spruce trees provided a barrier separating the lower meadow and training area from the rest of the camp. The bodies he'd seen standing guard duty were stationed in a line among the trees, standing with their AK 47's at port arms twenty-five yards away.

Drake dropped to the ground and low crawled to his right until he had a clear line of sight to the sentries. They were all dressed alike, dark colored berets, dark military fatigue jackets and pants and boots. He remembered the Black Panther look-alikes who had escorted him to meet the camp manager.

One sentry, taller than the others, walked slowly behind the line from one end to the other. He stopped occasionally and leaned his head close to the ear of one of his sentries, like a drill sergeant instructing his troops. He would be the one to target, Drake decided.

He slowly pulled his Kimber .45 from its holster. When his target moved between the two sentries closest to Drake, he took aim and switched on his laser.

The man took three steps before he stopped and dropped his chin to look at the red dot on the middle of his chest. It took a split second to recognize the red dot for what it was, and then he darted behind the closest tree and blew a whistle.

Drake scrambled back a couple of yards and took off running diagonally down the slope, dodging the tall rhododendron plants like a running back breaking clear of the scrimmage line. From behind the line of trees at the top of the slope, he heard multiple 4-stroke ATV or UTV engines firing up.

He reached the edge of the slope and ran into the cover of the spruce trees that bordered the meadow.

"Keep heading down," he heard in his ear bud, "and move deeper into the trees. They're coming down the trail in UTV's with lights blazing. They think you're still on the slope and they're trying to block your escape."

Drake ran on and joined Casey at the far end of the meadow. From there, they watched as four UTV's raced down and took position along the line of target stands of the shooting range. Each UTV had lights on its front brush guards and atop its roll bars. Facing the slope above, the combined candle power from all the lights lit up the area, casting tall shadows all the way up the slope.

One man in each UTV stood from the passenger side and sighted his AK 47 over the top of the roll bar at the slope above. The driver in each UTV kept the engine running, waiting to chase down the intruder.

"They were waiting for us," Drake said, when he'd caught his breath when he reached his friend.

"This isn't a boy scout camp," Casey whispered. "These guys are a well-trained as some unit."

"And well-equipped," Drake said, as he watched the driver in the first UTV down the trail step out with a bull-horn and walk out in front of the others.

"There's no place to run," he shouted. "You are trespassing, and we have the right to use deadly force against you. Come out now and we'll talk."

The man with the bull horn returned to his UTV and stood beside it. He remained there for another minute, and then walked back out in front of the line and raised the bull horn again.

"In three minutes," he announced calmly, "my men will begin shooting. Come out now or suffer the consequences."

Drake leaned closer to Casey and said, "Let's get out of here. They'll figure it out soon enough that I'm not up there."

Before they reached the road, they heard the AK 47's open up on full auto and keep firing until their 30 round magazines were empty.

When they reached their Tahoe, Casey stowed his rifle on the floor behind his seat and had the engine running before Drake slid in beside him. Both men kept their night vision goggles on, as they drove off without turning on the SUV's headlights.

"Let's keep the lights off until we're down to the paved road," Drake said. "We shouldn't run into a sheriff on patrol this far out."

"As soon as we're clear, we also need to get out of these clothes," Casey said. "Someone will report hearing the shooting. We'll be suspected of hunting at night if we're stopped. I'd rather spend the night back at our hotel and not in some local jail."

Casey drove down the dirt road as fast as he dared, until they came to the intersection with the paved country road that led to the city of Romney and the highway back to D.C.

"Mike, turn left. This road will run back to the highway about twenty miles east of Romney. Turning right takes us back through the town, and they probably have someone there spotting for them. They weren't surprised to see us tonight."

"Maybe they were hoping you'd bring Liz back with you," Casey joked, "all these horny adolescents cooped up out here."

Drake started to remind his friend of what they'd learned about the sexual practices of young men in Afghanistan and thought better of it. There was plenty to think about on the drive back, without polluting their minds with those thoughts.

Chapter Thirty-Six

MOHAMMAD HASSAN WAS in his office in the Evening Star building in D.C. when Rasheed Marcus reported in from the youth camp in West Virginia. He took out the burner phone he was using at the moment and listened.

"The trip north was successful. I'm home."

"I saw of your success," Hassan said. "Was your return uneventful?"

"Completely."

"What about the party when you returned?" Hassan asked.

"We were not able to celebrate as planned."

"Did your guest arrive?"

"He did but didn't stay long."

Hassan swore, set the phone down on his desk and paced around it. When he regained control of his anger, he sat back down and picked up the phone.

"Are you're sure it was the guest we expected?"

"My spotter at the truck stop recognized him when he stopped for coffee," Marcus answered.

"What did he see?"

"The training facility on the meadow."

"Nothing else?"

"I'm told that's all."

"Are you sure?"

"I met with each of my men separately. They told the truth."

Hassan knew how Marcus sought the truth from his men; with a gun to their head.

"Send four men to me at daylight. Have them call when they arrive. I'll locate your guest so they can deliver the party gifts he didn't stay around for," Hassan instructed and ended the call.

He looked at his watch, a new Patek Philippe Calatrava he treasured, and saw that he was late for his tryst with the lovely and demanding Layla Nebit. Knowing how the White House had reacted to the third jetliner being shot down was critical to his plan.

The president had followed the suggestion of John Prescott and pointed the blame for the acts of terrorism on Syria. The MANPAD launch tubes recovered from the first two downed jetliners had, indeed, provided evidence for that. The MANPADS were from the same lot smuggled out of Libya by the Brotherhood. They were not, however, the ones that had been sold back to the CIA for supply to the Syrian rebels. They were the ones that had been sold to the crazy Sheikh Qasseer in Bahrain.

The next step was to get the MANPADS traced back to Sheikh Qasseer, and not Syria, so that the U.S. would take a closer look at his relationship with Iran. While Syria was a puppet of Iran, its president was reckless enough to act on his own, without being told to do so by Iran. The endgame was to get the U.S. to wake up and get serious about Iran's nuclear weapons program. Saudi Arabia and the other Sunni Muslim nations in the region could not afford to have a nuclear Iran dominate the region.

It was a dangerous game, to be sure, but if a few hundred passengers on these jetliners had to be sacrificed to provoke the sleeping giant, so be it. They were, after all, *infidels* who would be sacrificed eventually when the *caliphate* was restored.

Before he left his office, Hassan made a quick call to a man only few knew served the cause as he did.

"Raul, do you recognize my voice?" Hassan asked. Raul was the cover name the man used.

"Yes," Carlos Mora, chief of security for the Venezuelan embassy in Georgetown, said.

"I need to have a man followed. He's staying near you in the Savoy Suites Hotel."

"How soon?"

"Tonight, if possible," Hassan said.

"It will be expensive. I'll have to pay my men personally."

"Your fee will be deposited in your Cayman account."

"Send his picture to me, and I'll see to it."

"A pleasure as always, Raul," Hassan said.

Hassan had met Carlos Mora through the man he knew as Ryan Walker, who facilitated the cooperation between the Islamic jihad movement and the drug cartels of South America. He was a banker like himself, and they both had offices in London. And he was the man who funneled money from the Muslim Brotherhood to various groups around the world, including the American Muslim Youth Camp Foundation that ran the camp in West Virginia.

He had considered, and then decided against, warning Walker about the need to sacrifice the foundation. The link from the youth camps to Sheikh Qasseer had to be discovered by the Americans. Walker was the best in the world at illicit money transfer and didn't need his warning to be careful. But it was still a risk, though. If Walker's link to the foundation was discovered, it would eventually lead to a money trail connecting most of the major terrorist groups and drug cartels in the world.

Warning Layla Nebit about the need to sacrifice the foundation was another matter. They had used her relationship with John Prescott to set up the foundation, as a conduit for funding the various Muslim Brotherhood front groups in America.

Prescott was omnipotent in Washington, as a lobbyist, and his reputation was above reproof. He might survive as a lobbyist and be able to insulate himself from the fallout when the true nature of the youth camps was discovered. If he didn't, he might have to be sacrificed along with the foundation.

Layla Nebit's influence and role as a trusted advisor of the current president in the White House, on the other hand, probably would not survive. As much as he enjoyed her beauty and the pleasure she gave him, he wasn't willing to risk his plan to save her position. And he wasn't completely confident that she would willingly sacrifice her position of power so that his greater plan could be successful.

Layla was committed to the Muslim Brotherhood's long-term goals for subverting America from the inside out, *the Project*, as they called it. He too shared the belief that America would eventually destroy itself from within, with its decadence and greed. But the events of the Arab Spring had advanced the time table for dealing with a greater threat to the vision of the Brotherhood, the resurgence of the Shia Muslims and Iran. Iran had to be dealt with, and the might of the armies of the West were, unfortunately, necessary to do that before it was too late.

He was humming Eric Clapton's "Layla" as he drove out of the basement parking floor on the way to Layla's condo for their weekly tryst. As sad as he felt about the woman's future prospects, he intended to make the best of the situation, at least for one more night.

He needed to know what the president was thinking of doing. So far, all the options the president had chosen had originated with her.

Chapter Thirty-Seven

MONDAY MORNING, after hearing about their exploits in West Virginia, Liz invited Drake and Casey to meet her for breakfast at the Tabard Inn on N Street NW. The 1880's town house had been converted into a hotel and restaurant and, according to Liz, remained one of the best places in Washington to enjoy breakfast and a little history.

When they were seated near a window at the far end of the main dining room, Liz was anxious to talk about the American Muslim Youth Camp Foundation.

"Relax, pretty lady," Mike Casey said as he studied his menu, "I need to decide what I'm having before I can pay attention."

Drake shook his head. "Mike's hungry, Liz, but I'm listening. What did you find out?"

"It's complicated, but I think the foundation may be a front for the Muslim Brotherhood."

"I'm not that hungry," Casey said, and put his menu down. "What makes you think that?"

"The American Muslim Youth Camp Foundation is a 501(c)3 non-profit foundation.," she explained. "It hasn't filed the IRS Form 990 tax forms as required for the last three years, so we don't know who its contributors are. But we do know that John Prescott was a lobbyist for the Muslim Brotherhood when it was in power in Egypt, and he receives a million dollars a year for serving as the foundation's board chairman."

"How do we know that?" Drake asked.

"His tax returns. Four of the other nine board members receive half a million dollars a year each for four quarterly board meetings. Three of the board members lead Muslim organizations thought to have ties to the Muslim Brotherhood, and the fourth is the president's closest advisor."

"Let me guess," Drake said. "The fourth board member is Layla Nebit. But does she have ties to the Muslim Brotherhood?"

Liz shook her head. "Not directly. She was born in Egypt and educated here. Her mother is a U.S. citizen, a former State Department foreign officer. Her father was a professor at the American University in Cairo. He left that position and came to the states when he fell under suspicion for being a member of the Muslim Brotherhood. He denied it, of course, but to admit it meant spending the rest of his life in an Egyptian prison, being tortured by the Mukhabarat, their secret police."

"I think you're barking up the wrong tree," Casey said. "There's no way someone with suspected ties to the Muslim Brotherhood would be allowed to serve as the president's closest advisor."

"Maybe," Liz admitted. "She's counseled the president throughout his political career, not just in the White House. So, he trusts her, and he gets to pick and choose his advisors. But look at the way our foreign policy has changed since she's had the president's ear. She's also the White House official who handles inquiries about the administration's position on Senator Boykin's bill, to restore the assets of the Muslim Brotherhood we've frozen."

Drake asked for more time to consider his menu when the waiter came. "Liz, let's say the foundation is a front for the Muslim Brotherhood, or has ties to it. Has anyone paid any attention to these so-called youth camps the foundation is operating?"

"I looked into that," she said. "Initially, the FBI put the camps under surveillance. They're all located in remote, rural locations.

The camps knew they were being watched. Then the Muslim lobby here in Washington raised a fuss about religious discrimination, and the FBI backed off."

"Unbelievable," Casey exclaimed. "There's nothing the government is doing to protect people from these nuts?"

"Until they directly act against us, there isn't," Liz said. "White supremacists operate paramilitary "survival" training camps all over America and the law allows it."

Drake had heard enough and picked up his menu. "We might not be able to do anything about the other camps, but there's no way we need one in Oregon. I'm advising my client to reject the foundation's offer. He'll have to find another buyer if he still wants to sell the ranch."

"Does that mean we go home?" Casey asked.

"If you think Congressman Rodecker doesn't need protection any longer, I guess we can," Drake said. "Has he made arrangements for a place to stay, or is he staying with Senator Hazelton?"

"He's staying with the senator for the rest of this week," Liz said.

"There's your answer, Mike. I'll pay the foundation attorney a visit today. We could leave tomorrow."

"But you're still coming for dinner tonight?" Liz asked Drake.

"I wouldn't miss it," he said.

Mike Casey started to ask if he could come along when his cell phone vibrated in his pocket. He excused himself and walked from the rear dining room to the covered entrance of the restored row house and stepped outside to take the call.

"Boss," Kevin McRoberts, his IT guru and company hacker said, "you asked me to look into that foundation in Washington. You won't believe what I found."

"Go ahead."

"You know the bank in San Francisco that was involved in that thing with Mr. Drake? All the contributions made to the American Youth Camp Foundation are made from accounts in a bank in London owned by the same banking conglomerate."

"How much are we talking about, Kevin?"

"The foundation received forty-five million dollars in the last calendar year. It's on a pace to receive even more this year."

"Did you try to get into the conglomerate's IT system," Casey asked.

"No, I didn't think you wanted me to."

"Good, let's hold off on that for now. Good work, Kevin. I'll talk with Drake and get back to you."

Mike Casey stood on the front steps of the Tabard Hotel and wondered what charitable work the nonprofit foundation was doing with forty-five million dollars, supplied from a dirty universal banking conglomerate they'd run into before.

As he turned to go back inside, he didn't notice the two Venezuelan secret service men watching him from a car parked across the street. Nor did he know they had been following him, from the time he left the Savoy Suites Hotel that morning with Drake.

Chapter Thirty-Eight

CASEY RETURNED to his table in time to order breakfast.

"That was Kevin," he said, as he looked to Drake. "Remember the Pacific First Security Bank of California in San Francisco."

"I remember the bank and the bank president, why?" Drake asked.

"The American Youth Camp Foundation got forty-five million dollars last year from the universal banking conglomerate that owns that bank," Casey said.

The previous fall, Drake had uncovered a plot to take down America's electrical power grid. The bank and its president had been involved, with the operation being run by a neo-fascist group out of a fortified basement in the bank president's home. The banker president had fled in a private jet bound for Cuba before he could be arrested, and was still being sought by the FBI and Interpol.

"Is the bank president from San Francisco involved with the foundation?" Liz asked.

"I don't know," Casey said. "I thought we needed to discuss it before I, uh, ask Kevin to look into it."

"You mean hack into the bank's system," Liz asked. "Can he do that?"

"I am not aware of the full range of my employee's skills," Casey said, "and I will not confirm such a plan to commit such an act."

Drake laughed. "No one is aware of all the skills young Kevin has, Mike. What I would be interested in knowing is who's involved with this banking conglomerate. Who owns these accounts contributing forty-five million dollars to the foundation? Do any of them involve our bank president from San Francisco? If they are, what's someone involved with neo-fascists doing sending money to a Muslim foundation here in America?"

"Not to get too far off topic," Liz said, "but the Nazis and the Muslims worked together in WWII. Both of them are technically classified as "fascist" due to their belief systems."

"That's all we need, Liz, getting those two groups back together again. Adam, are you okay with me asking Kevin to take a peek?"

"I'm not sure it's necessary, Mike," Drake said. "I'm advising my client to reject the foundation's offer for his ranch. This sounds like something Liz needs to get someone in the government to investigate. No need for you or Kevin to take any risks on my behalf. Enjoy your breakfast and let's wrap things up and go home."

AFTER BREAKFAST in the historic inn and restaurant, Liz left for her morning staff meeting in Senator Hazelton's office, and Casey left to have his Gulfstream ready for the trip home. Drake decided to walk the short distance to the Prescott Building to tell the foundation's attorney his client wasn't interested in selling his ranch so that could become a Muslim paramilitary training camp.

It was cold in the capital at ten in the morning, but still warm enough for Drake to enjoy walking down Massachusetts Avenue. He would have liked to have had time to visit the war memorials and the Smithsonian, but events of the week had kept him busy. Still, as he looked around at the busy center of government, there were places and institutions every citizen needed to see and know about.

He was looking down the broad avenue when he sensed a car slow behind him. As it passed to his left, he saw that it was a dark silver Chrysler 300C. The side windows were tinted, and he couldn't see who was driving the car, but he noticed that it carried foreign mission license plates.

Seeing a car in Washington with diplomat, consul or staff foreign mission license plates wasn't unusual; they were everywhere. But the way the car slowly drove past and then accelerated away had stirred an old sensation of danger.

The license plate had a blue border on top, a red border below and a white center with a large letter **S** followed by two letters and four numbers. Drake committed then to memory: **S LC 2254.**

He was three blocks farther down Massachusetts Avenue when the same car passed him again. This time it slowed just enough to get a good look at him and then continued on. He was being followed.

Drake took out his cell phone and called Mike Casey.

"Mike, I'm five blocks down Massachusetts Avenue from the Tabard Inn and I'm being followed. How far away are you?"

"Ten minutes. What do you want me to do?"

"Get on Massachusetts, somewhere between 10th St. and 9th St. and park. I'll walk on by and see if a silver Chrysler 300C comes by again. License is a foreign mission plate, **S LC 2254.**"

"Got it," Casey said. "Want me to follow them?"

"Yes, let's find out who this is. If they head back my way, let me know."

Drake continued walking, alert now to every car that passed. It was possible that someone at the youth camp had guessed who it was that paid them a visit the night before, but there wasn't any reason for them to be following him in a car with foreign mission license plates.

His phone vibrated in his pocket.

"You'll love this," Casey said. "The license number you gave me means it belongs to the Venezuelan embassy. **LC** is the two-letter designation on all their vehicles."

"What interest could Venezuela possibly have in me?"

"No clue. I'm parked between 10th and 9th. Stroll on down and let's see what these guys are up to."

Drake picked up his pace. Other than the crisis swirling around the city, caused by the terrorist attacks on the jetliners, his visit to Washington had been uneventful. Except for sneaking onto the youth camp, of course. Now there was a new element involved and he couldn't guess why.

Two blocks down the avenue, he spotted the white Chevy Tahoe waiting where Casey had parked it in the middle of the block. If the silver Chrysler kept to the same pattern of surveillance sweeps as before, it should be driving by any moment.

A car slowed he looked in his peripheral vision to see if it was the silver Chrysler. It wasn't. It was a black Chrysler 300C this time with foreign mission plates.

"Mike," Drake said hurriedly after hitting redial, "follow the black 300 just going by. Same embassy plates."

If they were using a two-car team to follow him, Drake knew there was something serious going on and it involved a foreign country that wasn't exactly a friend of ours.

Chapter Thirty-Nine

DRAKE KEPT WALKING down Massachusetts Avenue until Mike Casey called back.

"The black Chrysler pulled around the corner and let a guy out," he said. "He's headed your way. Five nine, dark complexion, black hair and dark overcoat."

"Any sign of the other Chrysler?"

"Haven't seen it. He may have dropped someone off as well. You probably caught them off guard by walking."

"Mike, Union Station's up ahead," Drake said. "I'm going to keep walking and then go inside and see if I can get photos of these clowns. When I call you, pick me up out front."

"If you need help, call me. Two against one isn't a fair fight."

"Who said anything about a *fair* fight?"

"Roger that," Casey said.

Drake picked up his pace and continued, until he crossed the street at North Capitol Street NW and kept walking down Massachusetts Avenue past the National Postal Museum. As much as he wanted to stop and see why on earth there was a national postal museum, he crossed First Street NE and entered Washington's Union Station.

Inside the national landmark, with its soaring vaulted entryway and spectacular 600-foot Main Hall, he played the role of a tourist visiting for the first time. Turning slowly to take in the statuary and the 96-foot-high white coffered ceiling shining with gold leaf, he took out his cell phone and began taking pictures.

Without focusing the pictures he was taking, Drake scanned the entryway he had just passed through until he spotted the man Casey had seen dropped off. The man was walking beside another man carrying a folded newspaper in one hand and a briefcase in the other. Both men turned and walked toward a kiosk in the middle of the East Hall. When Drake began slowly turning to complete a panoramic shot of the vaulted ceiling, both men turned away to study the offerings of the kiosk.

Moving on, Drake stopped beside the café in the center of the Main Hall and looked at a menu posted on the wall. In its glass-covering, he saw in the reflection the two men turn back toward him.

When they continued to stare at him, he focused his cell phone on the menu and whistled softly, as if the prices there were shocking, and fiddled with the focus setting. He also switched the camera icon to "selfie" mode and twisted just enough to frame the two men over his shoulder.

With a clear frontal shot of both men, he walked out of the Main Hall to the Amtrak ticket counter and stood looking at the posted schedules. After a minute, he put his cell phone to his ear and called Casey.

"Call me when you're out front," he said. "Let's see if we can lose these guys."

Three minutes later, the vibration in his pocket told him his ride was waiting.

Drake spun on his heel and walked quickly to the entryway and out to the white Tahoe parked at the curb. As soon as his door was closed, Casey quickly pulled out onto Columbus Circle and then accelerated down Louisiana Avenue NE.

Twisting around in his seat, Drake watched for one of the

Chrysler 300's or any other car with foreign mission plates following them.

"Looks like were clear, Mike."

"What now?"

"Let me think," Drake said. "I still need to talk with the foundation's attorney. Let's head there. I'll call Liz. She might be able to get someone to use facial recognition to identify these guys. While she's working on that, I'll see if the attorney's in."

By the time he had called Liz, told her what he needed and forwarded the picture of the two men to her, Casey had pulled up in front of the Prescott Building.

"I'll find a place to park where I can keep an eye on you when you come out," Casey said.

"I shouldn't be long," Drake said, as he was getting out. "How long can it take to say "no"?"

In the elevator on the way to the top floor, he ticked off the things he'd learned about the American Muslim Youth Camp Foundation and the reasons he'd give his client when recommending the rejection of the purchase offer. The foundation did, indeed, run what appeared to be paramilitary training camps for Muslim youth, if the camp in West Virginia was representative of the other camps and the camp it wanted to set up in Oregon. The foundation was doing more than just providing summer camp experiences for young Muslims; it generously funded a number of organizations that were thought to have ties to the Muslim Brotherhood. And perhaps most importantly, the West Virginia Camp manager fit the description of the man who beat up Congressman Rodecker.

When he gave the receptionist his name and asked to see Mr. Hassan, he was again asked to wait until she checked to see if Mr. Hassan was in. This time, however, Hassan's assistant came out to meet him before he had time to sit down and scan the latest news on the front page of the Washington Post.

"Mr. Hassan has a moment to see you before his next appointment," the assistant said and turned to lead him to Hassan's office.

"A moment is all I need," Drake said, to end this charade.

Chapter Forty

MARK HASSAN SAT behind his desk with his hands folded calmly in his lap. "Has your client decided to accept our offer, Mr. Drake?"

Drake sat down and mirrored Hassan's confident posture. "I advised him to reject your offer, Mr. Hassan."

Hassan turned his head to look out the window, and turned back with a tight smile on his lips. "Why would you do that?"

"I think you know why. I visited the camp in West Virginia. I met the camp manager who looks a lot like the man who put Congressman Rodecker in the hospital. I looked into your foundation and the organizations and causes it supports. And I learned a little about where your money comes from. In short, there's no way in hell I'd let you buy my client's ranch to run a training camp for some sheikh in Bahrain," Drake said, throwing in a mention of the sheikh he heard named by the two foundation men in Oregon, to see if Hassan would rise to the bait.

"Those are slanderous accusations you're making," Hassan said. "They have a way of being taken very seriously in this town."

"Truth is a complete defense to a charge of slander, Mr. Hassan. I don't think your foundation would like to test that in court."

"That's a decision the foundation's board would have to make. I might be willing to overlook your words today, Mr. Drake, but it would be dangerous for you to repeat them elsewhere."

Drake stood. "Is that a threat?"

"Take it any way you like," Hassan said, as he rose behind his desk and watched Drake walk away down the hall.

Casey was parked across the street in front of an old Methodist church when Drake walked out of the Prescott Building.

"How was the meeting?" Casey asked when Drake sat down in the passenger seat of the Tahoe.

"Remember how we poked the hornet's nest in West Virginia? I think I may have done it again."

"How'd you do that?"

"I told him there was no way in hell we were going to sell the ranch so the sheikh in Bahrain could run a training camp in Oregon," Drake said and smiled. "That's when he told me that repeating such an accusation would be dangerous."

"Dangerous like they might sue you?"

"I think he meant dangerous, Mike, as in dangerous. It was a warning."

"What do you want to do about it?"

Drake saw Mark Hassan walk briskly out of his building and head west on K Street.

"I think I want to know a little more about the man who just threatened me. There he goes," he nodded.

Casey turned and looked across the street. "Black hair, 5-9, in the blue suit?"

"That's the one."

The Tahoe was parked on the south side of a two-way street. Hassan was headed the other way.

"By the time we get turned around to follow him, we might lose him," Drake said. "Why don't you follow him and see where he's going? Once he's a block or so away, I'll turn around and pick you up."

Casey handed him the keys and crossed the street to follow Hassan.

Drake waited until he saw Hassan cross 10th Street NW before he got out and took Casey's place behind the wheel. When he saw that Casey had crossed the street as well, he drove east and looked for a place to turn around. Two blocks away, he found a parking garage on the other side of the street, pulled in far enough to allow him to reverse quickly and drive back up K Street.

Searching ahead on the sidewalk, he didn't see his red-headed friend on the block he was on, or as far as he could see on the next block. Now what, he thought. Casey could call him without alerting Hassan that he was being followed. Half the people walking on the sidewalk were using their phones.

Drake pulled to the curb in the first parking space he found and waited for Casey to call. He could always catch up with him when he learned where he was. What they did then would depend on Hassan. If he was going about his business as usual, watching him would be a waste of time. Discerning whether it was business as usual would be the hard part.

He was drumming his fingers on the top of the steering wheel when Casey called.

"Where are you?"

"Three blocks up K Street at the Hamilton Crowne Plaza."

"Is Hassan there?"

"He's waiting for someone, I think."

"Why do you think that?"

"He just ordered two drinks."

"You're in the bar?"

"They call it the 14K Lounge."

"What do you want to do?" Drake asked.

"Have a beer, have something to eat, see who he's meeting."

"You're enjoying this, aren't you?"

"Can't let you have all the fun."

"Only fair, I guess. I'm parked on the street a block away. If he heads this way, call me so I have time to move."

"Want me to bring you something?"

"Hang up and enjoy your beer."

While he waited, Drake called Liz. There was too much he

didn't know about Mark Hassan, and the work he did for the foundation.

"Liz, you have a moment?"

"Sure, where are you," she asked.

"Sitting in our rented Tahoe, while Mike's keeping an eye on someone who just threatened me, why?

"We need to meet. There's a lot going on you need to know about."

"When are you free?" Drake asked.

"Give me an hour. Meet me where we had dinner."

Drake sat back and waited, focusing his attention on the pedestrian traffic flowing by. He didn't have a solid reason for following Mark Hassan, just an instinct that the man's threat was one he needed to take seriously.

Hassan had been too calm when confronted with allegations about the youth camps being run by a sheikh in Bahrain, or that the camp manager resembled Congressman Rodecker's attacker. Calling it all "slanderous" was a lawyer-like deflection that fell way short of the vehement denial you would expect.

And it wasn't that someone had threatened him. As a prosecutor in the District Attorney's office in Portland, he'd been threatened by men he considered to be more dangerous than a lawyer like Mark Hassan. It was that the threat had been an inappropriate response to such an obvious provocation.

Drake's phone vibrated in his hand.

"Hassan's party just arrived," Casey said. "He could be Hassan's brother. Hassan's agitated about something and the other guy is trying to calm him down. No, back that up. The other guy is getting in his face. Hassan's looks like a schoolboy being disciplined by his principal."

"Can you get a picture of the other guy?"

"Just did, he's facing me three tables away."

"When the other guy leaves" Drake said, "Give me a heads up. I'm going to see if I can find out who he is. Finish your midmorning snack and I'll come back and get you."

Before Drake could find the right Sirius channel to check the latest news, Casey called back.

"He's heading your way. Hassan's right beside him."

Drake started the engine, ready to pull out and follow the other man. Casey was right, he saw. Two men walked out of the Crowne Plaza and they looked like brothers. Mark Hassan turned left and headed toward Drake and the other man turned right and walked to the intersection.

When he saw an opening in traffic, Drake pulled out and used a parked car to shield him from Hasaan as he walked by. The other man crossed the street and continued down 14th Street NW toward the White House.

At the intersection, Drake waited for the oncoming traffic to allow him to turn down 14th Street NW and turned left. The other man was a block ahead on the left and still walking.

Fortunately, the traffic this near the White House moved slowly enough that he didn't have to worry about being forced to drive by his target. Keeping up with him was the challenge.

At F Street, the man turned left for three blocks and then south again down 12th Street NW. Drake was just able to see him enter the Evening Star Building when he made the turn onto Pennsylvania Avenue.

There was no way he could park and hope to find which office the man entered, so Drake pulled down the underground parking ramp, forked over nine dollars for a one-hour parking pass so that he could at least find out who occupied the offices above.

On the second level down, he slowed and knew he didn't need to get out and check the office listings. It was too much of a coincidence for the man he'd been following to not be the owner of the black Gembala 911 Porsche parked in the space reserved for Wyse &Williams Investment Bank of London, Mohammad Hassan's firm.

Chapter Forty-One

DRAKE WENT BACK and picked up Casey, who was standing in front of the Prescott Building.

"Did you find out where he was going?" Casey asked, as he opened the door and got in.

"I did. I even know who he is."

"That was quick. Who is he?"

Drake turned to watch traffic and pulled away from the curb before answering. "He's the guy in the black Porsche, who followed me to West Virginia. His name is Mohamed Hasaan and he's a banker from London. Interpol thinks he might be a money man for the Muslim Brotherhood."

"What the hell!" Casey exclaimed. "What's he doing meeting with the attorney for the foundation?"

"I don't know, Mike. Maybe they're brothers. They look alike and both of their last names are Hassan. Maybe the Muslim Brotherhood is a big contributor to the foundation. I'm just glad I don't need to have anything more to do with any of this."

"We're going home? Now?" Casey asked.

"Liz wants to meet us in a bit. She has something she thinks we need to know. I'm having dinner with her to night. Tomorrow morning all right?"

"That works for me," Casey said. "I'll let my pilot and my wife know we're flying west."

Drake drove around the block and got on Massachusetts Avenue to meet Liz at the French bistro. When they drove past Union Station, Casey turned to see if they were being followed again.

"Déjà vu," Casey said. "The silver Chrysler 300C is three cars back."

"This is getting old. When we find a place to park at the bistro, let's introduce ourselves. I don't like being tailed."

Two blocks beyond Union Station, Drake turned left and drove around the block so he could park in front of the bistro. The silver 300C followed.

They were early for lunch and there were several parking spaces open on the street in front of the bistro. Drake drove down the block and chose an open space that left an open space for the 300C two spaces back. He hoped it would pull in so they could have a little chat.

As the Tahoe was coming to a stop, Drake saw in the rearview mirror that the silver car was parking two spaces back.

"You take the passenger side, I'll see what the driver has to say,' he told Casey.

Both men jumped out and quickly walked back. Before they passed the first car, the Venezuelan embassy car pulled out and accelerated down the street.

"Guess they didn't want to hear what you had to say," Casey said.

Drake shook his head. "I think they know what I wanted to say. If we see them again, I'll make sure they hear it."

They found Liz waiting for them in a booth in the bistro's wine bar.

Drake slid in beside her, leaving Casey alone on the other side.

"Thanks for coming," she said. "It's been an interesting morning."

"For us too," Drake said. "You go first."

Before she did, the waiter brought a small loaf of bread with garlic butter and left the menus. When he left, she said, "There's not much news about the terrorist attacks, really. The intelligence committee briefing we received this morning was about the same as the last one. The Air Force still can't explain why the drone didn't spot the shooter with the missile before it was fired. They're pretty sure it was fired from the back of a white delivery van or something similar, parked across the river. They think it must have had infrared shielding of some sort that prevented the drone from seeing the shooter inside."

"I thought it was supposed to be a secret that there were armed drones flying over our airports," Casey said. "How would they know to use infrared shielding?"

"It must have leaked somewhere," Drake said.

"It had to have been a pretty quick leak, because the president's decision to fly the drones was only made a couple of days before the third plane was shot down," Strobel said.

"Is that what you wanted to tell me about?" Drake asked.

"What I wanted to talk about is some pretty sensitive stuff," she said and leaned forward with her elbows on the table. "You said something earlier about the ranch your client has in Oregon that made me curious. Since you both have Top Secret security clearances from your time in Delta Force, I can talk about this, but it can't leave this booth."

Drake and Casey both nodded their understanding and leaned forward to hear what she had to say.

"The CIA has been working hard to identify the terrorists and find out where the missiles came from. A well-placed informant in Syria they work with to supply the rebel forces told them Iran, working through a proxy, is shooting down our planes," she said.

"Is this informant reliable?" Drake asked.

"They apparently worked with him before in Libya," she said. "He's Muslim Brotherhood and was helping them track down Gaddafi's missing MANPADs."

"What's he doing in Syria for the CIA?" Casey asked.

"Where do you think the rebels are getting their shoulder-fired missiles?" she said.

"From the CIA?" Casey asked.

"From Gaddafi's missing stockpile the CIA recovered, right" Drake said. "The informant is the CIA conduit."

"That's my guess," Liz said. "They won't confirm it, of course."

Casey sat, perplexed. "I don't get it. Why is the Muslim Brotherhood helping us? I thought we were on the outs with them, since they were overthrown, and we didn't do anything."

"They're helping us because they want to regain power, and they want their assets released," Drake said. "They want Senator Boykin's bill passed. But why is this something you thought we should know, Liz?"

"The informant didn't name the proxy, but the CIA put together a short list. Sheikh Qasseer's name is on it."

Drake and Casey exchanged looks.

"I met with the attorney for the American Muslim Youth Camp Foundation this morning. I told him, among other things, my client wasn't about to sell his ranch so some sheikh from Bahrain could run a training camp," Drake said quietly. "I threw it out to see how he would react, and wound up being threatened."

"And now we're being followed by cars from the Venezuelan embassy," Casey added.

The waiter approached their table and they all sat back.

"I think we need a bottle of your pinot noir from the Burgundy region," Drake told the waiter, pointing to the first wine at the top of the list.

When the waiter left, Liz asked Drake, "Do you think the foundation has something to do with these terrorist attacks? My God, some of the most powerful people in the city are on its board of directors."

"I don't know what to think, Liz. Mike saw the guy with the black Porsche that followed us to West Virginia meeting the foundation's attorney less than an hour ago. They look like they could be brothers, and both have the same last names, Hassan. If he's the money man for the Muslim Brotherhood as Interpol believes, there could be a connection."

"If there is," she said, "there's probably a money trail. But with the people involved with the foundation, no one's going to want to investigate it."

"They may not have to," Casey said. "I might have some information this afternoon that will help."

Drake approved of the wine he'd ordered when it was presented, and raised his glass when it was poured, "To interesting times."

After the others had joined in the toast, they discussed what they should do with their suspicions and finished off the bottle of wine and the loaf of bread.

Unnoticed by them while they were in the bistro, a man from the Venezuelan embassy's security detail planted a tracking device under the rear of the white Tahoe that Drake had parked outside.

Chapter Forty-Two

MOHAMED HASSAN CLOSED the door of his office in the Evening Star Building to take the call from "Raul", a.k.a. Carlos Mora, the chief of security for the Venezuelan embassy and head of station for the Venezuelan secret service.

"Raul, my friend, *que pasa?*"

"Your friend knew he was being followed," Mora said. "He even led two of my men into Union Station so he could take their picture. I put a tracker on his car."

"Where is he now?"

"He's in a bistro on Massachusetts Avenue with his tall friend."

"I need to know where he is tonight. I have something planned for him."

"No problem. Call me when you need to know."

The Venezuelans did good work, Mohamed knew. They'd been trained by the Cuban secret service and were able to afford the latest equipment with their oil money. Since Russia's resurgence and renewed ties with allies in the Caribbean and South America, including the jihadists training in the Tri-Border Area, Russia and Venezuela were powerful friends if you wanted to attack America.

Their hatred of America also made them useful fools. To

provide America cover for an attack on Iran that destroyed its nuclear weapons program, it had to be seen that America had been provoked and was justified in the eyes of the world for using its military might. If America was seen as attacking Iran in concert with Israel, as Israel continued to request, Russia would join the fight to honor the security agreement it had with Iran.

But if Russia and Venezuela believed they were merely accommodating Sheikh Qasseer's jihadist strike at America, they were more than willing to provide assistance. All he had to do was keep his real endgame a secret from both of them. Which was why he was going to have to think of a good explanation for the hit on the attorney from Oregon if Carlos Mora ever asked.

Hassan's next call was to Jameel Marcus at the youth camp in West Virginia.

"Are your men ready, Jameel?"

"They're ready. When do you want them?"

"Tonight," Hassan said. "Have them here in D.C., by evening. What will they use?"

"They have AK 74's, two with GP-30 40mm grenade launchers, and a supply of the Russian RGD-5 hand grenades. I'll send some of the PVV-5A plastic explosives if you think they'll need it."

"How have you trained them to do it?"

"They'll be in two cars, two men in each," Marcus said. "If he's driving, they'll take him in his car. If he's on foot, they'll make it look like a drive-by."

"Are they prepared to enter his hotel if necessary?"

"They are martyrs, Mohamed. They'll go after him, wherever he is."

"Good, good," Hassan said. "He can't be allowed to stop us. Call me when they get here."

Hassan took the SIM card out of the burner phone he'd used for the two calls and put it in a zip lock bag to be tossed down a drain later. Killing the attorney was necessary, but it was the most dangerous part of the plan for him personally. He knew the attorney may have identified him by tracing the license plate on his Porsche, and taking the car had been a mistake. But there wasn't any way he could be tied directly to the youth camp or the actions of Jameel Marcus and **Allah's Sword**, so far.

There were others that would need to be silenced as well, and he regretted that. But the threat of a Shia Iran with nuclear weapons was too great to let his cousin or his lover live and have the attacks ultimately traced to the Brotherhood.

He had one more task to complete before he left the office. Another demand letter from **Allah's Sword** had to be prepared for the president, to be delivered by courier to the Israeli embassy. It was time to turn up the pressure on the White House to act, and the Jews were the perfect people to do that. The Jews would clearly see the hand of Iran behind the attacks, because they wanted to. And when Iran was a smoldering patch of Persian sand, his ultimate mission would be accomplished.

Chapter Forty-Three

JOHN PRESCOTT WAS late in getting to his office Monday, after staying up past midnight the night before reading the secret file the CIA had on Layla Nebit.

Now Prescott was anxiously waiting for the packet of information on Nebit he had purchased from Ryan Walker. The London banker seemed to know a lot about a lot of things no one else knew. If his information supported the unsubstantiated musings of the CIA analysts, and the rumors of the lover she was keeping, he would have what he needed to break the hold she had on him. Correction, he would have what he needed to not only control her, but control to an extent what went on in the White House.

According to the CIA file, Layla Nebit was an Islamist at heart, who hid her true religious beliefs to further her political ambitions. It was known that she had been born in Egypt and that her father had been the Egyptian ambassador to the United Nations. It was not well known, however, that her movie-star mother had had a long-standing affair with the second-ranking man in the Muslim Brotherhood while she and her husband lived in Egypt. And it appeared that few people outside the CIA knew that Layla Nebit's real father was not the ambassador.

The lover Nebit entertained frequently in her expensive condo was the real dirt. He was the Muslim Brotherhood's investment banker, with offices in London and Washington, and an Interpol file. Like the CIA file on Nebit, Interpol hadn't been able to confirm its suspicions about him, but they were keeping an eye on him. The CIA file, however, was more convinced of the role he played in the war on terror.

According to the CIA, Mohamed Hassan moved Brotherhood money around the world to support its activities and causes. On the surface, his actions appeared to be legal. The Muslim Brotherhood did have enormous financial holdings in a number of countries and did make a lot of profitable investments that were entirely legal. Below the surface, however, evidence was piling up that the Muslim Brotherhood was the fount from which much of the world's terrorist activities flowed.

Mohamed Hassan was also thought to be one of the jihadi masterminds who orchestrated terrorist activity behind the scenes. He always maintained a distance from these activities, but he was believed to be the mind that created and directed those activities, nonetheless.

What wasn't clear from the CIA file was why there was nothing being done about the president of the United States closest advisor, who happened to be sleeping with the enemy. It was possible, he conceded, that Layla Nebit was working with the CIA to learn what Hassan was up to, but he doubted it. He had friends in the intelligence community, and knew there was no love lost between the White House and the CIA. The president didn't trust anyone outside the circle of his closest advisors, and rarely listened when he was briefed on matters by the CIA. When he had, in the past, the agency's intelligence estimates had been wrong, and he'd been embarrassed.

It was more likely the CIA was building a case against Nebit and her lover, so that it could use it as leverage at some later time. The same way he intended to use the information.

At ten minutes before noon, as promised, his secretary brought him a thin packet wrapped in brown paper. It was simply addressed to John Prescott, with no return address or other markings of any kind.

Prescott waited for his secretary to leave and used the antique silver Italian stiletto he kept in his desk drawer to open confidential mail delivered to him, as this was. Inside the brown paper was a plain manila folder with three pages copied from a dossier stamped *Secret* and two small photographs.

The first photograph was of a beautiful young woman, standing beside a smiling older man. The name written on the photograph next to the man identified him as Sayyed Qutb, the Egyptian theorist and philosopher whose writings created and inspired Islamist fundamentalism, the man who inspired bin Laden. The name written next to the young woman identified her as Layla Nebit's mother.

So, Layla Nebit's roots reached deep into the soil of Islamist terrorism. How in the world did she ever get the top-secret clearance that allowed her to sit in on every briefing the president of the United States received?

The second photograph was of a handsome Omar Sharif-look alike in his mid-thirties, in military fatigues with an AK 47 standing next to Ayman al-Zawahiri, the current leader of al-Qaeda. The younger man was identified as Mohamed Hassan, Layla Nebit's lover.

The three pages in the folder detailed Mohamed Hassan's activities on behalf of the Muslim Brotherhood. They also identified Layla Nebit's mission in Washington. She directed various Muslim front organizations to achieve cultural jihad and impose sharia law on America.

What the information the CIA file and the packet Ryan Walker provided him didn't answer, however, was what connection Layla Nebit or her lover had to Sheikh Qasseer's camps and the jetliners that were being shot down.

Prescott left his desk and stood at his office window to think, with his arms folded across his chest. With the information he now possessed, he could bring down the president, blackmail his closest advisor or wind up dead, depending on how reckless he wanted to be.

Whatever he did, it would have to be done very carefully.

Chapter Forty-Four

WHEN THE MEETING at the French bistro broke up, they each left with assignments to confirm their growing suspicions about the American Muslim Youth Camp Foundation and the youth camps it was operating.

Liz returned to her desk in Senator Hazelton's office in the Dirksen Senate Office Building, five blocks away. She was to direct her research staff to find any possible link between Sheikh Qasseer in Bahrain, and the foundation or the youth camps. Initial filings that created the 501(3)C nonprofit organization could be accessed, as well as any of the public records for the purchase of properties for the camps that were spread across the country. She also offered to reach out to her friends at the Department of Homeland Security to see what files they had on the youth camps.

Drake and Casey returned to their hotel. Casey was calling his IT guru, and young master hacker, at his company in Seattle to see what had been uncovered about the London bank and its account holders. He specifically wanted to know if Sheikh Qasseer had an account with the London Bank, and if the foundation had received contributions from the sheikh.

"Mr. C," Kevin McRoberts said when he answered, "I was just

getting ready to call you. I got into the system at the bank you mentioned. I have a list of the account holders and the withdrawals from all those accounts, if you want them."

"Slow down, Kevin. That's good work, but I don't need that much right now. I want you to see if a sheikh in Bahrain, Sheikh Qasseer, has an account there. If he does, can you tell if he's made contributions to the foundation we discussed?"

"I can't tell where the withdrawal went, but I guess I can match the amount of the withdrawals with the contributions received by the foundation and see if they match up. Would that help?"

"That should help, Kevin, but be careful," Casey cautioned. "This is becoming a little more complicated than I thought. How long will it take you to make the comparisons?"

"Already working on it."

"Call me when you're finished," Casey said, sitting at the work desk in the hotel room he shared with Drake.

Drake was sitting on the end of his bed talking with his father-in-law, Senator Hazelton. He wanted to let him know he was returning to Oregon the next day and needed to ask a favor.

"Have you told your mother-in-law you're leaving," Senator Hazelton asked.

"I will as soon as I hang up, I promise."

"She'll want to see you before you leave. Are you free for dinner tonight?"

"I'm not, sorry. Liz is having me over for dinner," Drake said.

"Maybe breakfast then, tomorrow. Have you concluded your business here?"

"Yes, we're rejecting the foundation's offer."

"How did that go over?"

"Not very well, actually," Drake admitted. "Senator, is Liz in your office?"

"She's working with her staff at the moment, why?"

"Ask her to tell you what we've learned about the foundation," Drake said. "Then, if you're comfortable helping us, I'd like to ask a favor."

"Go ahead, I'm listening."

"The attorney at the Prescott Group I'm dealing with met someone that Interpol believes is an operative for the Muslim Brotherhood. As the chairman of the Senate Select Committee on Intelligence, do you have access to any file the CIA may have on the man?"

"I can probably get a file like that," Senator Hazelton said. "Mind telling me a little more about this person?"

"If it's all right with you, Sir, I'll let Liz do that. It's complicated and may not be anything. There may be a link between this man, the foundation, its youth camps, and a sheikh in Bahrain. Apparently, he's on the CIA's list of possible Iranian proxies responsible for shooting down our planes."

"I see," Senator Hazelton said. "Let me talk with Liz. I'll see what I can do."

"Thank you, Senator."

Drake stood and stretched. "Mike, I think I'll go down and work out before I take off to have dinner with Liz. Want to come?"

"Loosening up for the big event?"

"Don't start that again. I haven't had any exercise since our visit to the camp in West Virginia."

"You could just wait until your date tonight."

Drake started to reach for something to throw at his friend, when Casey held up his hands in surrender.

"Okay, okay," he said. "I need to make sure my guys are ready to leave tomorrow and find a place for dinner. They want to try some good Thai before we leave. Then I'll come down and join you. What did the Senator say?"

"He said he can probably get the CIA file on Hassan, assuming they have one. This could all be a wild-goose chase, Mike. We really don't have anything except a string of coincidences."

"Yeah, but they're a pretty suspicious string of coincidences, you have to agree."

"Agreed, but the last couple of times I tried to get someone to do act on my suspicions, it didn't work out so well," Drake reminded him.

"And each time, you wound up preventing bad things from

happening on your own. You've got a good nose for things like this. That's why I want you to take over the legal work for my company. Keep me out of trouble and have the resources to do some good when you get involved in things like this."

"Create our own little special forces group?"

"More of a special section of one, to handle things for our clients when the government won't, or can't."

"Let me think about it, Mike. Right now, I just want to find out what these youth camps are all about and get home."

"And have dinner with a beautiful woman."

"Having dinner with a friend, who happens to be a beautiful woman," Drake said and grinned.

Chapter Forty-Five

IN THE HOTEL'S fitness center, Drake ran through his stretching routine, did a light free-weight workout, and hit the treadmill hard for thirty minutes. Dripping wet, he went back to his room just as Casey was leaving.

"Ron and Spencer found a Thai restaurant for dinner," Casey said as he tossed Drake a set of keys. "It's supposed to be the best in D.C., so don't worry about us not having a good meal."

"Worrying that you wouldn't find a place for a good meal is the last thing on my mind. What are the keys for?"

"The Tahoe we've been driving is low on gas, so take the other one. The Thai place is only a couple of blocks from here, so we'll walk."

"Where are you going?" Drake asked.

"Downstairs to the bar. Spencer's buying beer and promising to teach me the finer points of professional hockey. I've never understood the game. I made the mistake of admitting it to him, after he told me he played hockey in college."

"I don't think I'll be late, but don't wait up for me."

"Just be back before sunrise," Casey said, "we're leaving for the airport right after an early breakfast."

"You won't let it go, will you?"

Before he stepped out the door, Casey put an arm around Drake's shoulder and said, "Heh, you like her and she likes you. There's nothing wrong with that."

Half an hour later, he took the stairs down to the hotel's restaurant, selected a bottle of Napa Valley Cabernet Sauvignon he knew Liz liked and left for her condo in Camden Potomac Yard, driving the second of the two rented Chevy Tahoes.

After crossing the Potomac River on the Jefferson Davis Bridge, Drake turned south on Hwy. 1 and drove on to the high-rise condominiums Liz called home. A short walk from visitor parking and a quick elevator ride to the fourth floor brought him to Unit 421, where he stood ringing her doorbell.

"Hi Adam," she said brightly, as she opened the door and gave him a quick kiss on the cheek.

She had on a white scoop-necked cashmere sweater, a pair of fitted jeans and plain leather thong sandals and looked casually elegant.

Drake held out the wine gift bag to her. "I didn't know what we were having for dinner, but I know you like your Napa Valley cabernets."

"We might try it later," she said, as she led him toward the kitchen. "I thought you might like my Maryland crab cakes with a chardonnay I picked out to go with it. Would you like a drink first?"

"Wine is fine. This is a great place, Liz," Drake said, looking around.

And indeed, it was. Twelve-foot-high ceilings with crown moldings, a large balcony patio at the end of the living area and a kitchen any chef would enjoy. A soft white leather sofa faced a modern gas fireplace and the wall art featured abstract watercolor paintings in bright spring colors.

"It's not as nice as the old stone farmhouse on your vineyard, but I like it. Want to pour us some wine?" she said and pointed to a stone wine cooler on the kitchen counter.

Drake poured them each a glass of chilled chardonnay and joined her on the leather sofa. A platter of smoked salmon, cucumber slices and fresh dill on thinly sliced rye bread sat on the glass-topped coffee table in front of them.

He took a bite of the crunchy cucumber and salmon appetizer and smiled. "I think I'm in for a treat tonight, if this is any indication of how good a cook you are."

"Thanks. I hope you like Maryland crab cakes."

"One of my favorites."

"Good," she said, and then added with a slight pout, "Are you really going home tomorrow?"

"I need to get back, Liz. There's nothing more I can do here. Congressman Rodecker's out of the hospital and safe, staying with my in-laws."

"I know, I know. I was just hoping I could see more of you," she said, and leaned her head over on his shoulder.

Drake smelled her light floral perfume and leaned his head down and kissed the top of her head. Her hair still carried the fresh fragrant scent of her shampoo.

When she laid her hand softly on his thigh, he felt a stirring that jolted him. He was both surprised and excited by the rush of emotion he was feeling.

"Liz, I," he started to say, when she reached up and put her finger on his lips.

"Let me do this," as she slowly stood before him and then sat in his lap, straddling his legs. With her hands pressing him back on the sofa, she leaned down and kissed him gently. Her lips were soft and cool from the chilled chardonnay.

Their tongues touched lightly and then tentatively explored each other.

Drake put his hands on her waist and set her further back on his legs. Her hazel green eyes were searching his for a signal, and he knew what she was asking. Moving slowly, he slid his hands under her soft cashmere sweater and then up to her bare breasts.

Without a word, she stood and slowly took off her sweater.

"Would you like to see the view from my bedroom?" she asked.

Chapter Forty-Six

AFTER A LATE DINNER of crab cakes and a second bottle of chardonnay, Drake said goodnight and promised to call Liz before he flew home the next morning. Plans had been made for her to join him there in a month for some spring skiing at Mt. Bachelor.

It was nearly midnight when he parked next to the other rented Tahoe, and walked under the blue awning into the lobby of the Savoy Suites Hotel in Georgetown. One young woman was still working at the reception desk and two of Casey's men were sitting at the bar in the lounge.

"How was the Thai food?" he asked, when he reached them.

"Best I've ever had," Spencer Reynolds, the former Recon Marine said.

"You two ever settle the argument about who's tougher, Recon Marines or Airborne Rangers?" Drake asked, knowing the two had never stopped arguing the point, whenever they had the time and a few beers.

"No argument about it, sir," Ron Larson, the former Ranger said. "Recon can find the enemy, but then they call the Rangers in to fight them."

Before the good-natured argument escalated, Drake left and

took the stairs up to his room on the sixth floor. Casey was lying on his bed watching his favorite movie, SHOOTER, with Mark Wahlberg, when he got there.

"How was dinner?" Casey asked, with a smirk on his face.

"Her crab cakes were okay," Drake returned stoically. "How was your evening?"

"That's it? That's all you're saying?"

"That's all I'm saying? What more do you need to know about my dinner?"

Before Casey could interrogate his friend any further, his cell's ringtone started up.

"Boss, trouble headed your way," Spencer Reynolds said softly. "Four men wearing balaclavas and AK 74's are asking for Drake at the front desk."

Casey heard gunfire before Reynolds said, "Shit, they just shot the gal at the front desk."

"Where are you?" Casey asked.

"Behind the bar," Reynolds said. "I spotted them when they came in."

"Are you and Ron still armed?"

"Just the concealed carry .45's you issue."

"Are they taking an elevator or the stairs?"

"The stairs."

"You and Ron follow them up. Let's trap them in the stairwell," Casey said.

Drake was already taking his Kimber .45 out of his carryon and putting two extra mags in his pocket.

"Four men with AK's coming up the stairs," Casey said as he grabbed his .45 from his tote bag and rushed out.

Their room was in the middle of the hallway, thirty yards from the stairwell. Drake got there first, cracked open the door and heard footsteps pounding up the stairs.

"I'll let them get between floors and let them know we're here," Drake said and ran down a half flight of stairs. When he took a quick look, he saw the barrel of an AK 74 turn the corner below, before a face covered with black balaclava peeked around. The AK 74 had a grenade launcher slung under its barrel.

Drake fired one shot where he'd seen the first man's head and ran back up the stairs and took cover on the right side of the stairwell door.

"Grenade launcher," he whispered to Casey, as a burst of rounds from the AK struck the wall opposite from where he'd been standing a half flight below.

"Wait for them to come up, or keep them between floors?" Casey asked.

"They get this far a lot of people will get hurt. Keep them between floors."

The stairwell got quiet, and then they heard firing from below.

"Ron and Spencer must be drawing fire," Casey said.

"Before they figure it out, let's end this," Drake said, and ran back down a half flight of stairs.

When he reached the corner, he stood with his back to the wall with his gun raised in his right hand. Seeing in his mind where he'd seen the first shooter, he slowed his breathing and readied himself. The thousands of rounds he'd fired in the "House of Horror", the shooting house where he trained for close quarter battle as a Delta Force operator, had prepared him for just such a moment

Drake turned the corner and started down the stairs. The first intruder poked his head out and was knocked back with a 230-grain hollow-point round between the eyes. Continuing down, he saw the first man drug back and then another man jump around yelling "Allahu Akbar" and firing wildly.

Drake shot him twice in the head and stepped over his body to reach the landing between floors. When darted his head around the corner, he saw two more bodies sprawled on the stairs below.

"Spencer, Ron," he called out. "Are you okay?"

"Clear down here," was the answer.

Drake turned to make sure the second man he'd shot was dead and saw Casey doing the same with the first man on the stairs above.

"What the hell was that all about?" Casey asked.

"I don't know, but I'm sure going to find out," Drake said. "Did someone call 911?"

"The bartender did. Police should be here by now," Ron Larson said. "I'll go down and make sure they know we're the good guys."

"Mike, you'd better go up and make sure no one comes down the stairs," Drake said. "The police need a preserved crime scene. I'm going to look for ID on these guys."

Drake quickly searched the pockets of the four men and found none of them were carrying anything that would help identify them. But he didn't need a driver's license or a wallet to know who they were.

He could hear the police coming up the stairs and knew they might be able to identify them from their fingerprints, because they all had prison tattoos on the back of their hands in Farsi script. And he'd seen the same tattoos before, at the youth camp in West Virginia.

Drake joined Casey at the top of the stairs.

"I need to stay a couple more days, Mike. There's an attorney who told me it could be dangerous here in D.C. It's time he learned just how right he was."

Chapter Forty-Seven

MOHAMED HASSAN TOOK the call from Jameel Marcus in Layla Nebit's condo, standing on the balcony with a brandy snifter in his hand. He had eagerly waited for the call that would allow him to celebrate the death of the meddlesome attorney.

"Where are you?" he asked Marcus.

"In the parking lot at his hotel."

"And?"

"The police are all over the place and my men haven't come out."

"Is the attorney dead?"

"No way for me to know, because I'm not going in there," Marcus said.

"What happened?"

"Your information was bad!" Marcus shouted. "That's what happened. We waited for him to come out to the white Tahoe you tracked, but he never did. Then he drives up at midnight in a second white Tahoe and went in before we could stop him. I had to send them into the hotel."

"Leave and get back to the camp," Mohamed ordered. "We're almost finished, but I may need to use you one more time."

He stayed on the balcony, looking out at the symbol of all that he hated about America, its Capitol Building in the distance, and swore to Allah he wouldn't leave until the attorney was dead. There were things he needed to make sure happened, though, before he allowed himself that pleasure.

His Egyptian lover had confirmed that the CIA had the sheikh from Bahrain on its short list of suspected proxies working for Iran. It was only a matter of time before they found the money trail he had created that linked the sheikh to the MANPADs being used by **Allah's Sword.**

Then, with the president's closest advisor whispering in his ear that it was time to deal with Iran, once and for all, he could sit back and enjoy his accomplishment. He would be remembered as the warrior who single-handedly destroyed the Persian threat, and restored Shia Muslims to their rightful place as the true heirs of Muhammad, peace be upon Him. America would do what they lacked the might to do, for now.

When America's strike on Iran was underway, there were some unfortunate sacrifices that had to be made. His cousin, Mark Hassan, and his boss, John Prescott, would have to be killed. Indirectly, they both knew too much about him. They had been easy to manipulate; Mark with his eagerness to please the Muslim Brotherhood, and Prescott with his pride and insatiable greed.

The youth camps spread across America would also have to be sacrificed. It had been costly over the years to provide the resources that helped Sheikh Qasseer build up his army, but with the destruction of Iran, the Brotherhood would stand supreme in the Muslim world.

The real debate among the leadership was over the future of Layla Nebit. Her career had been carefully crafted and promoted, and her influence in America was greater than they had ever dreamed it could be. But, she knew too much about him and that was a threat to his own future. Despite the wishes of the council, he'd decided that she would have to die accidentally and untraceable to him.

Until then, he would enjoy a taste of the rewards he knew would soon be his.

Returning inside, he went to the bottle of excellent cognac on the side bar and refilled his snifter.

"Are you coming back to bed?" Layla said from the bedroom.

"In a moment, I have one last call to make."

Mohamed returned to the balcony and called the head of security at the Venezuelan embassy.

"Raul, it's me," he said. "You need to collect the tracker you were using before it's found. It didn't go as I'd hoped."

"So I hear. My information is that you lost four men and the target is still alive."

"True," Hassan admitted. "Thanks for your help. Allow me to return the favor."

"Oh, I will, my Muslim friend. We share a common enemy. I'm sure we'll find a way for you to return the favor."

Mohamed finished his cognac and headed to the bedroom. His work was not yet finished for the night.

Chapter Forty-Eight

AFTER HOURS of being questioned by first the Metropolitan Police and then by the FBI, Drake secured their release early the next morning by calling Liz Strobel and asking her to call in any favors she might be owed by the FBI or her former employer, the Department of Homeland Security.

Fortunately, her position as Executive Assistant to the Former Director of DHS and currently as the national security advisor for the Chairman of the Senate Intelligence Committee was enough to gain their freedom, with a stern admonition not to leave the city. But for her, they were told, they would have been held indefinitely.

Drake convened an after-action debriefing at all night diner nearby. When they all had coffee and were waiting for their breakfast orders to be delivered, he began by thanking Casey's two men for being alert.

"If you hadn't let us know they were coming, we wouldn't have made it to the stairwell in time. You saved a lot of lives last night," Drake said.

"We were lucky, that's all," Spencer Reynolds, the Recon Marine said.

"Luck had nothing to do with it," Drake said. "Mike hired you because of your training and experience. You're good at what you do."

"From what I saw, you and Mike handled things pretty efficiently as well," Ron Larson, the Ranger, added.

"Well, I'm just glad you're all safe," Liz said. "The FBI will probably call this drug-related or gang activity. Did you tell them what you thought was going on?"

"We didn't think that was a good idea," Casey said, "after our trip to West Virginia."

"Mike," Drake asked, "how well stocked is that armory you keep on the jet? I doubt we'll get any of our weapons returned any time soon, even though Puget Sound Security is licensed as a Private Protective Services company."

"And as such, we're well enough stocked to equip all of us with M45 CQBP's, if we need them. There's also a box of the CRKT G10 knives if anybody wants one."

"What now?" Liz asked. "It sounds like you are gearing up for war."

"Just being careful," Drake said. "We didn't ask for this but were not going to walk away from it either. There's a lawyer at the Prescott Group I need to see, and then we'll go from there. The police and FBI just want the shooters. I want to know who sent them and why."

After the adrenaline rush from the attack at the hotel, the four men attacked their food when it arrived as if they hadn't eaten in days.

With a forkful of steak and eggs halfway to his mouth, Casey asked, "Liz, did you find any connection the sheikh in Bahrain has to these camps?"

Liz shook her head. "Not yet. We know the first camp in New York was started by the sheikh, but it was later purchased by the foundation. The name has changed a few times, but the American Muslim Youth Camp Foundation picked up the ball and then expanded the project as a non-profit charitable program across the country. It's received awards for working with inner city youth, mainly from Muslim groups. But after his initial involvement, it doesn't appear the sheikh has been involved."

Drake raised his coffee cup to a passing waitress, asking for a refill, and said, "I imagine these same Muslim groups were the ones who complained about the FBI keeping an eye on the camps, and got the administration to cancel the surveillance."

"Probably," Liz acknowledged. "The administration has bent over backwards to reassure Muslims they aren't being profiled as terrorists, because of their religion."

"What'd you call training kids to be martyrs?" Casey snorted. "Will we ever pull our heads out of the sand and wake up?"

"I know, Mike, I know," she said. "But Muslim citizens have the same rights we do."

"No offense, Liz, but you're starting to sound like a Beltway politician," Casey said and attacked the last of his breakfast.

"All right," Drake interrupted, "let's focus on what we need to do next. Arguing the pros and cons of profiling isn't going to help us. Although, I think we could learn a lot from the Israelis about identifying the enemy."

"Liz," he continued, "I ask Senator Hazelton to see what he could find out about the guy driving the black 911 that followed us. Do you know if he's learned anything?"

"Not that I know of, but I'll check."

"Mike, you were going to see if Kevin could follow the accounts in the London bank to the foundation. Anything yet?"

"I'll check after breakfast, unless you want me to do it now."

"Let's finish eating," Drake said. "It's been a long night. I'm going back to the hotel and take a shower, before I visit Hassan Number One. We'll regroup this afternoon."

As they were leaving the diner, Liz put her hand on Drake's arm and pulled him aside.

"Mark Hassan threatened you, so please be careful," she said.

"I will. He may know something, but he's not the type to get his own hands dirty. I'll be fine."

"Make sure you are," she made him promise.

Chapter Forty-Nine

MOHAMED HASSAN LEFT Layla Nebit's bed early in the morning and drove to McLean, Virginia. Mark Hassan lived in a modest townhouse he'd leased for the last several years, and Mohamed wanted to arrive before he left for his office.

It was just a matter of time before the police or the attorney questioned his cousin about the young men killed at the hotel, after they discovered they were from the foundation's youth camp in West Virginia. His cousin was a true believer, but he was also a liability that had to be eliminated.

Mohamed parked his black Porsche on the street in front of the red brick townhouse, with its green shutters and white trim, and walked to the front door. Cousin Mark lived alone and didn't have a current lover that he knew of. He hoped this morning there wasn't a new one.

Mark Hassan wore a white shirt and tie when he opened the door, with a cup of coffee in his hand.

"Cousin," he said, "what are you doing here?"

Mohamed brushed past him. "We need to talk."

"Sure, would you like some coffee?"

Mohamed nodded and walked on to the kitchen at the back of

the first floor. While his coffee was being poured, he took off his coat and hung it over the back of a chair at the dining table and remained standing.

"Has the attorney from Oregon been back to see you?" he asked when his coffee cup was handed to him.

"He came to my office yesterday, why?"

Mohamed tasted his coffee and asked, "What did he want?"

"He informed me his client wasn't willing to sell his ranch so that some sheikh in Bahrain could use it as a training camp."

Mohamed choked on the coffee he was swallowing. "How could he possibly know that?"

"How should I know?" Mark Hassan said defensively and leaned back against the kitchen counter. "The sheikh's name was never mentioned."

Mohamed searched his cousin's face for any sign that he was lying and saw that he wasn't. And yet the attorney had found out that Sheikh Qasseer was involved. After last night, it wouldn't be long before he also concluded that Cousin Mark and the foundation were more than a charitable nonprofit working with Muslim youth.

"Mark, you put me in a very difficult position," he said and set his cup of coffee on the counter. "Jameel sent four of his best men to kill the attorney last night at his hotel. The attorney survived, but all four of Jameel's men were killed."

"What? Why would Jameel do that?"

"Because I told him to," Mohamed said softly.

He watched his cousin process the news.

"You're shooting down the planes, you and Sheikh Qasseer?"

"I've been planning this operation for three years," Mohamed said calmly. "The council approved the plan and put me in charge."

"But why involve me and the foundation?" Mark Hassan asked. "You could have left us out of your plan and worked directly with the sheikh? This will ruin everything we've worked on here."

"Sometimes it's necessary to sacrifice smaller plans, so that bigger ones can succeed."

"And does that mean sacrificing me as well?"

Mohamed moved in front of his cousin. "I'm afraid if does, Cousin."

"Is that why you're here, Mohamed?" Mark Hassan asked, standing up straight and glancing toward the front door.

Mohamed put his hands on his cousin's shoulders and answered sadly, "I wish there was another way. Your choice is to die for Allah this morning and go straight to paradise. Or you can wait to be arrested and waste away in an American jail until you eventually die. Then you'd spend time in hell praying for your sins before being allowed into paradise."

Mark Hassan slumped back against the counter and began sobbing. After several minutes, he regained his composure and asked his cousin, "Will you allow me to purify myself?"

"Of course."

After the rite of ghusi had been performed and Mark Hassan had washed his body in the required manner, he prayed and did as Mohamed Hassan directed.

Sitting in a chair in his bedroom upstairs facing Mecca, he put the pistol he was given to his temple and shot himself.

Mohamed Hassan rushed downstairs to a laptop in his cousin's study and prepared a suicide note. The note contained a confession for taking a small commission from money received from contributors to the American Muslim Youth Camp Foundation. The note asked forgiveness for interfering with the work and the goals of Sheikh Qasseer in Bahrain.

Chapter Fifty

DRAKE WAS the only person standing in front of the glass doors at 9:00 a.m. when they were opened, and he was allowed to enter the lobby of the Prescott Group. He asked to see Mr. Mark Hassan.

"I'm sorry, sir. Mr. Hassan isn't in yet," the receptionist told him. "Do you have an appointment to see him?"

"I don't, but it won't matter," Drake said. "He'll see me."

Drake sat and watched people pass through the lobby for an hour, reading the Post and all of the Sports Illustrated magazines, before he returned to the receptionist.

"Is he in yet?"

"Let me check," she said, and called Hassan's assistant. "He still hasn't come in, sir. Would you like to wait?"

"I don't suppose you'd give me his home address?"

"No sir."

Drake left the lobby and called Liz out in the hallway.

"Hassan hasn't come in yet. Is there any way you can find his home address for me?"

"Have you tried finding it on your smart phone," she asked.

"Too frustrated to think of that, sorry."

"It wouldn't have helped," Liz said after a minute. "His number is unlisted and there's no address."

"And the government with its vast data base doesn't know everything," he teased. "That's a relief."

"I didn't say I couldn't find it, smarty. He lives in McLean on Red Cedar Lane," she said, and gave him the address."

"Do I want to know how you found it?"

"Not if you're paranoid. Call me if you find him."

It took Drake forty-five minutes to find the red brick townhouse with green shutters and white trim in McLean. When he did, he had to park a block away and walk to the yellow rope barricade. He stood with the other onlookers for a couple of minutes, watching police come and go from the red brick house.

"What's going on," he asked a man standing next to him.

"Someone was shot in the house, according to one of the news guys."

"Do they know who?"

"He didn't know, but thought it was the guy who lived there."

Drake walked down the line of yellow crime scene tape to a Metro cop making sure no one got any closer to the house.

"Officer Carter," he said after glancing at the man's name badge, "a reporter over there is saying it's a homicide. That true?"

"Don't know what he's been smoking," the officer said. "More likely a suicide."

Over Officer Carter's shoulder, Drake saw two men wearing blue jackets with FBI in white across the back enter the crime scene, and stop at the front door to confer with another Metro cop.

Drake stepped away a short distance and called Liz again.

"Looks like I'm not going to talk to Mark Hassan," he told her. "The address you gave me is a crime scene. Someone's been shot inside. One cop thinks it's suicide, but the FBI just showed up. Can you find out what's going on?"

"I'll make a call," she said.

Drake continued to watch, as a medical examiner van pulled up. Ten minutes later, a body bag was brought out on a stretcher and driven away in the van.

"An FBI friend says Mark Hassan committed suicide," Liz said when she called back. "They're investigating it because his suicide note appears to be a confession to embezzlement. But it also mentions Sheikh Qasseer in Bahrain. As soon Metro police saw that, they called the FBI."

Two Ford Crown Victoria's arrived, and four more FBI agents marched to the front door.

"That confirms what we knew about the sheikh and the youth camps. But why would Hassan commit suicide?" Drake asked.

"If he was stealing from the sheikh," she said, "maybe he feared sharia law more than our law regarding embezzlement."

"Maybe but offing himself the morning after thugs from one of his youth camps come gunning for us is more than a little suspicious. I'm heading back to the hotel. I'll call you after I meet with Mike."

Now what, Drake thought, as he drove through the streets of McLean on his way to Georgetown and his hotel. With Mark Hassan dead, the people left that he believed were involved with the foundation and the West Virginia camp had just narrowed to include the camp manager and perhaps John Prescott himself, as the chairman of the foundation's board of directors. The other Hassan certainly had to be involved, as well as the mysterious sheikh in Bahrain.

As he stopped at the intersection ahead and sat waiting for the light to change, he let his mind wander. Connections were usually made when he let his mind slip into neutral and work freely, choosing paths of its own to draw lines from dot to dot.

Something he saw at the camp he wasn't supposed to see…

A honking horn from the car behind jolted his racing mind like a cattle prod. He drove on and pulled to the curb in the middle of the next block to think. What had he seen at the camp? Which time?

Chapter Fifty-One

JOHN PRESCOTT SAT STOICALLY in his office and listened to the FBI agent detail what had been discovered on Mark Hassan's laptop. And then the questions he had feared began.

"Did Mr. Hassan have access to the American Muslim Youth Camp Foundation account?" Agent Leslie Perkins asked.

"He was a member of the foundation's board of directors, but he had limited access to the account itself."

"Did that "limited access" allow him to direct expenditures from that account?"

"He was the director assigned by the board to monitor the account, yes?"

"And did "monitor" the account include arranging for financial auditing of the account?"

"It did."

"Were those audits performed by outside auditors, or were they internal audits he arranged?"

"I don't know the answer to that question."

"Mr. Prescott, you are one of the directors of the foundation. In fact, you're the board's chairman. As such, you have a fiduciary duty to oversee the foundation's financial matters. Are you saying that you don't know what type of financial auditing was done?"

"I don't know the answer because I don't remember, Ms. Perkins."

"Do you know if there was any evidence, in any of those audits that you don't remember, of missing funds or embezzlement?"

"Again, I don't remember. It looks like I won't be able to help you with these questions until I ask my staff about the matter. Until I have time to do that, I think we're finished for today," Prescott said and stood to indicate the meeting was over.

Agent Perkins remained seated, entering her notes on a small laptop.

"We'll need to conduct our own audit of the foundation's account, Mr. Prescott. For the time being, freeze the account until that's completed. I'm sure you're as interested as I am to know if a crime has been committed here. Good day," she said and left.

Prescott watched the FBI agent walk down the hall from his corner office and called Mark Hassan's secretary.

"Bring me all the files Mr. Hassan has in his office for the American Muslim Youth Camp Foundation. If he kept anything on his laptop, bring the laptop too," he ordered.

He wasn't worried about missing funds because he knew there weren't any. He couldn't believe Mark Hassan would indicate otherwise. What he was worried about were the campaign contributions from foreign contributors to the president's reelection campaign before the funds were deposited in the foundation's account.

And that didn't include the amounts that had been siphoned off for other candidates in the president's party who had needed to fill their coffers for difficult campaigns. A grand total of close to $250 million dollars had been dispersed from foreign contributors into various campaigns, and all of it had been a violation of federal election laws.

If the foreign money received by the foundation he chaired was discovered, online contributions from foreign contributors would also surely be discovered. That arrangement had been easier to set up because amounts under $200 dollars didn't have to be reported and there was no requirement that each contributor had to be verified to be a U.S. citizen.

If both schemes were exposed, the president and a lot of Washington heavy weight politicians would be dragged down in one of the biggest elections scandals the country had ever seen. And he would be right in the middle of it. He had to find a way to keep the records of the foundation's account out of the hands of the FBI auditors.

Prescott told his secretary he was leaving for lunch and left the office. In the privacy of his car in his reserved space in basement parking, he called Layla Nebit on her private line.

"Meet me at Hay-Adams for lunch," he said.

"I'm busy, Prescott."

"Get unbusy," Prescott ordered. "We have a problem."

"Did I not make myself clear? I'm busy."

"The FBI wants to audit the foundation's books." He waited while the news registered.

"I'll be there in ten minutes."

He was finishing his first martini when she made her way across the room, taking her time to acknowledge those who deserved to be acknowledged and ignoring the ones who hadn't earned the recognition yet.

Her cheeks were flushed from walking over from the West Wing when she sat down.

"What the hell happened," she demanded.

"Mark's dead. He apparently left a suicide note on his laptop, confessing to embezzling money from the foundation," he told her.

"Bullshit, John! We both know every dollar can be accounted for."

"Except for the money that never made it into the account," he reminded her.

"But there's no record of that. Besides, what does all this have to do with me?"

"You set the whole thing up, Layla," he said with a smile. "A lot of the money came from your friends in the Middle East. And a lot of that money that was off the books made its way to the Muslim groups here that you wanted blessed. And a lot of it went to getting your boss re-elected. I'm not in this alone."

"You can't prove we were involved in any of this," she said softly.

Prescott motioned to a waiter to bring his guest a martini and said, 'Layla, have a martini with me and listen for once. You are a director of the foundation, and you have a fiduciary duty to manage the finances, just like I do. We both have to find a way to keep the FBI out of the foundation's books."

She shook head. "No, John, as I said before, the books are clean. Mark assured me of that. You need to take care of this yourself."

The waiter stopped by with Nebit's martini and Prescott waited until he'e left to say, "I know all about you, Layla, and your mother and your lover. I have a copy of a secret file the CIA has been keeping on you. I'll share it with the world, before I take the fall for this."

Chapter Fifty-Two

LAYLA NEBIT CLOSED the door of her office in the West Wing and sat at her desk, stilling her body so that her mind could find a way out of the quicksand that was about to pull her under.

With all the effort over the years to carefully craft a career and relationships that put her at the side most powerful man in the world, who valued her advice on every speech he gave and every new program he proposed, she was about to lose it all; her position of power and influence and her good name.

Prescott's concern about the FBI's audit of the foundation's books didn't worry her. Money flowed freely in Washington for all sorts of agendas that might trouble the average citizen, and had throughout the life of the republic. Rumors of foreign money being used by presidential candidates had been around for at least the last three or four elections and nothing had been done about it. Prescott should know that as well as anyone.

And if rumors began circulating about the president's campaign contributions for his reelection, she would quickly put an end to them. She controlled access to the White House and the president, and by virtue of that she controlled the media.

What she feared most was losing her position at the pinnacle of power, due to her mother's past indiscretions with the philosopher of modern terrorism, and her lover's secret life. She could probably survive if it was just her mother's past that was exposed, but she knew her fall would be fast and furious if her relationship with Mohamed was exposed.

Her mother had seemed to be young and naïve to her fans, and probably had been easily influenced as she struggled to be noticed early on as an actress. But that wasn't the truth, of course. Her mother was brilliant and had known exactly what she was doing when she joined the cause and began her fight for a truly Muslim Egypt.

But Mohamed was another story. She knew he had a secret life as a freedom fighter and she didn't care. He was exciting and dangerous, and it thrilled her to be his lover. He was young and virile and passionate about a cause they both shared, the submission to their religion by the entire world.

If her relationship with him was discovered, she knew she would lose him, as well as her relationship with the president, and she couldn't let that happen. What she didn't understand was why the CIA hadn't done anything if they knew he was sharing her bed. She'd been vetted and given the highest security clearance there was, next to the president's.

If they were worried about her, that wouldn't have happened. Unless, of course, they were afraid of how the president would react if they tried to take down his closest advisor and friend. The president didn't conceal his distrust of the intelligence community, finding them neither intelligent nor reliable.

So, the immediate problem was keeping the FBI out of the foundation's books and dealing with John Prescott and his threat to expose her. She knew how to deal with the FBI. One whisper in the president's ear that the FBI's threatened audit was an affront to every American Muslim would get his attention. He was very protective of every constituent group that had supported him.

Dealing with John Prescott was another matter, and one that she should discuss with Mohamed before she did anything.

"Could you come to my place in an hour?" she asked Mohamed when he answered her call.

"You sound upset. Is something wrong?"

"Yes."

"Are you okay?" he asked.

"Yes, but we need to talk. I'll see you in an hour."

For the next thirty minutes, she postponed her scheduled meetings and sent a text to the president saying she wasn't feeling well and needed to go home.

By the time her chauffeur stopped in front of the high-rise condo, she had developed and rejected several ideas for dealing with John Prescott. Her first thought had been to quietly blacklist him so that his lobbying clients would run from him, as if he had a communicable disease, and then run him out of town. While the thought was immensely satisfying, she knew that course of action would only guarantee her exposure.

The other options, besides simply making him disappear, focused on making sure the FBI never got close to the financial records of the American Muslim Youth Camp Foundation. When she let herself in her condo, she decided that was her best hope.

With the president's blessing, she would call her man in the Department of Justice and have him take over the investigation of the foundation. As long as there appeared to be an ongoing criminal investigation, they could decide at some later time how they wanted to put together a case against Mark Hassan. That would satisfy the FBI and keep the sensitive financial records protected until they could be altered or erased.

She was outlining her plan on her iPad on the green granite countertop of the kitchen's island when she saw Mohamed closing the front door.

"Tell me everything," he said, as he approached with his arms wide.

As she prepared him a cup of Shay Khamsina, the Egyptian tea with mint, he loved, she told him about the FBI's questioning of John Prescott and the suicide note left by Mark Hassan, his cousin.

"I learned of Mark's death on my way here," he lied, "and I

can't believe it. I saw him yesterday and he was fine. You say Prescott told you Mark left a note and confessed to embezzling money?"

"That's what the FBI told him," she said, "But it's not true. There's no missing money."

"Does Prescott know that?"

"I think he does, Mohamed. He trusted Mark. He's more worried about an FBI audit discovering his foundation funneled money to campaigns from foreign contributors."

Mohamed finished his tea and sat quietly for a moment and took her hand. "I have an idea," he said. "Before you call in the Department of Justice, let me talk to Prescott. There's a way to make this all go away without getting you involved."

Chapter Fifty-Three

MOHAMED RETURNED to his office in the Evening Star building and got to work. For the last three years, he had recorded all of the financial transactions for the **Allah's Sword** operation on an encrypted Excel spreadsheet.

From the first $1,000,000 he had received from the sale of the 50 MANPADS to Sheikh Qasseer in Bahrain to the $9,000,000 the Brotherhood had provided to fund the $10,000,000 budget he had created for the operation, every dollar had been accounted for and every disbursement listed.

He had created a code for the spreadsheet that only he could understand, and with a few simple changes he made it appear that John Prescott had been the moneyman for Sheikh Qasseer out of a separate account he alone controlled. With a transfer to an encrypted Ironkey drive for secure transport, all he had to do was plant the spreadsheet on a computer Prescott used and make sure it was discovered.

And the discovery of the altered spreadsheet would be almost immediate because he had decided that John Prescott needed to die that night. Coupled with Layla's plan to get the FBI to back off an audit of the foundation's financial records, the investigators should be satisfied for years to come. Their final report would conclude that John Prescott's treachery aided and abetted the latest terrorist attack on America and its citizens.

Mohamed did a quick search on Google and found Prescott's home address. With the help of Google Earth, he was able to study the neighborhood in Arlington where Prescott lived to plan his route in and out of the exclusive area. Roving security patrols were to be expected, but he would be driving a car registered under a false name he kept for occasions like tonight. He had met Prescott on several occasions and didn't expect to be turned away at the door.

The only serious problem he faced was making sure he didn't leave any trace of his visit that could identify him. What he planned for John Prescott had to appear to have been caused by Prescott's own hand.

When the spreadsheet finished downloading to a new encrypted Ironkey drive, Mohamed told his secretary he was leaving for the day and drove to the one-bedroom apartment he'd purchased at the Watergate West for his visits to America. Aside from the wonderful waterfront view, it allowed him to meet and mingle with people who held important positions in the city.

It was dusk by the time Mohamed reached his apartment and poured himself a glass of chilled white Bordeaux to go with the goat cheese and fig appetizers on flat bread he'd stopped to buy at the deli in the complex. Layla would want to prepare something for him later that night when he went to her condo, but for now he needed a light snack for his work that night.

He walked to the window and stared at the river below while he savored the goat cheese and cold, crisp wine. He had no reservations about killing Prescott. It was necessary, and something he had done many times. But he regretted the need to kill his cousin. If the attorney had been killed as planned the night before, it wouldn't have been necessary. Before he returned to London, he would have to visit his cousin's parents to pay his respects.

He would also find a way to make sure the attorney would pay for his family's loss. The Law of Retaliation allowed a "life for life" and he would willingly make sure the debt was paid.

When Mohamed finished eating his light dinner, he went to his bedroom and took a black ballistic nylon duffel bag down from the top shelf in his closet. From it, he took out a Ruger 22/45 Lite with a SWR Warlock suppressor and loaded a magazine with ten rounds of .22 LR ammunition. Next, he selected two pairs of surgical gloves and a small Ziploc bag he'd filled with bleach germicidal wipes and put all of that in a gallon Ziploc bag for cleaning up any mess that he made.

Mohamed put his tools for the night in a slim black carbon fiber attaché, gathered his wool topcoat and prepared to leave. With a last look around, he turned off the lights and headed out.

It took ten minutes to walk to a nearby parking garage where he kept a three-year old emerald green Range Rover. He rented the parking space by the month when he was in Washington, D.C., and the rest of the year kept it in a leased garage when he was in New York. Each time he used the vehicle, it carried a different license plate from his stolen license collection. Unless he was stopped, the car was virtually impossible to trace back to him.

Giving the Rover a minute to warm up, Mohamed entered Prescott's address in the GPS/NAV system and set off to Arlington, the wealthiest county in America. As he drove over the Theodore Roosevelt Memorial Bridge, he thought of the old Rough Rider and his favorite saying; "Speak softly and carry a big stick." He hoped that the public outrage over the jetliners that had been shot down would give the current president the courage to do the right thing when he learned that Iran was responsible. If the feckless foreign policy the man had followed since his election was America's response, his plan would miserably fail.

Mohamed followed the GPS directions and drove past Prescott's house. He saw there were no cars in the driveway as he continued past for another two blocks, and then pulled into a driveway and retraced his route. Several cars were parked on the street in front of an adjacent massive red brick Georgian-style home, and he slowed to a stop behind the last car.

Directly across the street was Prescott's slightly smaller classic colonial style home. Mohamed sat quietly and looked for signs of a security system. Two small bullet security cameras peaked out from under the roof of the covered front porch, one beside each of the white pillars on either side of the porch.

He took his black wool fedora from atop his attaché on the seat beside him and adjusted it down low over his eyes. From the center console, he chose his black leather driving gloves. Before he stepped out, he opened the attaché and slipped the pistol in a left side under shoulder holster and stuffed the Ziploc bag in the pocket of his topcoat. Mohamed opened the door of the Range Rover and walked across the street carrying the attaché in his right hand.

As he walked up the steps to the front porch, Mohamed kept his head down and moved with purpose, an employee bringing papers at night to his boss.

"Who is it?" a woman asked over the intercom speaker beside the door.

"Mrs. Prescott, I'm from the office. I have some papers Mr. Prescott needs to sign."

As she opened the door, she asked, "My husband is in the library, follow me."

Mohamed walked behind her through the foyer, with a staircase just beyond leading up to his right and a formal living room to the left.

Mrs. Prescott knocked softly on the next door to her left and said, "John, there's someone here from your office."

Mohamed took his suppressed Ruger pistol from a nylon hip holster on his left side and waved the woman into the library.

"I'm afraid Mr. Prescott wasn't expecting me," he said and shot her in the forehead, above eyes widened in surprise.

"Or maybe you were, Prescott. I'm Layla's lover. Keep your hands on top of the desk. We need to talk."

Chapter Fifty-Four

"WHAT DO YOU WANT?" Prescott asked calmly.

"I want you to be grateful that I killed your wife, Prescott. Now you can continue your affair with your office manager without feeling guilty for cheating on your wife."

"How did you…?"

"Mark Hassan is my cousin. He kept an eye on you for me."

"What am I supposed to do with her body? I can't just carry on as if nothing has happened."

"You'll think of something. Before we discuss a proposition I want you to consider, why don't you pour us some of that forty year old Laphroaig sitting on your desk."

Prescott started to get up.

"Stop," Mohamed ordered.

"If you want a drink, you'll need a tumbler. It's in the cabinet above the wet bar."

"Sit back down. I'll get it," Mohamed said and moved to the wet bar set in the middle of the floor-to-ceiling bookshelves on the left side of the library. When he opened the cabinet door, he found a Glock 36 lying on the bottom shelf.

Mohamed picked up the slim compact pistol in his left hand.

"You know how to use this?" he asked, as he put the pistol in the left pocket of his topcoat.

Prescott nodded.

Mohamed returned to his place in front of the desk and motioned with his pistol for his host to pour their drinks.

Prescott poured them each a generous amount and pushed one tumbler across the desk.

"Here's to your good fortune," Mohamed said and tried the Scotch. "Excellent, you live well, Prescott. I hope you're smart enough to keep doing so."

"What's your proposition?"

"In exchange for letting you live, I'll dispose of your wife's body, so it won't be found, if you'll give me the CIA files you told Layla about."

Prescott smirked and finished off his drink. "They're not here."

That's unfortunate because I'm not leaving here without them. While you reconsider your answer, I'll pour us both another round."

Mohamed took Prescott's tumbler and moved it beside the bottle of Laphroaig. He set his tumbler down next to it and shifted his pistol to his left hand. With Prescott's eyes glued to the deadly suppressor on the barrel of the Ruger 22/45, he slipped a small white pill into Prescott's tumbler and quickly poured him another two fingers of Scotch.

With another sip of Scotch, he said, "You have a choice to make, John, and it should be an easy one. Give me what I want, and I'll let you get on with your life. I'll take your wife's body with me and keep my mouth shut about how your foundation is supporting the terrorists. Refuse me and I'll put your body on the floor next to your wife, and make it look like a murder suicide."

He watched Prescott take a big swallow of Scotch. The small white pill that he'd put in his drink was a lab-modified version of Flunitrazepam, or Rohypnol. It acted within minutes and wasn't traceable in a person's system two hours later.

Prescott blinked his eyes several times, as the first of the drug's symptoms were felt. The visual disturbance was quickly followed by confusion.

"Layla doesn't know where the files are, so why should I tell you. Besides, you'll never find my safe. I hid it where no one will ever find it." Prescott shook his head from side to side and chuckled. "My wife didn't find it when she searched all over my library."

"So, it's here in the library?" Mohmad asked.

Prescott lifted the tumbler toward his mouth and spilled Scotch all over his starched white shirt. "I don't remember where, though."

"Do you remember the combination, John?"

"Never do," he said, his speech slurred as the full effect of Flunitracepam intoxication took hold. "Why I write it inside drawer."

When Prescott's head slumped down and the tumbler dropped from his hand, Mohamed returned the Ruger to his holster, took off his driving gloves and put on the surgical gloves that were in the Ziploc bag.

He moved behind Prescott and rolled his chair back. On the bottom of the middle drawer of the desk, he found the six-figure combination of Prescott's safe that was hidden behind the cabinet above the wet bar. When he'd opened the cabinet door to get his tumbler, the cabinet had pushed back slightly, like a handle less cupboard door would. Prescott had also looked nervous as he approached the wet bar.

Sure enough, the entire cabinet swung out and a small black wall safe was hidden behind it. Mohamed spun the dial on the safe, using the combination Prescott never remembered, and opened the safe door. Two passports, insurance policies, a deed, five stacks of $20's in bank wrappers and the CIA file.

He left everything in the safe except the file, closed the door and returned the cabinet to its place above the wet bar.

Prescott was snoring gently when Mohamed pushed his chair back behind the desk. He unscrewed the suppressor from the threaded barrel of the Ruger and placed it in Prescott's hand, with his finger on the trigger. Without resistance, the gun was raised to Prescott's temple and fired.

Mohamed stepped back and looked for blood spatter on the hardwood floor that would indicate there had been someone standing there when Prescott was killed. As he expected, there was no blood even around the entry hole the small .22 caliber bullet made, much less any blood splatter. The bullet had entered Prescott's brain and remained there.

With the Ruger that had killed his wife on the floor beside the tumbler he'd dropped, the police would conclude that Prescott had murdered his wife and killed himself. The only thing left to do was to download the encrypted Excel spreadsheet onto Prescott's laptop and his work would be finished for the evening.

Mohamed waited patiently while the Ironkey drive downloaded the spreadsheet. When it was finished, he opened the spreadsheet, left the laptop on for the police to examine when they arrived and left the quiet house to call 911.

Chapter Fifty-Five

DRAKE AND CASEY spent the afternoon and early evening being grilled by FBI Special Agent Kate Perkins about the shootout at their hotel, and what they knew about the Muslim youth camp in West Virginia. It was 8:15 p.m. by the time they left the FBI headquarters on Pennsylvania Avenue and returned to the Savoy Suites lounge to debrief the day.

Sharing a large pizza and a pitcher of beer, they sifted through the information they had learned from the FBI agent and Casey's young hacker at Puget Sound Security, Kevin McRoberts.

"She didn't tell us anything we didn't already know about the boys at the camp," Casey as he finished his second piece of pizza before emptying his first glass of beer. "They were young prison converts to Islam, suspected of a number of crimes in and around the youth camp."

"I'm not buying the camp manager's story that those four left the camp months ago," Drake said. "I recognized one of them from my trip there last Saturday."

"Good thing she doesn't know about that midnight visit, or we'd still be at FBI headquarters or in jail."

"What I don't understand is why Mark Hassan committed

suicide, number one, and why he would confess to embezzling from the youth camp's foundation. Why mention Sheikh Qasseer at all? Even if he took the money, why mention the Sheikh, and get him involved in an investigation?"

Casey plucked a couple of black olives from the top their shared pizza and ate them. "He was going to be involved at some point, anyway. Kevin was able to find the Sheikh's account at the London bank, and he transferred $9,000,000 dollars to the American Muslim Youth Camp Foundation. A lot of that occurred in the last two years. Kevin looked to see when the properties for the camps were purchased, and they were all purchased for cash way before the $9,000,000 was deposited with the foundation. That's a lot of money to account for if you're not buying more land for additional camps."

"The foundation's a nonprofit, there should be financial audits that will show where that money went," Drake said.

"Agent Perkins has probably checked the audits. We should ask her without letting her know we know about the $9,000,000."

"John Prescott, the chairman of the foundation's board of directors should know about the audits. He has a duty to keep an eye on the foundation's finances. I'm not sure he'd talk to me about the audits they have, but it's worth a try," Drake said.

Casey ordered another pitcher of beer to help them finish the pizza. "What about the guy we saw meeting with Mark Hassan? Did the Senator get anything else on him?"

"I forgot to ask Liz," Drake admitted. "I'll step out to the lobby and call her."

Standing next to a tall indoor palm tree in the lobby, he waited for her to answer her phone. There was something he was missing. Something they'd just been talking about was important, raising its hand for him to pay attention.

"Are you coming over?" she asked when she finally answered.

"Not right now, Liz. I spent the afternoon with Mike being interrogated by Special Agent Perkins. We're having a late bite to eat while we try to figure out what's going on."

"Was it Kate Perkins?"

"Yes, you know her?"

"She's with the FBI's Counterterrorism Division. I worked with her several times when I was at DHS."

"What's the CTD doing investigating a suicide and embezzlement case?" Drake asked.

"Would you like me to ask her?"

"That'd be great. Was Senator Hazelton able to get any more information on Mohamed Hassan?"

"The CIA isn't sharing. He's asked for a meeting with the Director tomorrow. As chairman of the Senate Intelligence Committee, he should get some answers," she said.

"Liz, I think I'd better take a rain check tonight. I'd be lousy company."

"I doubt it, but I understand. Call me tomorrow."

Drake returned to the lounge and sat down at their table.

"Mike, something we were talking about before I called Liz started to ring a bell. We were talking about Agent Perkins and what little we learned about the four from the camp."

"Let me think. We agreed we didn't learn much, that you didn't buy the camp manager's story that the four left months ago because you recognized tattoos, and we…"

"That's it! Those guys were trying to keep us from talking about something we'd seen at the camp. Something worth the risk of shooting up a hotel to silence us."

Casey refilled Drake's glass. "Okay, but the only thing we saw was an army-style training layout and guys who weren't afraid to shoot us."

"No, it's something else."

"Maybe it's something you saw when you were there with Liz."

Drake replayed his trip to West Virginia and visiting the camp in his mind. They were escorted to the camp manager by four Black Panther looking guys with the tattoos he'd seen again, Quonset huts, a barn with a white delivery van a couple of guys were working on, a camp manager who wasn't glad to see them.

The white delivery van.

"Remember Liz telling us the MANPAD that shot down the last

plane came from a white delivery van across the river," Drake said. "I saw some guys working on a white delivery van at the camp when I was there with Liz."

"There are a lot of white delivery vans around, though. What were they doing on the van?"

"Hanging sheets of something on the walls. I didn't look that closely, but remember Liz also said they were surprised that the drone didn't detect the missile launch. If those sheets were something that prevented a drone from detecting what was in the back of that van, the van I saw could be the one the terrorists used."

"But we didn't learn the president was flying drones over major airports until after the second plane was shot down. How would terrorists know to install shielding in the van?"

Drake and Casey said it together. "They have someone inside!"

"I've got to call Liz," Drake said as he took out his cell phone. "We need to know who to tell about seeing the white delivery van at the camp."

"Liz, I changed my mind. I'm coming over."

Chapter Fifty-Six

DRAKE DROVE to her condo in Arlington and got there in twenty minutes.

"Hope you don't mind seeing me in sweats and a T-shirt," she said when she opened the door. "When you said you weren't coming, I went for a short run."

Her cheeks were still pink, and her hair was pulled back in a ponytail and she looked great barefoot.

"You look great. I like the ponytail."

She led him to the kitchen and asked over her shoulder, "Would you like a beer or a glass of wine?"

"I've been drinking beer with Mike, I'm fine for now?" he said, as he took off his coat and laid it over the arm of her white leather sofa. Remembering the last time they'd been on the sofa, he turned to the kitchen where she was pouring herself a glass of wine and took a seat at the kitchen counter.

"Remember when you told me about the white van across the river when the plane in Philadelphia was shot down, and that the drone hadn't been able to spot the missile in time?"

"Yes, the drone had thermal imaging and should have seen

inside the van," she said and leaned a hip against the other side of the counter. "Why?"

"What could have prevented the thermal imaging from detecting the missile and whoever launched it?"

"I suppose some kind of infrared shielding could have been used."

"And what would that look like?"

"From what I remember from briefings at DHS, NASA developed Infra-Red blocking technology. Commercial applications use two sheets of polyurethane with an inner layer of insulation to prevent conductive heat flow. It comes in sheets of the material."

"Liz, that's what we saw at the camp in West Virginia!" he said. "Remember that white van we walked by? They were putting up sheets of something in the back of that van. I think that was the van the terrorists used in Philly."

"Oh my God," she said. "If you're right, we've found them."

"There's something else, Liz. If they were shielding that van on Saturday when we were there, they knew the president was putting drones up over the airports. I don't recall hearing about the drones until after the second plane was shot down. How did they know about it on Saturday?"

"Let's see," she said. "Senator Hazelton was briefed on the president's decision on Friday. Other than the Air Force and the people around the president, it was a pretty small group."

"Then they have someone inside," Drake said. "If I'm right about the van at the camp, who do I tell? I haven't had much luck in the past getting anyone to listen to me, even you."

"That was before I got to know you," she said with a smile, "and you turned out to be right. How about Special Agent Perkins? I know her, she'll listen to me and she's with the Counterterrorism Division."

"If you think she'll listen. Is it too late to call her tonight?"

Liz looked at the time on her microwave. "It's only eleven, early in D.C. Let me call her again. I left a message for her when we wanted to know why CTD was involved in a suicide or embezzlement investigation, and she hasn't called me back."

Drake watched her enter the FBI agent's numbers on her iPhone with one hand and let her hair loose from the band holding her ponytail with the other. The ease with which women multi-tasked always amazed him. He was admiring her silhouette as she stood at her balcony window holding the phone when she turned to him with a puzzled look on her face.

"She wants to know if we can meet her tonight?"

Drake nodded yes, and when she ended the call, asked, "What'd she say?"

"She's been busy with another "suicide". John Prescott apparently killed his wife and them himself."

Special Agent Kate Perkins was sitting in a booth at an all-night diner in Arlington when they arrived. She wore a blue half-zip pullover with a small FBI logo in gold and when she stood, they saw she had on khaki pants and blue Nikes.

"Thanks for meeting me here," she said, "I didn't have time for lunch or dinner, and I'm starved."

"Are you working the Hassan case and now the Prescott case as well?" Liz asked.

"I'm not the Agent In Charge on either of them. I'm reviewing them for CTD. You guys want something to eat?"

"I'll have coffee," Drake said. "You want anything, Liz?"

"Coffee and cream, thanks."

"Agent Perkins, why is CTD interested in Hassan and Prescott?" Drake asked.

Perkins turned to Liz. "I don't know a lot about Mr. Drake, although I have heard some of the stories about him. From now on, whatever I tell you, Liz, is being provided as a courtesy to you as Senator Hazelton's advisor on matters of national security and his chairmanship of the Senate Intelligence Committee, is that understood?"

"Understood," Liz said.

"I was called in when Hassan's suicide note mentioned Sheik Qasseer. We keep an eye on organizations we believe are fronts for the Muslim Brotherhood or allied with them. The American Muslim Youth Camp Foundation has been under investigation as a

Muslim Brotherhood front for some time. We wanted to know more about the money flowing through the foundation."

"Have you examined its books?" Drake asked.

"I met with John Prescott earlier today and requested copies of any audits that had been done of their finances. He stalled me. Tonight, I learn he's dead."

"So, your interest in the foundation is to see if it's a front for the Muslim Brotherhood. Are you involved in the search for Allah's Sword and finding the missiles they're using?" Drake asked.

"Not directly, why?"

Drake checked with Liz, and she nodded to go ahead. "We visited the foundation's youth camp in West Virginia last Saturday. I noticed a white delivery van and two guys hanging sheets of something in its cargo bay. I think it was the van that was used in Philadelphia to shoot down the second plane."

"What did the stuff they were hanging look like?" Agent Perkins asked.

"Silver sheet off a roll, about four feet wide. They weren't tacking it up or using a staple gun, so it must have had an adhesive backing of some kind."

"Did you see it too, Liz?" Agent Perkins asked.

"I didn't pay as much attention to what they were hanging as Adam did, but I did see them doing it."

"There are two kinds of infrared blockers commercially available. It could be either one of them. That would explain why the drone didn't spot the missile. These products will reflect about 80% of solar energy when it's installed in the windows of buildings. It would do the same with thermal imaging, keeping the heat from bodies being identified by thermal imaging."

"Adam also wondered how the terrorists knew to use shielding, when it wasn't public knowledge that the president had ordered drones to protect our major airports," Liz added.

The FBI agent sat back to process what she was hearing. "With your experience at DHS, Liz, do you think there's enough evidence to warrant a raid on this camp?"

"It fits, Kate. Sheik Qasseer is a radical Islamist. I understand he's on a short list of proxies for Iran the CIA thinks might be responsible for the attacks on the jetliners. He's contributed a lot of money to the foundation, and he has a small army of followers in these youth camps all around the country."

Agent Perkins started to get out of the booth when she saw the waiter bringing her breakfast. "Looks like I'm not going to get anything to eat right away. I need to report in and when I'm gone, stay out of my food."

Chapter Fifty-Seven

DRAKE DROVE Liz back to her condo after Agent Perkins returned to the diner. She told them she was going back to the FBI headquarters to assist in the planning of a raid on the camp in West Virginia, based on the information they had provided about the white delivery van. They would be contacted later to provide a recorded statement about what they'd seen at the camp.

Before she got out of the Tahoe and went inside, they sat in front of the Camden Yard Potomac building and talked a little longer.

"When is Senator Hazelton meeting with Director Willard tomorrow?" Drake asked.

"Eight o'clock. He's invited to have breakfast in the Director's private dining room, next to his office."

"Why the special treatment?"

"Willard's a gifted politician, not a career intelligence officer. The CIA is always lobbying to remain at the top of the intelligence community food chain."

"Will Willard give the senator what he's asking for?"

"Probably, Senator Hazelton has a lot of influence as the

chairman of the Intelligence Committee. Willard needs his support."

"Will you call me as soon as he gets back to your office?"

"Of course," she said. "Will I see you tomorrow?"

"Of course," he smiled. "I'll be around until we know what Agent Perkins finds at the West Virginia camp. Mike has agreed to stay a couple more days, and I've developed a hunger for crab cakes."

It was Liz's turn to smile. "I'm glad you liked my cooking," she said and kissed him before jumping out and running inside.

Mike Casey was still in the lounge at the hotel when he got back, watching a hockey game being played on the west coast.

"Thought I'd stay up and see when you made it back," Casey grinned.

"I didn't know you liked hockey," Drake said as he sat down.

"I don't. Don't know the rules, can't find the puck half the time, but I like the way these boys fight. Did you know they had a hockey team in Phoenix?"

"Sure, the Coyotes," Drake said. "Liz and I met with Special Agent Perkins. She got called out on a murder/suicide after she finished with us. Guess who's dead now?"

"You want a beer?" Casey said and waived to the bartender as he kept watching the hockey game. "Who's dead?"

"John Prescott, the chairman of the board of the American Muslim Youth Camp Foundation. They say he killed his wife and then shot himself."

Casey turned his back to the flat screen carrying the hockey game. "A man like that does not shoot his wife. He makes sure he has a pre-nup, and then divorces her. First Mark Hassan, the head of his Middle East Division and now the head man himself. This must be related to the foundation and the camps they run."

"Or terrorists using MANPADS to shoot down jetliners," Drake said. "The FBI is going to raid the West Virginia camp sometime today."

"You think they'll find anything? After losing four of their guys when they came gunning for us, they'll have cleared out and relocated somewhere else."

"Yes, but maybe they'll find something at the camp. If nothing else, they'll see the shooting range and the training facility and take a little more interest in these camps."

Two glasses of beer and a bowl of peanuts were delivered to their table.

"Cheers," Casey said, and then asked, "Did Agent Perkins say anything about the other Hassan, the one we saw meeting with Mark Hassan?"

"She didn't mention him and neither did I. Why?"

"When I watched them sitting together, dead Hassan seemed to defer to live Hassan. They got together as soon as you left dead Hassan's office. Live Hassan's the man we need to talk to."

"Let's wait and see what Liz and my father-in-law find out about him," Drake said. "Senator Hazelton is having breakfast with the Director of the CIA tomorrow. I'd like to know as much about him as possible before we take him on."

"You want me to have Kevin see what he can find? If he is a moneyman for the Muslim Brotherhood, his financials will be interesting."

"Good idea and have him take a look at his firm too. If it's buying Gembala Porsches for all their guys, I might have to see if they have an opening," Drake joked.

"Is that what it's going to take to get you take me up on my offer to become chief counsel for my company?" Casey asked.

"Hmm, I hadn't thought of that. Let's finish our beer and get some sleep. My eyes are getting heavy. I'll dream about my new Porsche and see if that persuades me."

"I have a feeling a new car won't be the only thing you'll be dreaming about tonight."

"There you go again," Drake said, mimicking President Reagan.

Chapter Fifty-Eight

WEDNESDAY MORNING WAS COLD, with another storm front promising more snow for the capital and another day off for federal employees. Drake and Casey opted for a good workout in the hotel's fitness center and breakfast, before tackling their individual assignments for the day.

Casey's task was to work with his young employee, Kevin McRoberts, and hack into the London-based investment firm of Wyse & Williams and learn as much about Mohamed Hassan as possible. They wanted to see if his financial transactions would tell them who the man really worked for, his firm or the Brotherhood.

Drake's assignment was to see if Senator Hazelton, had pried anything out of the CIA about Mohamed Hassan. He left the hotel at 9:00 a.m. and drove to Capitol Hill, where he was lucky to find a parking space in the underground parking garage four blocks from the Dirksen Senate Office Building.

After a brisk walk under lowering clouds, he passed through a vigorous security screening and finally reached the senator's office on the second floor. Liz was waiting for him.

"They let me know you were coming," she said, and led him to her office.

Drake followed, nodding to each of the secretaries, who looked up and smiled as he passed them. From the unspoken greetings he was receiving, he suspected they either knew he was the senator's son-in-law or that he enjoyed being in the presence of the woman he was following.

There were yellow and red tulips in a vase on her desk and the famous lithograph of Washington at the Battle of Trenton on one wall.

"I haven't been here long enough," she said when she saw him standing and inspecting the lithograph, "to bring in some of my own. The senator loaned me that until I do."

"It's nice," he said. "Washington at Trenton is fitting for the work you're doing."

"Were you able to get some sleep?"

The mention of sleep prompted an involuntary yawn and a smile. "Not much, I couldn't shut off my mind. We're overlooking something."

"About the foundation and the camps?"

Drake waited for her to sit and then sat down in the chair in front of her desk. "That, and the deaths of John Prescott and the head of his Middle East division. Both were smart and experienced men. If they were involved with terrorists, they were smart enough to have stayed in the shadows and not risk being caught. Why kill themselves?"

"Traitors aren't always smart," she said. "Aldrich Ames lived well above his means, and was caught. He should have known sooner or later the CIA would notice his lavish lifestyle."

"Has the senator come back from his meeting at Langley?"

She pushed a button on her phone console and asked her assistant, "Sheila, has Senator Hazelton returned?"

"Just now," Drake heard over the console speaker.

"Does have a minute to see us?"

"His next appointment is in fifteen minutes. Come on down."

Drake walked beside her as they walked to the large ceremonial office, where Senator Hazelton stood behind his desk reading a file.

Without looking up, he waved for them to come and kept reading.

"Director Willard said he'd have this delivered by the time I got back to my office. It just arrived. Close the doors, so we can talk," he said.

They sat in the two dark brown leather chairs in front of his desk, as he continued to stand and read from the file.

"Tell me again, Liz, where you saw this man," he said.

"I haven't seen him, but I saw the car he owns. It followed us to West Virginia last Saturday."

"But you've seen him," he asked Drake.

"Yes sir. I went to see Mark Hassan at Prescott's office two days ago, the day before he died. He met Mohamed Hassan a couple of blocks away in a hotel lounge right after I left. Mike was there and took photos of the two on his cell phone."

"You were following him?"

"We were," Drake admitted. "After he warned me that D.C. could be a dangerous place, I wanted to know more about the man who had just threatened me."

Senator Hazelton laughed. "He didn't know much about you, did he? Well, from what I see here, you were right to be suspicious of him. Mark Hassan's cousin *is* Mohamed Hassan, and the CIA has a file on them. Director Willard made me promise I wouldn't provide Mohamed's file to anyone, but I'll tell you the high points. Mohamed Hassan is more than just an investment banker. He's an operative of the Muslim Brotherhood."

"By operative, do you mean a moneyman for them?" Drake asked.

"No, I mean the CIA believes he's a regular James Bond. They attribute several assassinations and bombings to him, or associates he directs. They agree with Interpol's assessment, but don't have independent evidence of their own."

"If that's all they have on him, why is their file so secret?" Liz asked. "I learned that much from one of my contacts."

"Because that's not all they have, Liz," Senator Hazelton said and sat down. "They've discovered that his lover here in D.C. is Layla Nebits, the president's advisor,"

In the silence that followed, the synapses in Drake's brain fired off and made the connections; Layla Nebits would have known the president was ordering drones over the airports. Mohamed Hassan could have learned about the drone protecting the airport in Philadelphia. Nebits to Hassan, Hassan to the terrorists at the West Virginia camp, who knew to shield the delivery van with infrared thermal imaging before launching a missile at the jetliner.

"Assuming Mohamed Hassan is working for the Muslim Brotherhood and hears pillow talk from the president's advisor, and if my hunch is correct that he's somehow involved in shooting down the jetliners, what does the Muslim Brotherhood stand to gain? Nothing would kill their chances of getting their assets released and being restored to power in Egypt quicker than being proven to be terrorists," Drake said.

"Adam's right," Liz agreed. "It doesn't make any sense."

"And there's something else that doesn't make any sense," Drake added. "The youth camps are linked to Sheikh Qasseer in Bahrain. He's contributed a lot of money to the foundation. He's a Shia Muslim. The Muslim Brotherhood is Sunni Muslim. Those two branches of Islam hate each other, as much as they hate Israel and America. Why would they be working together?"

Senator Hazelton sat back and rested his chin on steepled fingers. After a moment, he said, "Maybe we're missing the bigger picture. If Sheikh Qasseer is responsible for killing Americans, the president will send a fleet of drones to kill him with the blessing of Congress. And if Qasseer is acting as a proxy for Iran, how long will it be before the president goes after Iran, either alone or with Israel. The Muslim Brotherhood might have sacrificed some of their assets, but they would have succeeded in eliminating the biggest obstacle to their supremacy in the Middle East."

"Making us innocent tools of the Brotherhood," Liz summarized. "So, what do we do about it?"

"Nothing at the moment," Senator Hazelton said. "I'm going

back to Langley and run this by the Director. Let's see what the FBI find at the camp in West Virginia. If it's possible that we're being manipulated into a war, we must be very careful if there's a fox guarding the hen house."

"As in the White House?" Drake asked. "If it's true, I'd call it treason."

Chapter Fifty-Nine

BEFORE DRAKE LEFT the senator's office, Liz got a call from Special Agent Perkins.

The FBI had raided the West Virginia youth camp at dawn. Two SWAT teams from the FBI's Critical Incident Response Group (CIRG) were flown from D.C. in modified Sikorsky UH-60 Black Hawk helicopters for the raid.

Agent Perkins reported that they found the camp deserted. Forensic teams were being flown in to search for evidence of explosives and any evidence that would help identify the occupants of the camp. No delivery van had been found, but tire tracks for such a vehicle were located where Drake had seen the white van.

Nearby residents were being questioned, and several were reporting that two busloads of young men and an 18-wheeler truck and trailer left the camp early in the morning two days ago.

The FBI was expanding its search for the buses and the 18-wheeler, Agent Perkins reported, and was preparing raids on other American Muslim Youth Camps in nearby states.

"They knew we'd be coming for them," Drake said.

"If they anticipated that, then they must have had a plan to hide sixty men, buses and a semi somewhere," Liz said. "How far could they get in two days?"

Drake shook his head. "They wouldn't need to hide the men. They could just drop them off along the way and let them disappear. The FBI needs to focus on finding the semi. They've taken everything from the camp that would incriminate them."

"But what does that leave us with?" Liz asked. "The FBI has resources to find the semi, but that doesn't prove they've been shooting down the planes?"

"It leaves us with Mohamed Hassan and his lover," Drake answered. "I'm going back to the hotel. Mike might have something that will help us find him. I'll call you after I've talked with him."

Mike Casey was in their room when he returned to the hotel, studying the information his young hacker had forwarded to him.

"Pull a chair over and look at this with me," Casey said, sitting at the bedroom desk with his laptop open. "Kevin hacked the server at Wyse & Williams here in D.C."

Drake joined him at the desk. "What am I looking at?"

"All I've been through so far is investment-type memo's he sent to London. There's nothing in his emails and or expense account records that tell us anything, except that he entertains a lot."

Drake watched as Casey scrolled through a series of memos. "Since Kevin was able to penetrate the IT system at the firm's home office in London, can he get into any of his personal accounts over there?"

"And who says you aren't computer savvy!" Casey said. "That's what Kevin's working on now. Using the passwords he uses here at his office in D.C., he thinks he can come up with the likely password he uses there. He'll let me know when he's found a way in. What did the senator say?"

Drake got up and sat on the end of his queen bed. "The CIA thinks he's an operative for the Muslim Brotherhood. But the big piece of the puzzle is that he's sleeping with Layla Nebits, the president's advisor."

Casey shook his head. "The granddaddy of all terrorist organizations has found a way to get close to our president. Does the CIA think she's an *agent of influence* for the Brotherhood, or just a *useful idiot* that doesn't realize that she's helping them?"

"The senator didn't say, but my guess is she's the one who tipped Hassad off about the president ordering armed drones to fly over the airports. Whether it's pillow talk or actual espionage doesn't really matter. That information allowed the terrorists to go undetected and bring down another plane."

"So why doesn't the CIA do something about her?"

"This is Washington, Mike. The president doesn't trust the CIA or the military. Maybe the CIA is keeping its powder dry until they need to expose her and embarrass him or let him know they know when they need his support on something."

"That's cynical. Americans are dying and the CIA's playing politics?"

"We both know how bureaucrats operate. That's why we left the Army."

"It's still criminal," Casey insisted. "You'd think anyone that close to the president would be vetted and sent home, even if they did so quietly."

"Not if she's an advisor the president personally vouches for. Who's going to tell him he doesn't get to choose his own team?"

"She's off limits. We can still go after Mohamed, can't we?"

Drake smiled. "No one's stopping us. We know where he works and what he drives. Did Kevin find out where he lives here in D.C.?"

Casey picked up his cell phone. "I'll check. While I'm doing that, why don't you call down and order us a couple of burgers and fries so we can work through lunch."

Drake did as his tall, lean and bottom-less pit of a friend asked. By the time he was finished ordering room service, Casey wrote Mohamed's address on a note pad and passed it to him.

Watergate West, how appropriate Drake thought, as he read Casey's note. A suspected terrorist and operative of the Muslim Brotherhood is living in the D.C. landmark.

Watergate had been built, he knew, by an Italian company, backed by Vatican money, and was known for its luxurious digs, its international flair and air of political intrigue. Mohamed had style and wasn't afraid to operate out in the open.

Which meant that he was both a confidant and dangerous man, if he had done all the things the CIA suspected he had.

Chapter Sixty

DRAKE WAITED while Casey finished talking with his young employee.

"Ready to go find Mohamed?" he asked.

Casey stood and leaned back on the low dresser across from his bed and said, "Kevin got into Mohamed's account in London. He received a million dollars from the sheikh in Bahrain. He transferred that amount the same day to the foundation's coffers here in Washington."

"Qasseer contributed nine million dollars directly to the foundation," Drake said. "Why route a million through Mohamed's account?"

"I have no idea," Casey said. "Why don't we ask him?"

They decided to try his office in the Evening Star Building first. Casey drove the Tahoe to the iconic landmark located between the U.S. Capitol and the White House on Pennsylvania Avenue.

"Mike, let's take a turn through the building's underground parking and see if his black Porsche is here," Drake said. "It was in one of the reserved spaces on the first level near the elevators when I was here."

Casey paid the one hour parking fee and drove down the ramp.

As soon as they made the first turn, Drake said, "Over there. He's in the car and the tail lights just went on. Pull in behind and block him."

The Tahoe accelerated with a squeal of its rear tires and then slid to a stop behind the German Gemballa 911 supercar.

Drake held up his hand to stop Casey from getting out. "Let's wait and see what he does."

They couldn't see the driver through the darkened windows of the Porsche, but they only had to wait for a couple of seconds before he started honking to get them to move.

When they didn't move on, an angry young black man, who wasn't Mohamed Hassan jumped out, and stormed to the driver's side of the Tahoe.

"Move the damn car, man!" he shouted at Casey.

Casey lowered his window. "Where's the owner, Mohamed Hassan?"

"Don't know no Mohamed Hassan. Now move your car!"

Drake got out and walked around the front of the Tahoe. "Then why are you driving his car?" he asked and moved to the man's right while Casey slid out and blocked to the left.

The driver backed up and raised his right hand to show them the car's keys. "Hey, I was hired to drive this car to New York. You have a problem with the owner, go talk to him."

"Is he in his office?" Drake asked.

"How should I know? Car transport service I work for, sent me over to get the car for transport to New York."

Drake and Casey exchanged looks. "Give me the number of your company. Go stand by the car while I verify that," Casey said.

Drake walked to the passenger side of the Porsche and looked in. He could just make out a small red duffel bag with a water bottle on top of it in the passenger seat.

"Who ordered the transport?" he heard Casey say.

Casey listened and then put the phone in his pocket. "Mohamed told them he was returning to London and wanted it transported to New York. They don't know where he was when he called them."

They turned and got in the Tahoe as the driver began a creative tirade about their lineage.

"Where to now?" Casey asked.

"Find a place to park and let's go see if he's in his office."

The receptionist for Wyse & Williams, Investment Bankers of London, politely informed them she didn't expect to see Mr. Hassan that day. When asked if he'd be in the next day, she directed them to try his London office and gave them his business card.

"Do you think he's gone back to England?" Casey asked when they were in the elevator.

"If he's involved in shooting down the jetliners, now would be a good time to leave. Let's make sure and check his apartment."

They were driving west to the Watergate Complex on the Potomac, when Drake got a call from Liz.

"Special Agent Perkins came to see me after you left," she said. "She shared what they found on Prescott's computer, and you're not going to believe it; the whole terror plot was his doing."

"What do you mean the whole plot was his doing?"

"He had a spreadsheet that listed payments that were made for the whole operation; from round-trip airline tickets to Pakistan for "missile training", to shipping costs of the missiles from Bahrain to America."

"And all of this was on his computer for anyone to find? I don't believe it."

"It was encrypted, Adam. Not everyone could have broken the encryption like the FBI did."

"Even if it's true, it doesn't tell us who else is involved," Drake said. "Where are the guys from the camp? What was Mark Hassan's role? What about Mohamed Hassan and Layla Nebit? They're involved, I'm sure of it."

"The FBI thinks it has its guy," Liz said. "Apparently the president's satisfied as well. He'll reach out with a drone for the sheikh, and the FBI will roll up the rest of it. Let it go, Adam. There's nothing more for you to do."

"Liz, I'm with Mike and he's exhibiting road rage driving in your city's traffic. I'd better go. I'll call you later."

Casey turned and asked, "What road rage? We're sitting at a stop light!"

"I needed to get off the phone before I said something I would regret. The FBI found something on Prescott's computer that makes them think that he's the guy responsible for shooting down the planes. The president now gets to take his victory lap and tell America to relax and fly the friendly skies again, that it's all over. I don't buy it."

Casey pulled forward when the light changed and said, "Why don't you think Prescott's behind this?"

"Because, if he's smart enough to put this together, he wouldn't leave a spreadsheet on his computer. First Mark Hassan kills himself for taking money that no one knew was missing. Then Prescott conveniently decides to kill his wife and commits suicide because he feels bad for killing her. If he's just killed two plane loads of innocent people, he's not going to feel remorse for killing his wife?"

"If Prescott isn't responsible, then who is?"

"My money is on Mohamed Hassan. Drive on, James. Let's find him and see if I'm right."

Chapter Sixty-One

MOHAMED TOOK a last look at the Potomac River that flowed past his Watergate West apartment. He had purchased the corner unit on the tenth floor for its view and would miss the feeling it gave him to find such pleasure in the heart of the country he hated. He was here, undetected, and had commanded a deadly strike at the enemy, while enjoying the best the decadent place had to offer. And that included the bed of the lovely woman who advised the president.

Layla Nebit had sent a text message, in the code they had devised, that the Pentagon was preparing a joint plan with Israel to attack Iran's nuclear facilities. The strike would also reduce its Parliament Building and Presidential Palace to piles of rubble. His plan had worked.

And, he had done it all without one of his Sunni brothers having to sacrifice his life or fire a single shot directly at America.

His plan had been simple; provide the crazy and arrogant Shia Sheikh Qasseer with the 50 MANPADS after he had boasted that was all that he needed to bring America to its knees. The rest had been easy; funding the mission through the foundation the sheikh had established for his camps, getting the missiles smuggled across

America's unprotected northern border, and making sure the sheikh's favorite camp commander carried out the strikes as planned.

Which Jameel Marcus had done perfectly, except that he had failed to kill the attorney. Even that had worked out well, with the FBI raiding the camp in West Virginia in response and beginning a manhunt for the jihadists and the rest of the MANPADS.

Eventually they would track down all those who had been dropped off from the buses, along the way to the neighboring camp in Pennsylvania.

And, when they tracked the buses, they would find the missiles in the underground bunker in Pennsylvania. To their dismay, they would discover that the missiles were the very ones America had recovered in Libya and provided to the Syrian rebels at the request of the Muslim Brotherhood.

Of course, that news would be denied by the CIA. But he had a plan. An anonymous source would leak the information. The world would know just how two-faced America's leaders had been in their support of the Arab Spring that they liked to take credit for.

Would the greatness of his cunning never stop amazing him, he wondered, as he turned from the balcony windows and surveyed his apartment. He was leaving nothing behind that would tie him to the attacks in any way. The laptop with the encrypted spreadsheet that he had planted on John Prescott's computer was in a dumpster in Falls Church, Virginia, missing its hard drive, which was in another dumpster in Fairfax, Virginia.

The encrypted Ironkey drive was in his pocket, where it would remain until he got back to London. The only other loose end was his lover, and he had a plan for dealing with her.

Layla Nebit loved exotic flowers and he had arranged for her to receive an arrangement of one of the rarest of them all, Flame Lilies, or Gloriosa Superb, with her that night. He also had a small vile of colchicines, the poison that each Flame Lily contained. Three drops of the liquid would kill a good size dog, and he had 10ml of the poison in a small glass vial.

It was more than enough for the fatal dose he planned on

putting in her favorite night cap of heated Dom Benedictine B&B. Symptoms wouldn't develop for ten to twelve hours and would be attributed to an overdose of pills from the half-empty bottle of colchicines medication, commonly used for gout, that would be found in her medicine cabinet. Since she was a proud and vain woman, the fact that she had a bottle of gout pills that she purchased online, from a pharmacy in Canada that didn't exist, might never be questioned. At least, not before he was out of the country.

    Mohamed checked his watch and saw that he had thirty minutes until his appointment for a haircut and style at his favorite men's grooming lounge. He was feeling so good about the way the day was going, he thought he would have a massage and manicure as well, before shopping for the perfect wine to compliment the rack of lamb he'd been promised for dinner. Life was good when Allah smiled upon you, he reflected, and congratulated himself again as he left the apartment.

Chapter Sixty-Two

LAYLA NEBIT WAS UPSET by the call she received in her West Wing office, but she complied with the request to leave in the middle of the afternoon and go home. The hand-delivered note, and the business card that accompanied it, was something she could not afford to ignore.

The world knew the man she was summoned to meet as the distinguished senior journalist for the Times of London. His reporting on war and turmoil in the Middle East was a staple for diplomats the world over.

She knew the man as her uncle, and the chairman of the Muslim Brotherhood's Western Intelligence Action Committee. He was sitting in the back of her limousine when it pulled up in front of the West Wing of the White House.

Khaled Ibrahim handed her a note and motioned for the driver to raise the privacy window.

"We don't have much time," he said. "Read the instructions and then we'll talk."

The note was handwritten on stationery from the Hay-Adams Hotel.

Mohamed has been too clever and will be caught. His actions
cannot be traced back to us. He must be eliminated and made
to disappear tonight. The council has selected you to do it.

"Surely someone else can do this, Uncle. Why me?"

"Because he is in your bed, Layla, and he plans to leave tomorrow. There isn't time to get someone else close to him."

"How? How am I supposed kill him? I'm not a killer."

Her uncle took a vial from his coat pocket and handed it to her. "Put this in his drink. It will act quickly and then call the number on the back of the card I gave you. We will remove his body."

Layla settled back in her seat and rested her head on the cool leather. It wasn't a question about whether she would kill Mohamed; she didn't have a choice. No woman had ever played the role she was playing for the council as their eyes and ears at the highest level of the American government. But even that would not protect her if she disobeyed this order.

The question swirling around in her mind was whether she would be implicated in whatever Mohamed had been doing. She hadn't been seen in public with him, although the doorman and her security service knew him by name.

Was there something she had done or said that would come back to haunt her? Something she had let slip when John Prescott had confronted her. And then it hit her, right between the eyes.

Prescott knew about Mohamed from the secret CIA file!

The president would protect her from the CIA, of course. He already knew about her mother's past and hadn't been concerned. But had Prescott shared the file with anyone else? Or had the file been discovered by the FBI when they searched his house, after he'd killed his wife and committed suicide…the same night Mohamed had told her he'd go talk to Prescott?

Layla turned to her uncle and asked, "Mohamed killed John Prescott, didn't he?"

"Get the CIA files from him tonight before you kill him. We need to know how much the CIA knows about the two of you," he said and knocked on the privacy screen.

When the screen was down, he told the driver to take Ms. Nebit to her condo and let him out at the next corner.

Chapter Sixty-Three

CASEY DROVE down the ramp to underground parking for the Watergate complex at 2600 Virginia Avenue NW and paid for an hour of parking.

"High rent district," he said to Drake, as he put his wallet back in his pocket.

"The Watergate or the District of Columbia?"

"All of the above, plus the surrounding counties."

When they walked out of the stale air of the parking structure into the cold afternoon and the light scent of cherry blossoms, Drake pointed to the imposing gray building to the west.

"It looks like an ocean liner about to sail down the Potomac," he said.

The sharp angles of the building and the alternating bands of windows and balconies did, indeed, have a nautical look about it.

"Not the prettiest building I've ever seen," Casey said, "But I guess I could get used to it."

They followed the path through the terraced courtyard, in between the curving walls of the two more recognizable buildings of the Watergate Complex, and continued to the entrance of Hassan's building, 2700 Virginia Avenue West.

Inside, they were greeted by a doorman who politely asked who they were there to see.

"Mohamed Hassan," Drake said.

"Was he expecting you?"

"He asked me to stop by for a drink when I was in town. He's looking for a new security firm for his investment bank, Wyse & Williams," Casey improvised and held out one of his business cards.

The doorman took the card and read it carefully before handing it back. "I'm sorry that you missed him, Mr. Casey. He's returning to London tomorrow. Would you like me to tell him you stopped by?"

Casey took a twenty dollar bill out of his wallet and wrapped it around his business card. "It's important that I talk with Mr. Hassan tonight before he leaves, if possible. Would you have him call me at the number on my card when he returns?"

"Certainly, Mr. Casey," the doorman said with a smile and slipped the gratuity and card in his pocket."

Outside, Drake said, "You know he'll never call you."

"It doesn't matter. We know where he'll be."

It took Drake a second to read the Cheshire grin on his friend's face before he said, "His last night in town, with his lover, Layla Nebit."

"I'll have Kevin find out where she lives and after dinner with your in-laws tonight, we'll go see if we're right."

"Sounds like a plan."

After a quick shower back at their hotel and a change of clothes, Drake and Casey were ready for the dinner Meredith Hazelton had insisted on before they returned to Oregon.

"Mom tends to go a little overboard when she has me over for dinner, so be prepared," Drake said, and then added, "not that that would bother you."

Casey stopped in front of the white brick row house in Georgetown that Drake pointed out and defended himself. "You make fun of the way I can eat, but I know you envy me. Never gain a pound and I don't have to work out."

As predicted, Casey thoroughly enjoyed a feast of Tournedos of

Beef in mushroom and red wine sauce, an onion-potato gratin, and asparagus.

"Mrs. Hazelton," he said, when the last speck of the gratin was gone, "that was terrific! Drake said you are a great cook, and I totally agree."

Drake had noticed that Senator Hazelton was unusually quiet during dinner.

"Liz told me the president is satisfied that Sheikh Qasseer in Bahrain is responsible for shooting down our two jetliners as Iran's proxy. Do you agree with his conclusion?" Drake asked.

Senator Hazelton took a moment to refill his wine glass and locked eyes with Drake, as he considered his answer.

"I've been fortunate to have been involved in Intelligence oversight for my last two terms on the Senate Select Intelligence Committee," he said. "I have a close relationship with several senior officials in the intelligence community. They tell me there is evidence that the sheikh shipped fifty MANPADS here, and that Iran knew about it. I'm not convinced, however, that the sheikh carried out the attacks at the request of Iran."

"Is there a difference between knowing about the missile shipment and ordering that they be used against us?" Drake asked.

"I think there is, for two reasons. Iran will always be happy whenever anyone attacks us. They danced in the streets on 9/11. Saying Iran knew about the attacks and may have approved of the plan isn't a stretch.

"But they have too much to lose if they provoke us. Iran's real proxy, Hezbollah, is fighting for its life in Syria. They're calling it *the Grand Battle* that was promised by the Prophet 1,400 years ago. Shia Muslims fighting Sunni Muslims, in a battle that's to be a prelude to the return of their Mahdi, a prophet who disappeared a 1,000 years ago, that leads to the establishment of a world-wide Islamic state.

"I just don't see Iran inviting an attack by us, or Israel, that would harm its ability to provide support to Hezbollah in Syria."

"If it's not Iran, Senator, then who do you think is behind this?" Casey asked.

"Well, I don't believe John Prescott was," the senator said

emphatically. "I have known John for over twenty years. I can't believe he would do something like this. He represented a lot of clients from the Middle East and would do just about anything to lobby successfully for them, but he wasn't an Islamist."

"I know there are things you can't discuss with us, but you haven't answered Mike's question," Drake said. "Who do you think is behind this?"

Senator Hazelton looked down and watched the red wine he was swirling in his glass. "Since the Muslim Brotherhood was overthrown in Egypt, it's been behind most of the unrest in the Middle East. With the way it has lobbied for us to restore it to power and flexed its muscle and influence here in Washington without success, it's possible they're playing a long game, maneuvering us to take out Iran and make them the preeminent power in the region."

"How would you prove that?" Casey asked.

Senator Hazelton looked directly at Drake. "By finding the guy who's orchestrating the whole thing for the Brotherhood."

Chapter Sixty-Four

DRAKE AND CASEY left Senator Hazelton's row house a little after 9:00 p.m. FBI Special Agent Kate Perkins was leaning against the driver-side door of their rented Tahoe outside.

"To what do we owe the honor, Agent Perkins?" Drake asked. "Or have you just been following us, I guess I should ask??"

"Should I be following you, Mr. Drake?"

"Why are you here?" he asked.

"Liz called me. She said she was worried about you. She asked me if I could return the handguns we took from you after the shootout at your hotel. She said you were returning to Oregon tomorrow. Why is she worried about you, Mr. Drake?"

"She probably gets that from my mother-in-law. They're close. How are you coming with your hunt for the rest of the MANPADS, and the people using them?"

"We're still looking, but we'll find them. We know who financed the operation and where the money went," she said. "It's just a matter of time."

"So, you believe John Prescott's your guy," Drake said. "Have you discovered why he would do something like this?"

"I suppose you have a theory?" she challenged.

"I don't believe he's your man. A person doesn't kill two plane loads of innocent people and take his life after shooting his wife. Killers don't think like that."

"And you know how killers think?" she asked.

"I've prosecuted killers," Drake said simply. "And I do know a little about how they think, Agent Perkins. Is there another reason you're here, besides telling me that Liz is concerned?"

Kate Perkins pushed away from the Tahoe and stepped inside Drake's personal comfort zone. "I did a little research on you and found that you have an affinity for going after terrorists and bad guys yourself, instead of letting us do our job. You're still playing Delta Force soldier without the uniform, and I think you're doing the same thing here in Washington. Am I right, Mr. Drake?"

He looked down at her aggressive posture and smiled. "With or without the uniform, every citizen has a duty to protect his country. Sometimes a helping hand from us citizens, even if we're not wearing a uniform, can be useful."

Agent Perkins held his gaze for a long moment, and then turned and walked to the back of an unmarked black Suburban and raised the lift gate. From a cardboard box, she removed two handguns and returned to stand in front of Drake and Casey.

"Mr. Casey, I believe the Colt CQBP is yours and the Kimber .45 belongs to Mr. Drake," she said as she handed the guns to them. "If you discover something you think might be useful tonight, Mr. Drake, call me. My number is on the card I gave you at the diner."

Drake and Casey watched her get in her bureau car and drive off.

"Is she setting us up, returning our handguns?" Casey asked.

"More like she's telling us to go find something that will be useful, without saying it," Drake said.

Before they drove away, Casey checked his iPhone and found a text from Kevin McRoberts.

"Kevin found Layla Nebit's unlisted address," he said. "She lives in a luxury condo, not far from Mohamed's apartment."

"Then let's go see if she's entertaining him tonight," Drake said.

"Along the way, we need to come up with a plan to get past security. We didn't do very well at the Watergate."

Casey entered the address in the GPS and drove off in the direction indicated on the navigation screen. "A place like this will have 24/7 security, and with the security clearance she'll have there, she may have her own private security as well. We're not going to talk our way in."

"Maybe, maybe not," Drake said. "What if we get her to invite us in?"

"She doesn't know us, why would she do that?"

"Because the chairman of the Senate Select Committee on Intelligence asks her to."

"Will the Senator do that?"

"He might, if I tell him that Layla Nebit might know something that will lead us to the guy he told us to find."

Chapter Sixty-Five

MOHAMED HASSAN KNEW something was wrong before they finished the first glass of the 2000 Château Margaux he'd selected for their last dinner together. Her quick peck on his cheek at the door lacked the hungry passion he was used to.

And she hadn't mentioned the display of Flame Lillies that were sitting on the end of her granite-topped kitchen island.

"Layla," he said, "the lamb smells wonderful. Did you come early just to prepare our dinner?"

There it was again, the quick look away as she tucked her legs under herself on the sofa, before answering.

"I wanted the lamb done the way you like it, Mohamed. Besides, the president can get along without me for one afternoon."

"I doubt that, my dear, but I appreciate your devotion. How is the president doing, with all the problems he's dealing with?"

"He's coping, looking for a way to save face with the terrorist attacks."

"Will he go after the sheikh?"

"Oh my god," she hissed, "That's what my uncle meant. You're involved in these attacks."

Mohamed watched calmly, as she stood and stared at him.

"When did you talk to your uncle?" he asked.

"What have you done, Mohamed?"

"What I was ordered to do, Layla. Now sit down and answer my question. When did you talk to your uncle?"

He watched as she fell back onto the sofa, her eyes blazing in anger.

"Today," she said defiantly.

"Is he here, in Washington?"

He waited for her to answer.

"He's here in Washington, then. What did he tell you?"

"That you'd been too clever and would be caught."

"And what else did he tell you?"

As smart as she was, Layla Nebit had never been trained as an agent. Her glance toward the small black clutch on the glass-topped entryway table gave him the answer to his question.

Mohamed got up and kept an eye on her as he walked to the entryway.

"Did he tell you to kill me?" he asked, as he picked up the clutch and held it out to her. He saw her eyes widen in fear and looked to the kitchen island, where he dumped the contents of the clutch out on the cold gray surface.

"One leather fashion wallet with credit cards, some cash, lipstick and an iPhone," as he recited the inventory of the clutch, "and a clear glass vial containing what, Layla, poison?" The vial went into the pocket of his gray blazer.

"Did you kill John Prescott, Mohamed?" she asked softly.

"And Mark Hassan as well," he said. "They were "loose ends", as you Americans like to say."

"Am I another loose end as well?"

"Just as I am, it seems. What I don't understand is why your uncle, the chairman of the Brotherhood's Intelligence Action Committee, would sacrifice me? My plan was developed years ago, and the council approved it."

"Why would the council approve such a reckless plan?" she asked.

"Because America drew a line in the sand and didn't enforce it,

Layla. Your precious president promised the world Iran would not be allowed to develop nuclear weapon capability, and then stood by and watched them do it. Do you really believe Iran just wants to destroy Israel? It wants to destroy its oldest enemy, Layla, all of us who are Sunni Muslims. We've been at war since the Prophet died 1,400 years ago, without clearly naming his successor. Iran must be destroyed, and we needed a way to get America to do it for us."

"So you convinced Sheikh Qasseer to use his followers here in America to shoot down jetliners to get the president to attack Iran?" she cried. "The sheikh isn't Iran, Mohamed. Why would the president do that?"

"But the CIA believes he's Iran's proxy, Layla." he said. "I made sure of that."

Layla shook her head in disbelief. "What now, Mohamed?"

"Come, let's have the lamb you fixed for me, finish this expensive wine and we'll see if there's a way we both can get out of this alive."

When she went to the kitchen to serve the first course of their dinner she'd prepared, Mohamed refilled her wine glass and added a healthy dose of the Flame Lily poison when she wasn't looking.

Chapter Sixty-Six

DRAKE WAITED for the security guard to buzz them into the lobby of Layla Nebit's elegant luxury condominium. Walls of glass and curving wrap-around terraces for each floor gave the place a futuristic promise of über luxury.

"And I thought the Watergate West was swank," Casey said.

"The perks of being a powerful civil servant," Drake responded.

When the tall glass door with its discrete gold numbers clicked open, they confidently approached the guard's desk.

"Ms. Nebit is expecting us," Drake told him.

Without taking his eyes off the two of them, the guard announced their presence to his well-known resident over the condominium's intercom system. "Ms. Nebit, there are two men here to see you. They say you're expecting them."

"Your names, please?" he asked.

"Mr. Drake and Mr. Casey, on behalf of Senator Hazelton," Drake answered.

The guard visibly tensed as he listened with the phone to his ear. "She says she doesn't know what you're talking about."

"Tell her to expect a call from the Senator in the next several minutes," Drake said, and moved away to call the Senator and have him ask her for a few minutes of her time to deal with a matter of national security.

Casey stood beside Drake and said, "If Mohamed's there, he's got to be suspicious of an after-hours visit."

"Nebit's probably used to couriers, bringing her things that can't wait until tomorrow. If Mohamed spends much time here, he'll have seen this before."

"Let's hope your father-in-law can make this work."

IN HER PENTHOUSE six floors above, Layla Nebit returned to the penthouse dining room after receiving a call.

"I'm sorry for the interruption, Mohamed. There are two men downstairs saying the chairman of the Senate Select Intelligence Committee sent them to see me. I may need to talk with them."

"Were you expecting something from this Senator?"

"No, I wasn't."

"Do you know these men?"

"No, I don't."

Mohamed pushed his chair back from the table and stood, as Nebit's cell phone on the kitchen island started playing "Hail to the Chief". "Go ahead, Layla, take the call."

While she dealt with the call, he retrieved the small Glock pistol from the pocket of his overcoat he'd taken from John Prescott's safe, and slipped it inside the waistband in the small of his back. He didn't need his plan for their evening to be interrupted, especially if she was being called back to work and would be out of his grasp.

Nebit listened to what the Senator had to say, then told him that she had a guest, and they were just starting dinner. When the senator said he was sorry, but that it was important that she see them tonight, she agreed to allow them five minutes, given the recent attacks on the country.

"I need to talk to these men, Mohamed, just for a few minutes. Senator Hazelton is a powerful member of the opposition and he'll owe me a favor. Why don't you wait in the upper living room."

Her penthouse had an upper level for entertaining and a rooftop terrace with a spectacular view of the Potomac. The spiral staircase leading up to it was just off the entry and from above, he'd be able to listen to what the men had to say.

Mohamed took a position leaning against the black cast iron railing at the top of the staircase, so he could just see the faces of the men below and waited for their arrival. They would probably be a couple of young Senate staffers, and with Layla's imperious manner, she would have them back out the door in no time.

Few men had ever seen the submissive side of her, as he had. Egyptian women had always been granted a high, if not equal, status with men since ancient times and they were proud of their heritage as the first true feminists. But the way she could intimidate others when it suited her had still fascinated him. It was a gift he admired.

He heard the muted doorbell chime and then Layla opened the door. Two men entered and were greeted with condescending cordiality.

"I trust this is as important as Senator Hazelton made it sound," she said, as she let them in.

He was just able to see the top of the first man's head and his red hair, when the other man he couldn't see yet said, "Is Mohamed Hassan here tonight, Ms. Nebit?"

When the second man came into view, Mohamed recoiled and stepped away from the staircase railing. It was the attorney they failed to kill at his hotel.

Chapter Sixty-Seven

"I'M CALLING SECURITY," she threatened. "This isn't about national security and Senator Hazelton is going to regret disrupting my evening."

"Oh, this is about national security, Ms. Nebit," Drake said. "Did you tell Mohamed Hassan the president was ordering drones over the airports before the second jetliner went down?"

"How dare you!" she hissed. "No one accuses me and gets away with it."

While Drake was going toe-to-toe with the most powerful woman in Washington, Casey had been looking for any sign of Mohamed and saw a movement above, at the top of the spiral staircase.

"Adam," he said, and pointed up.

Drake started to step around Layla Nebit to reach the staircase when she grabbed his arm. "Get out of my house this minute! You have no right to be here."

"He's up there, isn't he?" Drake asked.

Her eyes darted upward, just before she tugged at his arm to get him away from the staircase.

"Keep her here, Mike," Drake said and drew his Kimber from its holster before heading up.

Mohamed's first shot grazed the top of Drake's head above his left eye, as his first step up the staircase moved him slightly to the right. The second shot missed as well as he rushed up the stairs.

Drake fired one shot at the gray form as it pulled away from the top of the staircase railing. When he poked his head up for a quick look, he saw a long, wide hallway leading to a terrace at the other end. The hallway widened just before the terrace into a room with floor-to-ceiling windows with a view out over the city's skyline.

There was no way for Drake to know if Mohamed was waiting in the room or had ducked out onto the terrace. If he was still in the room, the hallway was a kill zone with no cover to shield him.

When he'd trained in the live-fire shooting "House of Horrors", acting quickly and decisively to attack a shooter was often the only option. But here, a round that missed could sail through the windows of the terrace and hit the building next door.

Without knowing if there was a way to escape from the penthouse terrace, waiting him out until the police arrived to investigate the reports of guns being fired, meant Mohamed could escape. That was not something Drake could allow to happen.

"Mohamed, when did a Muslim warrior run from a fight? You're taught to embrace death, but you're hiding like a little girl."

When there was no response, Drake tried again. "It's over, Mohamed. We know about the camps and the missiles and the foundation. Why not die as a martyr so someone will remember you?"

"Oh, I'll be remembered, don't worry about that," Mohamed shouted from the other end of the hallway.

"For what, getting young boys in these camps to kill for you? Or did you lure them there for another reason? Is that what this is about, Mohamed? You like young boys?"

Drake saw a pistol thrust around the corner at the end of the hallway and ducked as two shots were fired wildly at him.

"I'll tell you what, Mohamed. I won't tell anyone you prefer boys, if you'll walk down the hallway and try to kill me like a man.

Otherwise, the world's going to know the truth about you and how you enjoy boys and goats and…"

Drake sprung to the top of the stairs just before Mohamed roared something in Arabic and charged down the hallway firing rapidly.

Two shots from Drake's Kimber .45 hit Mohamed in the chest and knocked him on his back, as if he'd been clothes lined by a WWA wrestler.

"Drake, you okay up there?" Casey shouted.

"Be down in a minute. Make sure she doesn't go anywhere. I have a few questions for her before the police get here," Drake answered.

He ran to Mohamed's side, kicked a small Glock pistol out of his hand and felt for a pulse. Mohamed Hassan was already flirting with his virgins. A quick search of his pockets produced an empty glass vial in his right blazer pocket, another glass vial in his left pocket filled with a milky fluid and a gray USB flash drive.

When he came down the staircase, he saw that Casey had herded Layla Nebit into the dining area. She was sitting at the opposite end of the table set with two plates of uneaten salad on silver chargers.

"Mike, call Liz and ask her to call Agent Perkins. I think the FBI will want to talk to Ms. Nebit before she dies," he said, holding out the empty glass vial labeled "*Gloriosa*".

"Have you had anything to drink since he arrived?" he asked her. "The colchicine poison that comes from any part of a Flame Lily, like those on your kitchen island, is always fatal. He brought you flowers so a coroner would conclude you poisoned yourself."

Layla Nebit, the president's closest advisor and the most powerful woman in Washington, threw her head back and began laughing. When she finished, she dropped her chin to her chest and said, "Now both loose ends are tied up."

Chapter Sixty-Eight

LAYLA NEBIT HAD RETREATED into a far corner of her mind and hadn't said a word, while they waited for the police or the FBI to arrive. She appeared to be in shock and continued to stare at the empty chair at the other end of the dining table.

Drake and Casey stood between the dining table and the door leading out onto the lower terrace if she decided to end her life on her terms, instead of the painful death her lover had chosen for her.

"How much do you think she knows about the role Hassan played in shooting down the jetliners?" Casey asked.

"Hopefully, we'll find out before that poison kills her," Drake said.

"How soon will that be?"

"What I remember from our jungle training is eight to thirty six hours. It's a pretty ugly way to die; seizures, shock, and ultimately respiratory failure."

"How'd you get Hassan up there?"

"The hallway was a kill zone. I had to make him come to me."

"You baited him?"

"I insulted him, taunted him about liking young boys."

When the FBI arrived, Special Agent Perkins quickly assessed the scene and demanded to know what had happened. She started with Drake, separating him from Casey and leading him upstairs.

"What made you come here?" she asked, as they climbed the spiral staircase.

"Ms. Nebit was Hassan's lover. I thought he might be here because he was returning to London tomorrow."

"Do I want to know how you knew he was leaving?"

"I went to see him at his Watergate apartment. The doorman told me."

At the top of the stairs, Agent Perkins stopped and faced Drake.

"Before I ask you to walk me through what happened, tell me why you went looking for him," she said and pointed to Hassan's body lying halfway down the hallway.

"It's a long story. You sure you want to hear it?"

For the next ten minutes, Drake told her about his client with a ranch in Oregon that the American Muslim Youth Camp Foundation wanted to buy, the attack on Congressman Rodecker who had tried to block the sale of the ranch and opposed the Senate bill to restore the assets of the Muslim Brotherhood, and being threatened by Mark Hassan the day before he committed suicide.

"Mohamed Hassan followed me in a black Porsche when I drove to the foundation's youth camp in West Virginia. When I saw him huddled with Mark Hassan the same afternoon after I'd been threatened, I followed him to his office and recognized the Porsche in the building's underground car park. When I learned that Interpol had a file on him, I wanted to satisfy my curiosity."

He didn't mention the late-night return to the youth camp with Casey and being chased by the jihadists-in-training, or hacking into Hassan's banking account in London and finding that it linked him to the sheikh in Bahrain.

Drake showed Agent Perkins where he'd been standing when Hassan charged at him, and how he had defended himself.

"So, you cornered the guy in her penthouse and killed him in self-defense, is that your story?" she asked.

"That's what happened, Agent Perkins. Mike Casey will confirm it."

"I'm sure he will. What about Layla Nebit, will she confirm it?"

"She should, but who knows," Drake said. "She's been poisoned by Hassan. If she was working with him, she might try to convince you that she's the victim here. She might be innocent, but with her position on the foundation that owns these youth camps, and the deaths of John Prescott and Mark Hassan, I suspect there's more to it. I wouldn't wait too long before you question her. She might not be around much longer."

Agent Perkins led Drake downstairs, where medics were attending to a subdued Layla Nebit. Mike Casey was being questioned by another FBI agent. An FBI Evidence Response Team (ERT) was unloading gear and two officers from the Metro Police Department were standing guard at the door, monitoring personnel coming and going.

Drake waited as the FBI agent questioned Casey, and then approached Agent Perkins, who was instructing two members of her team about what she wanted done with Layla Nebit.

"Sorry for interrupting, Agent Perkins," Drake said, "I forgot to give these to you."

He handed her the two glass vials, one empty and one full, and the USB flash drive.

"You may want to see what's on this flash drive. It was in Hassan's pocket."

Chapter Sixty-Nine

DRAKE AND CASEY spent the rest of the night and half of the next day at FBI headquarters, answering questions until Special Agent Perkins and her superiors were convinced they had mined every nugget of information from them and that no crimes had been committed while they were in Washington.

When they were allowed to leave, Liz was waiting and offered to take them to their hotel or lunch, if they preferred.

"A good cup of coffee and whatever you want to eat sounds good to me," Casey said. "Special Agent Perkins tortured us all night with bad coffee instead of water boarding."

"Have you heard how Layla Nebit's doing?" Drake asked, as they waited in the cold, but refreshing air, to cross Pennsylvania Avenue.

"She's in the ICU at Georgetown University Hospital," Liz said. "She's vomiting and having a lot of abdominal pain, but she's cooperating. Kate Perkins doesn't think she knows much about what Mohamed was doing, but he told her he killed Mark Hassan and John Prescott. She doesn't know anything about the terrorists shooting down the jetliners, but she suspects Mohamed may have been involved."

The light changed and they started across the street.

"Where are we going?" Casey asked.

"We're walking to the Capitol," she said. "Senator Hazelton is having lunch in the Senate Dining Room and said to bring you over if you were hungry. He's anxious to hear about last night."

"Have they found the rest of the MANPADS?" Drake asked.

"Not yet, but the FBI is searching the youth camps all over the country to find them."

They walked three abreast down Pennsylvania Avenue to the Capitol building, where Liz used her Senate Staff ID to get them into the Senate Dining Room. Senator Hazelton was sitting alone at a table for four.

The senator waved them over and rose to greet them.

"You survived a night with Hoover's best, congratulations you two," Senator Hazelton said, as he pulled out a chair for his staff intelligence advisor.

"Always a pleasure to serve our country," Casey quipped, "but I would have enjoyed it more if they served Seattle's Best coffee."

Senator Hazelton laughed and said," The coffee's pretty good here, Mike, and the food's not bad either. Before we order, though, was Layla Nebit really poisoned?"

"Her boyfriend gave her a dose of poison from the Flame Lily," Drake said. "There's no known antidote for the poison. She won't live for more than a day or so."

"Do we know what she did to deserve being poisoned?" the senator asked.

"No, and we may never know the whole story, unless she makes a dying confession soon. But when I told her she'd been poisoned, she just laughed and said, "Now both loose ends are tied up". I believe she was working with Mohamed Hassan, or at least knew what he was doing."

"But we still don't know that Mohamed was the one responsible for these attacks on our airlines, do we?"

"No, Senator, but we do know he received $1,000,000.00 from Sheikh Qasseer, the man the CIA believes *is* responsible. The sheikh also contributed $9,000,000.00 to the American Muslim Youth

Camp Foundation the year before the first jetliner went down," Drake said.

"How do we know that?" Senator Hazelton asked. "Were you briefed on that, Liz?"

"Officially, we don't know that yet, sir. But I'm sure the FBI of the CIA will be able to trace the money when they audit the books of the foundation and investigate Mohamed Hassan's financial dealings," Drake suggested presciently.

Senator Hazelton studied his son-in-law's poker face and nodded. "I see. Will that information be forthcoming in time to consider its impact on the president's decision concerning the sheikh, and any role Iran had in all of this?"

"If you look in the right places, sure," Drake said. "Mike might be able to help Liz get her friend, Special Agent Perkins, started on that."

"Take a look at your menus, gentlemen, and let's get some food out here for you. I have an Intelligence Committee meeting at 2:00 p.m. and I need to make a few calls before then, it seems."

As they were looking at the day's lunch menu, Liz's cell phone buzzed. She excused herself and left the Member's Dining Room to take the call.

When she returned, she said as soon as she sat down, "Kate Perkins wanted you to know, Drake, that the encrypted flash drive you found in Mohamed's pocket had the same spreadsheet, detailing the finances for the terror plot, they found on John Prescott's laptop. They now think Mohamed probably killed Prescott and made it look like suicide."

"If he killed Prescott," Casey said, "he probably killed Mark Hassan as well. I saw both Hassans together, just after Mark Hassan threatened Adam. Both Mark Hassan and John Prescott would have known about the money flowing in and out of the foundation."

"Did you tell that to Kate Perkins?" Liz asked.

"No, I didn't. His suicide made sense with his suicide note saying he'd embezzled money from the foundation. I didn't have a reason to connect them."

"I'll tell her you saw the two Hassans together when we leave," she said. "Anything else I should tell her?"

Drake looked to the senator and asked, "If Layla Nebit was working with Mohamed Hassan, or aided and abetted him in any way, that's treason. At what point do you question the president's role in all of this? Nebit is his closest advisor. With her whispering in his ear, he's made foreign policy decisions concerning Egypt and the Muslim Brotherhood that have been curious, to say the least. Does Congress or the FBI need to investigate the president's role in aiding and abetting an enemy now that the Muslim Brotherhood is again considered to be a terrorist organization?"

Senator Hazelton looked across the dining room for a long moment at the stained-glass window that memorialized George Washington on a white horse.

"If what Layla Nebit said is true, that "both loose ends were tied up", it might be difficult to prove treason if articles of impeachment were approved by the House and presented to the Senate. I hope to God I never have to judge a president for treason, but there's another matter Congress may have to consider. There have been rumors, after both of his election victories, that his campaign received money from foreign contributors. If there's evidence that foreign contributions were received from a terrorist organization like the Muslim Brotherhood, that would be an impeachable "high crime or misdemeanor".

Chapter Seventy

BY NOON THE NEXT DAY, the FBI had advised Drake and Casey they could leave Washington and they checked out of their hotel. Drake had stopped by to say goodbye to his mother-in-law the night before and taken Liz to dinner. Now they were on their way to Washington Dulles International Airport with the sky clear and bright spring blue.

"You realize we've only been here a week and a day," Casey asked, "and been shot at three times?"

"It could have been worse," Drake pointed out. "We could have flown commercial and been in one of those jetliners."

"Point taken," Casey conceded. "I guess that bullet Mohamed bounced off your head is pretty insignificant, in comparison."

"Hey, don't minimize my wound. That little red mark on my head has been worth a kiss or two."

"And I'll bet your mother-in-law wasn't the only one to feel sorry for you."

"Better me than you, Mike. Your wife would banish me from your life forever if you came back injured."

Casey took the exit off the Dulles Toll Road and drove down Autopilot Drive to the Landmark Aviation Service hub, where the company Gulfstream G450 was serviced and refueled for the flight home.

The two PSS employees, Spencer Reynolds and Ron Larson, who had provided security for Oregon Congressman Rodecker, were already onboard the company jet. When Casey and Drake passed through Customs and joined them onboard there, they raised two Bloody Mary's and saluted them.

"We like the way you travel, boss," Spencer Reynolds said. "It sure beats flying around in a C-130."

Casey moved down the aisle to the aft galley to mix two Bloody Mary's and waved Drake to the executive chairs nearby.

Before he sat down, Drake's cell phone vibrated in his pocket.

"Hi Liz," he said, standing next to Casey and signaling for another pickled green bean to be added to his drink.

"Kate Perkins just called top let me know they found a cache of MANPADS in an underground bunker at a youth camp in Pennsylvania," she said. "The FBI thinks they were sold to the Syrian rebels by the CIA, and then used against us. The CIA isn't saying anything at the moment.

"I guess that's good and bad news. Do they think that's all of them?"

"They think so. Layla Nebit told them, before she died last night, that she received a demand letter after the first plane went down from something calling itself *"Allah's Sword"* claiming they had 50 of the MANPADS. They found 47 in the bunker and one more with the guy they killed who was guarding the bunker."

"I didn't hear anything about *"Allah's Sword"*, did you?"

"Not until now. The FBI thinks Mohamed Hassan was *"Allah's Sword"* and gave her the note, knowing she'd give it to the president."

"Knowing all of this, is the president still planning to hit Iran?"

"The briefing this morning for the Senate Intelligence Committee confirmed that a strike at the sheikh in Bahrain is planned, but he's holding back on Iran until there's clear evidence Iran ordered these attacks," she said.

"I'm glad he's willing to listen to someone other than Layla Nebit."

"One more thing before you jet out of here, Adam. Congressman Rodecker asked me to thank you and Mike for taking care of him. He also wanted you to know he's working with some young Turks in Congress to draft a resolution of impeachment of the president. Someone provided them with a preliminary audit of the American Muslim Youth Camp Foundation. A lot of money seems to have made its way to the president's campaign committee."

"It's good we're getting out of town before that bomb goes off," Drake said, "Are you still taking me up on my offer for a week of spring skiing at Mt. Bachelor next month?"

"Count on it, I might even bring you some crab cakes."

He could hear her smiling. "Love your crab cakes," he said.

"Be safe, Adam."

"You too, Liz."

Drake sat down and found that Casey had a smirk on his face when he handed him his Bloody Mary.

"What?" Drake asked.

"Just wondering what it is you just *luv* about her crab cakes?"

Drake returned a smile to his friend's smirk.

Casey got up and opened the cockpit door to tell his pilot it was okay to take off. When he returned, he asked, "Have you thought about coming to work for me?"

"Mike, I love you like a brother. But I have an office in Portland, a secretary with a husband who just had prostate surgery, and an old vineyard to restore. I can't move to Seattle."

"Who said anything about moving to Seattle?"

"What exactly do you have in mind, then?"

"I want you to be Special Counsel for Puget Sound Security and head up my Special Investigations Team. We have clients who ask us to conduct fraud and corporate espionage investigations for them. We provide counsel when there are ransom demands when someone's been kidnapped. I have security teams and VIP protection details that deal with law enforcement from time to time. Keep your office and farm in Portland. Commute to Seattle when I need you.

Keep doing the things you've been doing for Liz and the senator. Just do those things for PSS on a generous retainer. I'll even provide a company car, so you don't have to put a lot of miles on that old Porsche of yours."

"I don't know, Mike. Let me think about it."

By the time the pilot told them to prepare for landing in Seattle and they started descending through thick white clouds, Mike's offer had been all he'd thought about during the cross country flight.

Drake looked out his window when they broke through the clouds and saw the waters of Puget Sound and the city of Seattle below.

"What are we doing in Seattle, Mike?"

"We had to come here first, sorry. I'll get you home."

Drake had been looking forward to getting home before dark, and now it looked like he wouldn't be there until later in the evening. Even though Mike Casey was his best friend and brother-in-arms, he should have told him they were flying to Seattle instead of Portland.

When the G450 taxied and stopped in front of Puget Sound Security's hangar at Boeing Field, Drake silently followed Casey out and down the stairs of the plane. Parked twenty feet away was a beautiful new anthracite gray Porsche Cayman GTS.

Drake walked around the car, admiring its flowing lines and peeked in a window at the sports seats with the letters "GTS" embroidered in the headrests. "Your pilot has good taste," he said to Casey.

"Glad you like it. I said I'd get you home."

Drake turned, not understanding what the pilot's car had to do with getting him home in Oregon.

Casey was standing between Spencer Reynolds and Ron Larson with a set of keys dangling from his fingers. They were all smiling.

"It's your new company car, if you want it," Mike Casey, the CEO of Puget Sound Security offered.

"You drive a hard bargain, my friend," Drake said with a big smile and took the keys.

SCOTT MATTHEWS

. . .

THE END

Next in the Adam Drake series

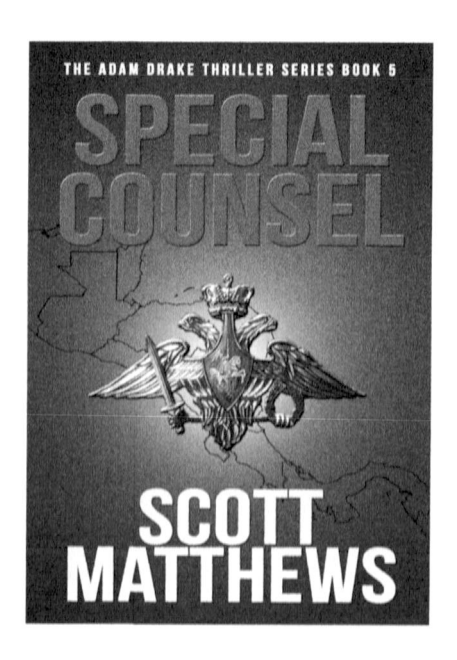

Our enemies have joined forces to launch an EMP attack that will annihilate America.

Operating from a base in the Southern Hemisphere, Russia and Iran are training Hezbollah to deliver a death blow to their common adversary.

When an armed convoy leaves the Nicaraguan terminal headed north, with blue containers loaded on Russian army flatbeds, and the military attaché at the U.S. embassy won't listen to him, Drake knows the convoy had to be stopped before it gets within range of America.

How he's going to make that happen is the problem.

Printed in Great Britain
by Amazon

47552167R00158